A TALENT FOR TROUBLE

A Spirited Spinters Sweet Regency Romance

ROBYN CHALMERS

JOIN MY READERS GROUP
https://www.robynchalmers.com/newsletter

CHAPTER 1

IN WHICH VISCOUNT BEAUFORT FANTASIZES ABOUT DRAWING A CORK

J ust as Leo Astley, Viscount Beaufort, reached Portman Square, the skies opened, and it started to rain. Large drops, soaking his fine merino coat and splashing his boots, turning the world gray and miserable.

As a staunch Londoner, he should know to carry an umbrella in May. Now his perfectly tied cravat would pay the price and give his valet another reason to raise his eyebrows.

Beau looked up, bemused, at the thunderous sky. He'd been sure the sky would stay clear. But then, positivity was his besetting sin, wasn't it?

Positive of blue skies, *positive* he'd repay the family debts in record time.

Ha. London tended to rain on that idea, too. If their current streak continued, he'd be running gambling parties in the ballroom until he had one foot in the grave.

He reached the house as thunder clapped overhead, and the rain started in earnest. The glossy black door led to a haven, even if it was a millstone around his neck.

The door swung open, and Merrick, his major-domo, ushered him inside. "I'll take your hat and coat, my lord."

"You mean the one that now has the charming aroma of *Eau de Wet Sheep?*"

Merrick lifted the coat to his nose and grimaced. "I'll give it straight to Postlethwaite."

"Send my condolences with it."

He was about to make his way to the kitchen to see what was warm and fresh, when Merrick caught his arm.

"You have *guests*, my lord." His hushed tone suggested they were not the welcome kind. "I put them in your study as her ladyship is in the drawing room and we don't want her seeing those sneaky coves."

He scanned the older man's face, taking in his pinched brow and the worry lines around his flint-gray eyes. As an ex-pugilist, it took a lot to make him show worry, and that could mean only one thing—Beau's moneylender and accompanying underlings had arrived.

Why that coxcomb thought he had visiting rights was beyond him. He would rather sit down to tea with the night soil man than Mr. Jinx. Of course, given his current—some would say dire—situation, he couldn't afford to offend the moneylender. At least, not *too* much. He took a deep breath. "My thanks. Do not call for tea."

Merrick nodded. "I will stay around should you need me to plant him a facer."

There was far too much relish in his voice.

"And perhaps have Anthony join you." The more muscle, the merrier. It was yet another time he was happy to have employed men from the regiment on his staff. They knew trouble when they saw it.

Merrick bowed and strode off, no doubt to find Anthony,

but likely Derek as well. They would support him if the need arose. *When* the need arose.

Beau opened the door of the study to find Jinx sitting at *his* desk, with two brutes standing on either side. The money-lender looked up and slammed a drawer shut, a wry smile lifting the corners of his mouth. He flipped that infernal gold coin he loved over the top of his hand like a magic trick.

Informants told Beau that Jinx's many London properties were obtained through a combination of blackmail and extortion. He was building an empire, and the odds he had No. 20 Portman Square on his list of things to acquire were not worth taking. And if he couldn't win it through Beau defaulting on his loan, he'd likely find a criminal way to get it.

All things Beau had not known on that infamous day five years ago when he agreed to Jinx's moneylending terms to combine all his father's debt in one place. At twenty-two, and in the depth of grief, one tended not to think clearly.

"I generally don't allow people to sit at my desk," Beau said lightly, closing the door behind him and leaning on it, crossing his arms over his chest. How satisfying would it be to draw his cork? Would Gentleman Jackson approve? Beau spent the next moment in a quiet fantasy of the idea.

At first glance, Jinx looked like a gentleman. His cravat was snowy white and simply tied, his hair cut in a fashionable Brutus crop. But his coat was ill-fitting, and his waistcoat was a gaudy yellow and puce stripe, inappropriate for a morning call. You could dress the ruffian as a gentleman, but he still wouldn't know when to wear the proper rig at the right time.

Jinx smiled, displaying golden canines. "It will be *my* desk soon, and I think we both know that."

"Do we?"

Jinx shrugged. "You've missed your payment this month. You agreed to the terms. You know the consequences."

Beau shrugged a shoulder. "I would never have thought my Faro bank would be broken twice in one week, but there you have it. And I have not missed the payment. It is only the fifteenth. I have another sixteen days before you can truly say I've missed it."

"You always pay by the second week."

"And I am always two weeks early." Beau flicked a piece of non-existent fluff off his arm. Much as he would like to do with Jinx. "And surely the extra amounts I have paid should cover this payment?"

The ruffians chortled, their beefy shoulders shaking with mirth.

Jinx leaned back in Beau's chair, making it creak in protest. "The extra you paid is *your* problem. Your contract only requires a steady payment each month. Surely you've figured out by now none of the extra payments have reduced your interest?" He picked up the white jade phoenix that sat on the desk and turned it over in his hand.

"Yes, I figured that. Would you like to take the phoenix as payment for this month?"

It was Liao Dynasty and solid white jade, but more than that, it represented his dreams for the family, to rise from the ashes of the debt his father had sunk them in. To be resplendent once more. But for the sake of paying down the debt, he'd let it go.

Jinx inspected it and then dropped it into his pocket like it was a penny he'd found on the street. "More like a little insurance. You can have it back when your payment is made."

Beau flexed his hand as rage itched under his skin. Oh, to pull Jinx by the knot of his cravat and shake him like the sewer rat he was. For almost five years he'd had to deal with one disastrous event after another, and now Jinx thought he could just walk in and take whatever he wanted? "No."

"No?"

The henchmen stood a little straighter and the one on the right cracked his knuckles.

Beau *wanted* it to come to fisticuffs, if he were being honest. Was spoiling for it. This was just one in a long line of unnecessary visits with barely veiled threats. "Take it as payment or give it back. My loan has always been unsecured."

Jinx stood to his full five feet five inches and patted his pocket. "I'll keep it. You want me happy, I'm sure."

"Not particularly." Beau pushed off the door and opened it. "Leave it on the desk or I'll have Bow Street come and fetch it for me. The choice is yours."

Jinx's dark eyes glittered dangerously. "You don't want me as an enemy."

"And you don't want me as one, either. You are nothing but a means to an end." He yawned, though tension—the readiness to fight—vibrated through every inch of him. "And, as always, I tire of you. Please leave."

Jinx huffed and put the phoenix down on the desk as though it meant nothing to him. And Beau was sure the object itself did not. But lifting something from a viscount and watching him squirm as you played with him? That was what Jinx lived for.

Beau held the door open and waved his hand in invitation. Jinx and company sauntered out as though they had all day. Merrick was already stationed at the open front door, Beau's two footmen flanking him.

"Oh, and Mr. Jinx?"

Jinx turned. "Yes, my *lord*?" He always said the title as though it were a joke.

"That waistcoat is more suited to a night at Vauxhall, and even then, I would think twice. A morning visit calls for more subdued attire. Perhaps my payments should be an hour of sartorial advice per month instead of cash? I hear you are trying to woo a young lady." *Lure* would be a more appropriate term. "You'd best be up to scratch."

"Says the man who lost his fiancée two weeks before the wedding." Jinx looked at his friends, who dutifully laughed like the hyenas they were, then frowned down at his waistcoat. With puce fabric and yellow flowers, he should by all rights have been blinded instantly.

Beau looked down at his fob watch. "Sage-green or a slate-gray would be more appropriate."

Jinx scowled, then strode from the house, followed by his men.

Beau watched to make sure he left, then met Merrick's gaze. "That was easier than I expected. Thank you for your support, as always."

"I am glad of it, sir, and happy to be of service." Merrick bowed but as usual, did not smile. "Her Ladyship has asked if you have a moment for her, my lord."

From one person to whom he owed a debt, to another.

Life was always demanding a payment.

As Beau entered the room, Viscountess Beaufort, who was in her sixth decade, but nobody knew exactly how far, turned from her position looking out the window over the garden, her face brightening. "Here you are! The tea is entirely cold now. Call for another pot, will you?"

Beau pulled the rope, ordered the tea, then sat on the worn but comfortable chair. "I was in a meeting. Sorry to keep you."

Her drawing room was a crowded jewel box, away from the gambling, and a resting place for the ghosts of their wealth. She sat next to a petite walnut table, with an ormolu clock on it. In the corner, a Sevres vase sat atop a marble column; and the walls were jammed with the gilded paintings she could never part with. And if the moss-green flocked wallpaper was a little faded near the windows, it still looked handsome enough. Not that many visited her in her own drawing room these days.

It was the price they paid.

"I hate to bring this up, but do you know what today is?" She sat a little straighter and splayed her fingers across her skirts, inspecting her rings.

What was today? Tuesday? It wasn't his birthday or anyone else's that he knew. "I confess I do not. Pray tell, what is today?"

"It is precisely five years to this day that we started our gambling parties." She wrung her hands, shooting him a worried look. "And three years after you assured me we were close to finishing."

"Ah, yes. I did indeed. It would seem I was precipitous." He allowed a small smile to play around his lips, but he was anything but amused. With takings falling and the bank he used at the Faro table broken more than he could cover, they were going backwards. He couldn't tell her that. It was his fault and not her burden to carry. He just had to fix it.

"I have not complained, and I am not now," she said. "You have brought us back from the brink of disaster. But I have

Emmeline to bring out next year and it must be done with, it *must*. I am tired of having Emmeline and Benedict live with your Aunt Theresa. You *promised* this would be of short duration."

"The word *short* is subjective," he said gravely. "For me, five years is acceptable if we settle the debt Father left us. And we are close. But we could still be running our card parties four years hence." *Although I hope not.*

She drew in a shocked breath. "Never say it, Beaufort."

"What else can we do? The debts are not paid."

She lay back on a cushion and lifted a gilt container of smelling salts to her nose. "Who do we owe all this money to? You have no consideration for my nerves."

"Just one last creditor." One horrible, enormous last creditor for an earth-shattering twelve thousand pounds. A figure that haunted him in his sleep. "And I believe your nerves to be up to any challenge presented. You are strong and have been an enormous help to me. I am in your debt."

She stared at the ceiling. "I mean my nerves regarding the parties themselves. I fear we have turned our home into a thieves' den where fortunes are lost in the blink of an eye. I can barely meet anyone's gaze when I venture out now."

He pulled at his cuffs. Her words had a horrible ring of truth to them. "Nobody loses their fortune here, as you well know. We do not allow vowels to be swapped. You gamble with the money in your pocket and when that's gone, you drink champagne and dance." It was part of what had made their parties so popular. Ladies and gentlemen alike knew the rules and there was no danger of gambling your entire estate away on the roll of a dice.

"That's not what I'm hearing. It's why I asked to see you."

It wasn't what he heard, either. Whispers of foul play,

clients leaving in great dudgeon, people he wasn't familiar with bearing keys of entry. Nothing concrete but enough to have the bright stars of suspicion join up like so many dots.

But as always, he had a plan. "I hear you, and I will investigate. We cannot turn a blind eye to foul play. I don't know how it's being done, if it is organized or random. But I will."

It felt like everything was spiraling out of control. Jinx, the Faro bank breaking, cheating on the floor. It was a horrible way to live. Usually he liked Faro and Hazard. The bank always won. But currently the bank *wasn't*. He'd been watching like a hawk and couldn't see why. He was checking the cards every night and hadn't seen telltale pinpricks or coloring that marked a swapped-out deck.

His mother sat up; her shoulders pulled back in the proud way he knew so well. "If you can, you will have us out by the end of the year, correct? There's many a young heiress who would love to marry you. You don't need to do this."

What a wonderful bargain for his bride. To be married for her golden coffers. No, thank you.

"I am trading on our family name enough already. I hope we are not so far gone that I need to sell myself entirely." The thought of lumbering an heiress with the job of rescuing him was appalling.

"Many do, is all I am saying. I know you're proud, but sometimes we must push that aside. Will you consider it?"

What was worse, he *would*. By Jove, he would even *do* it. Against his better judgment and wishes. "I have a meeting tomorrow with a man to help us make our parties more profitable. With a few good months, I can pay out the debt. Then, with the rent from the estate and Huntingdon Abbey, we can keep ourselves afloat. It won't be grand, but we'll be out."

"We'll be out," she echoed, as though the words themselves

9

were a balm. They'd be out even quicker if bills from the mantua-maker and milliner stopped arriving with such regularity. But nobody knew better than Beau that looking the part was half the battle.

The tea arrived, and she poured them both cups, resting a macaroon on the side of his saucer. "Give this man whatever he asks for, if he can help us."

They needed Mr. Harry Townsend's help more than the man in question could imagine. Beau knew better than to indulge in hope, but he couldn't help himself. Like everyone else in the Ton, he'd read Townsend's book *Winning at Whist*. But he saw something they did not. A sharp mind and a passing mention of cheating that suggested an intimate knowledge of the shadier side of card play. That's what he was interested in.

He had enough blunt to pay Mr. Townsend to ferret out these people like the vermin they were.

If it was the last thing he did.

CHAPTER 2

IN WHICH MISS TRUCHARD DOES NOT LOOK
A GIFT BOOK IN THE MOUTH

M iss Harriet Truchard allowed the footman to open the door of the Temple of the Muses and stepped through, breathing the new-book smell deep into her lungs. Leather, paper and ink.

Nectar of the gods.

Her velvet drawstring purse jangled with coins. Here, it didn't matter who you were. Even the daughter of England's most infamous card cheat could buy a book. A truly egalitarian experience. But books were not why she was here. *Concentrate, Harriet.*

Viscount Beaufort, likely an aging card roué, had asked to meet the author of *Winning at Whist* to hear a mutually beneficial proposal. The very idea of it still had her stomach flitting like a hummingbird's wings, ever since her publishers had forwarded the letter to her. She couldn't ask Mother about him, because her ears would prick up like a veritable terrier on the hunt.

It had only taken three lies to get here. One to Mother, saying she was going for a walk in Hyde Park. The second to her brother Bertie, so he would not accompany her; and the third to her mother's maid, who questioned why she wore her best walking dress to traipse around the grass.

But it was a small price to pay for nobody interrupting this meeting.

It was a perfect May morning, the chill in the air mitigated by sunshine streaming into the airy space. Harriet walked past the magnificent stretch of windows, to the towering bookshelves that overflowed with books. Tall ladders leaned against each bookshelf, with assistants scaling up and down them, restocking the shelves. No wonder they had such magnificent calves.

Apparently, nine in the morning was an unfashionable hour, because the bookshop and circulating library was deserted. As in, one could wheel a cannon through the large front doors and blast away without hitting a single soul. The shop was even more impressive for it. Harriet sighed in satisfaction. The perfect place for a business rendezvous. The lack of shoppers meant Harriet would spot her quarry easily. But even if it were crowded. aristocrats had a way of standing out like the preening peacocks they were.

And of course, seeing her book on the shelf was always glorious. The *ten* sweet copies sitting there warmed her heart. Perhaps the pipe dream of setting up her own establishment with Bertie was not *entirely* unrealistic.

She ran a finger down the spine of the book she had written, and pulled the slim volume from the shelf. The publisher had chosen cheap green board as the binding, suggesting her work would not live long on people's shelves. She did not care.

"A very popular choice, miss. Especially if one enjoys the game."

Harriet turned to see a young gentleman with tight curly brown hair admiring her book. *Oh, you dear thing!* His black tailcoat and buff breeches marked him as a store assistant.

The smile that spread across her face was obviously unexpected, for his eyes widened and he blinked, a flush of red appearing on his neck above his limp cravat. He nervously averted his gaze to the book in her hands.

"It was only published last year, but has already gone back for three reprintings. Not that anyone would admit needing help with their Whist. But I vow I sell a copy each and every day!"

Heaven help her, tears welled in her eyes. It was one thing to receive the irregular royalty payments from Thomas Egerton, Publisher and Bookseller, quite another to hear of copies being sold every day, and that people found it useful. "I'm sure my game is far beyond help. Could you point me toward the novels?"

The assistant led her to the fiction shelves. "And don't forget that if you would like to peruse the book, you can take it to the lounging area just up that wide staircase. If you need me, I am at the circular counter in the middle."

"Thank you." The fiction area was a good vantage point to watch for Lord Beaufort. She had a notion why he wanted to meet her. He thought there might be other secrets she had not divulged within the pages of the book, and perhaps would be willing to pay a good sum for them. A smile played across her lips and a delicious feeling of cleverness overcame her. Yes indeed, she would.

Finally, another way to earn money that did not involve fleecing some foolish innocent, as her parents would have her do.

The front door opened, and a tall man stepped inside,

taking in the entire room in one long glance. She blinked. His dark coat sat snugly on broad shoulders. The points of his white shirt were high, but not ridiculously so. Her gaze traveled quickly down his form, not wanting to stare, but eager to drink him in. Long and shapely legs were highlighted by tight breeches and hessians that were polished to within an inch of their lives. His valet had done him proud. His hair, longer than fashionable in 1812, was light brown with wondrous shafts of golden highlights illuminated by the sunlight.

He's like a beautiful lion. Please be Beaufort. Please be Beaufort.

She made her way back to the shelf where her book resided, their arranged meeting point, chuckling internally at life throwing her an unexpected pair of aces.

What fun to converse with such a magnificent creature. Of course, as soon as he opened his mouth, she would be disillusioned, as she always was by the aristocracy. However, it never hurt to dream.

His gaze landed on her for a moment, but then moved around the room. Considering she had agreed to meet him at the place where her book was shelved, she was not surprised to see him make his way to the counter and ask to be directed.

Soon, he was walking her way with the delicious saunter of a man for whom time meant nothing. Harriet watched him approach, her heartbeat banging away in time to the click of his shiny hessian boots on the wooden floor. She pretended to inspect the shelves as he came and stood beside her. He took her book from the shelf and she turned to him. "Lord Beaufort?"

He started, his gaze snapping to hers. His eyes were the color of a soft caramel, warm and with golden flecks throughout. *Oh my.* The dark brows above them pinched together. "Are we acquainted?"

"Only if you are here to meet the author of *Winning at Whist.*"

He tilted his head to one side and inspected her from the tip of her bonnet to the chin she defiantly pushed forward. "And that, I presume, is you? Or did the author send you here to meet me in his stead?"

"No, it is me."

His gaze dropped, and he frowned. Perhaps because now he would have to play by a different set of rules. Now he couldn't take her to his favorite chophouse and talk cards over a thick steak and ale. She would never know.

"You seem disappointed."

He smiled ruefully. "It does somewhat put a spoke in the wheel of what I was going to offer you."

"Please feel free to offer it, anyway. You may be surprised." *I will likely do anything legal, if it means accumulating more funds.*

He raised his eyebrows and shrugged. "I need help with the ways people might cheat in games of chance, and your book suggests you might know."

He wanted to learn to cheat? Dear, deluded aristos. They pretended to be so honorable, but inside they were a seething mess like the rest of society.

She scoured her memory for where she'd mentioned cheating. She'd tried so hard not to let her family's training or inclinations color her manuscript. "But my book is about winning, with only the barest mention of cheating."

"True, true." He motioned to the wide staircase on the other side of the room. "Come, shall we go to the lounge area upstairs? I assure you it is one of the few places in London that we can happily be in each other's company without a chaperone."

The thought of her needing a chaperone was laughable. If

anything, *he* would need one to protect *his* virtue. Such was the reputation of the Truchard family.

He did not offer her his arm. "I am astonished to find the author is a lady too young to have gathered the knowledge the book has in spades." He looked at her sheepishly. "Pardon the pun."

She groaned. "You are pardoned, but only this once. What is less forgivable is your assumption that either my youth or my gender renders me incapable of intelligent thought."

He started up the sweeping staircase that led to the lounge. "There is a world of difference between intelligence, and the jaded but superior knowledge in your book."

Her lips curved upward and before she knew it, she beamed, her joy radiating outward. "You think me intelligent? And so much so that you have sought me out for ..." She frowned. "*Cheating.* Now where in my book did I mention I would be *au fait* with such matters?"

At the peak of the staircase, they stepped into the lounging area. Furniture was scattered around the room and books were already in disarray on the nearby tables. He led her to a pair of blue chairs that overlooked Finsbury Square. "If memory serves me, there was a small section toward the back where you stated that one could never win against a cheat, no matter how much one learned and that you had faced many."

Oh. She had said that, because it was an eternal truth. She could memorize the cards until the numbers swam in her head, but if her opponent had a counterfeit ace tucked up his frilly sleeve, she was never going to win.

"Ah, yes." As usual, she was fascinated by the lengths people would go to to change their odds. "But why are you investigating cheats? Or do you want to become one?"

"I find I have the greatest abhorrence of people who break

the code of honor and cheat for their own gain and the ruin of others." There was a tic in his jaw and his expression was as sharp as daggers. *Fascinating.* Normally, the aristocracy settled such things on a lonely field at dawn, not by chasing down the author of an obscure book.

"I am sure that if you have read my book, you know there are many ways to gain an advantage that do not fall into the territory of cheating. I myself am adept at all of them."

They stood in front of their chairs. The moment stretched out with him bowing his head forward as though waiting for her to do something.

Oh. He couldn't sit until she sat, and was waiting.

He quirked an eyebrow, as if entertained, and she dropped into the chair. "As you can see, I am not accustomed to gentlemanly manners."

He lifted his coattails and arranged himself in the chair, one muscular leg crossed over the other. "There are worse things to get used to. But we're here to talk about the less gentlemanly activities that I have noticed on occasion."

"Pray tell, where have you noticed these anomalies?"

"Vingt-et-un, Faro, and Hazard."

"My, you are *quite* the gamester." Her heart sank a little. There you had it. Disappointment *always* followed any kind of admiration of the nobility.

But he shook his head. "Quite the opposite. I detest gaming in all its forms. It is the province of fools and dreamers."

Surprise lifted her eyebrows, although she could not help but agree wholeheartedly with his sentiment. Indeed, her family's income was built on this very premise.

It didn't mean she liked it or that she wouldn't move heaven and earth to escape it. And drag Bertie with her. If this man was of a similar mind, then they had more in common than he knew.

"Some people use gambling as their entertainment. Do you take issue with that, too?" She searched his face and could see nothing but derision written there.

Was he a puritan? Surely not. His attire alone firmly entrenched him in *le bon ton*. And that was before a person knew he was a viscount.

The way he effortlessly conversed with her, a complete unknown, hinted at an easygoing nature. But the way he ran his fingers along the armchair's brocade suggested something more hedonistic entirely. She was grateful for her parents' lessons in paying attention to small clues while playing cards; these minute details captivated her.

"I have no issue with people using gambling as entertainment. Indeed, it is these people I aim to protect. Knowledge is power, don't they say?"

"Yes, definitely. The more people understand how little regard many gamesters have for the code of conduct, the better everyone will be." She blinked, thinking. If Viscount Beaufort was interested in the machinations of cheating, would others be too? Could this be her second book? Would it be more of a hit than her first, or would it just give a whole generation of fools information they had not the wit to think of themselves?

"You think it is that entrenched?" His voice was wistful as he looked out the window.

"I know it is." *Careful, Harriet, don't give yourself away.* "The only question is, how much of my knowledge and time do you need?"

He looked at her steadily, unblinking, and she had the powerful impression that *he* was not a man who played fast and loose with the truth. "I cannot take advantage of you. I hoped to employ the author to spot foul play at the gaming tables. But you being a young lady, unmarried, I presume?" He steepled his hands in front of him, gazing at her over the top of his fingers, questioning.

"Distinctly unmarried," she replied primly.

"Means that there can be no question of you accompanying me."

He nodded as though his statement was the end of the argument. Harriet inwardly rolled her eyes. He was likely one of those gentlemen for whom decisions, once made, were cast in stone. Why did men think they had the right of everything, even in snap decisions that weren't necessarily logical?

But he would *not* take away her bright glimmer of hope, either for the research into this new book, or the opportunity to make a goodly sum and push her own ambitions forward.

She leaned back in her chair and smiled lazily at him, as though he amused her with his rigid proprieties. "Now then, let's not be hasty. While I may not stand shoulder to shoulder with you in a gaming hell, my services are still valuable. I could, for example, play with you while cheating in every way I have in my repertoire—"

His eyes widened. "You have a *repertoire* of cheating methods? I don't believe it."

"I have many methods that are both underhand and aboveboard. Luckily for the gamesters of London, I never gamble myself." She patted down her skirts and looked at him expectantly.

"You expect me to believe, with that arsenal and your intellect, you don't put it to good use?"

She liked the idea that he admired her mind. Because, as

Mother and Mariah were gentle to point out, she did not have her looks to recommend her.

"The definition of *good use* is subjective in this case. I am much too particular about who I play, even with fair methods. They must deserve a trouncing. A fleecing. They must need to be humbled in the worst possible way. They must be arrogant and rude. And since all those traits reside mostly in the aristocracy, where I have no entrée, you can see my quandary. Oh, I have some fun beating cits, but it palls after a time. They rage and curse at being beaten by a young dab of a thing, and then I must allow them the opportunity to recoup their losses, which only leads to deeper and deeper losses, more anger and more cursing. I may line my pockets, but it is *exceedingly* tiresome."

His eyes twinkled, and his lips curved upwards. "I should be thoroughly glad you have never graced my card parties."

She felt a spark of electricity as his gaze met hers. Her breath caught in her throat. *Concentrate on the facts, Harriet.* He was *not* a disinterested bystander or somebody who sought to do good. He was a man protecting his investment, for if she knew anything, the phrase *card party* meant a *highly organized gambling establishment run for profit.*

Her heart sank again, this time lower and with a resounding thud.

He was, in many ways, just like her parents. Both made their money off gullible gamblers, although at least he must gain a point or two for not wanting cheating to prosper. Unless it was his own cheating, of course.

"Would I be correct in gathering that your card parties have been the subject of foul play that has reduced your profits?" She looked at him as steadily as he had looked at her. He didn't shirk away from her comment—the fact he chased profit—something most nobles would consider unpardonably rude.

He nodded, with a slight smile being the only admission that the question was too direct. Searching around, his gaze lighted on a couple close enough to eavesdrop. "Come, let us walk around the store."

He led them back down the stairs to the main floor, where he picked up a basket and trailed after her, as though they were shopping together. "My Faro bank has been broken twice in the past ten days and I've heard rumors of guests losing larger amounts than normal in circumstances that left them curious. My parties are exclusive. One must be in possession of a specially made key to attend. They are also known amongst the Ton as unequivocally fair. These happenings are an assault on my honor and one that I will fight with everything I have." He spoke softly, but the ferocity in his voice caused the hairs on her arms to rise, even though she had committed no crime.

He might look gentrified, but apparently he was more like a lion when protecting his own.

She picked up a copy of *The Surprising Adventures of Robinson Crusoe* and flicked through the pages. "Perhaps my lack of social connections can be used to our advantage. I could be your greatest ally. Nobody knows me. I have no reputation to harm."

An image flashed in her mind of Mariah, bucking the Truchard trend by marrying her baronet. There was a *chance* somebody at Viscount Beaufort's card parties knew her brother-in-law, or indeed that Charles himself might attend. But it was unlikely. However, it *was* a risk. There might not be a lot of love lost between Harriet and her sister, but that did not mean she meant her any harm.

She put *Robinson Crusoe* back on the shelf, and he promptly put it in his basket. "There is no question of you attending alone. Although you might be right, perhaps we can still work together. Would you help me from afar? Perhaps come and see my gaming rooms tomorrow? I assure you my mother will be home to receive your visit. Nothing more respectable than visiting Viscountess Beaufort for tea."

"That does sound lovely. I assume you have taken your mother into your confidence about the problems?"

He shook his head. "Not completely. It is enough of a charge on her that I hold these parties at all. Knowing that I am losing wealth rather than creating it would be too much for her to bear. Her sacrifice would be for nothing."

"Perhaps you should either tell her or stop your parties altogether. If there is one thing I know, people who cheat in games of chance don't give up easily. You must confront them. There is no gentlemanly way around this. She will find out eventually."

He tilted his head and studied her intently, his eyes narrowed. "How do you know of these scoundrels?"

"I hear stories." She picked up Byron's *Hours of Idleness* and then another novel, and each time she put them down, they went into his basket. *What was he doing?*

There was a short silence between them. He was staring at her in a way men never did. Like she was interesting. "There is an air about you of someone forged in fire."

She laughed, delighted at the silly compliment. "What a lovely way to say I'm as jaded as my book suggests. My, you have a silver tongue." She dared not pick up another book, for he would think she was going to buy it, and she did not have enough money for what was already in the basket. But how lovely it felt to put them in the basket as though she could.

Dash it, she would, even if she had to leave them at the counter.

"I am not known for my compliments, so you should take that and put it in your purse with the coins I can hear jangling and begging you to buy some books. Shall I send a carriage around for you tomorrow, say eleven?"

She shook her head, panic rising in her chest at the thought of him knowing where she lived. "No need. Mayfair is not so big that I cannot walk."

"You live in Mayfair?"

"For the season." In a rented house with barely any servants and no horses or carriage. "Then we shall return to the country."

"And your name. I gather it is not Mr. Harry Townsend."

"Obviously," she said with a laugh. That was her pen name. The cover to hide her femininity and the surname that many in London would abhor.

She really didn't want to tell him her name. But there was every likelihood if she withheld the information, it would only make him more determined to find it. "Miss Truchard. But I hope that if you ever have occasion to meet my family, with the exception of my brother Bertie, you will not mention that I have a *nom de plume* and have written a book."

He smiled broadly, and it took her breath away. "I do like a good secret."

"I only care that you can *keep* it."

"It won't be much of a secret if I don't. However, I should tell you that knowing the author of *Winning at Whist* would be wonderful currency in my situation. Everyone is agog to know who the author is."

She clutched her reticule in her hands. "Be that as it may, *you* will not tell them. Are we clear?"

He raised an eyebrow. "Are you telling me what to do?" *A peer of the realm, no less?* "You amuse me."

"Make no mistake about it. And if you want my help, you'll do as I request." She stared at him, unblinking, unsmiling. He needed to know she was in earnest.

"I think I like you, Miss Truchard." His accompanying grin suggested he was not taking her even slightly seriously.

She ignored him. "Where is your residence, my lord?"

It was curtly said, because what did he mean he 'liked' her? What had she done? Or was he just funning with her? This needed to be purely business, or the thrill of meeting such a fine specimen of manhood would go to her head. Life had turned up a high card in his offer, and she was determined to finish this hand in her favor.

"We are on Portman Square. Number 20."

She curtsied. He bowed in return and carried the basket to the circular counter. It now had at least ten books, where she had coins enough for one.

"The lady would like to purchase these," he said, hearing her sharp intake of breath. "But you can put them on my account."

"Oh no, my lord, I couldn't possibly." If she took them, she would spend the entire night worrying about what it meant.

"Put them on my account," he said, handing over his card, his title printed on it in strong bold font.

The sales assistant did not take the card, and instead shook his head. "No credit here, my lord, I'm sad to say."

Lord Beaufort looked taken aback for a moment, then fished a pouch out of his pocket, putting a pile of guineas on the counter. "Count it out, there's a good chap."

"I truly cannot accept a gift from a gentleman, especially one I have just met. This is most inappropriate." Never mind how she was going to explain it to Mama when she got home. But oh, how she wanted them. She hadn't had a new book in years and the old ones had all been sold.

He stopped, as though her words finally sank in. He blinked. "Truly? You don't want them? I promise there are no strings attached. It just seemed like fun."

Pounds and pounds worth of books, a year's worth if she was lucky, and it was just *fun*.

"Very well." She could not find it in her heart to refuse.

While they waited for the assistant to wrap the package, he talked about Byron, and how he was a frequent visitor to his parties and invariably lost all his blunt and had to be rolled into his carriage roaring drunk.

The assistant returned, and Harriet picked the package up by the strings. "If you like to waste your blunt on a perfect stranger, far be it from me to argue. I don't look a gift horse in the mouth." Clutching her prize to her chest, she swung around. "I shall see you tomorrow."

She didn't wait for him to reply, but heard him say softly. "An *utterly* perfect stranger."

CHAPTER 3

A SURPRISE INVITATION

Harriet knew it was an ambush the moment she stepped into the drawing room.

The first clue was that Mariah was there, and she never visited without an invitation. Her sister was dressed in a bang-up red riding habit that made her look like she'd just inspected the troops and found them wanting.

The second clue was the look Mariah shot Harriet when their eyes met for a split second. Smug triumph and a dash of excitement sparkled in her eyes.

Dash it. She should have gone directly to the park after her meeting at the Temple of the Muses.

Seeing her elder sister perched on the sofa with a saucer on her lap was not the unmitigated delight it should be. Mariah had never recovered from the sibling rivalry that made Harriet's childhood a misery. One would think that marrying a baronet, definitely above their touch, would have sealed the competition once and for all. But all it made Mariah do was deal one smug anecdote after the other, hoping Harriet would finally see how superior she had *always* been.

Mother, of course, either didn't see this, or hoped it would inspire her to make an even more eligible match.

If only Harriet cared.

She paused at the door. That was not *quite* true.

If she could find a man to love who would love her as she was, Harriet would embrace the married state in the blink of an eye.

Escaping her parents' clutches must always be the grand plan.

But, so far, the men presented to her as eligible only wanted her skills. A wife who used her God-given talent for their increased wealth. Sitting at a card table all evening memorizing the cards and winning for them. A golden goose to have in their roost.

Her brain was such a tiresome thing, and her talent was nothing but trouble of the first order.

She did not even use it for her *own* personal gain, so why should she use it to line their pockets?

"There she is," Mother said. "I told you she could not walk in the park forever. Goodness, why on earth are you wearing your best frock?"

"Whimsy," Harriet replied. She could not tell Mother she had been visiting the bookstore, for that would only bring down the 'you are turning into a bluestocking' lecture that had ceased to become amusing some years ago.

"And I could walk in the park forever if you would let us have a dog." Harriet replied, never one to miss an opportunity. "Imagine the gentlemen that would be introduced to me if I were walking one. Men love dogs." Harriet looked down at her fingers. "I met a dear little whippet there the other day. Gray as a pigeon and sweet as a dove." The kind of dog who would curl up at the end of the bed in a snug circle of velvety softness.

Mother sighed and picked up a shortbread, nibbling a small bite and putting it on her saucer. "You know as well as I that our lives are not conducive to pets. It never ceases to amaze me how you refuse to give up asking for one."

"It's because I think our life would *expand* if we got a pet. It would enrich us." *And give me a friend.*

"*You* could enrich us if you tried or cared."

Harriet stilled and took a deep, steadying breath. Then another. It was an ancient argument and barely registered as an insult. But it was still an exasperation. One that had been itching under Mother's skin since Harriet had decided to never again play cards for high stakes, when she'd discovered that one never knew what the stakes of your opponent *actually* were; sometimes they were life and death.

Not that her parents cared. As far as the entire Truchard clan was concerned, if someone was stupid enough to bet their money, they deserved to lose it. A very black-and-white approach to something quite nuanced. But it enabled them to make their living entirely on the proceeds of gambling. Whether it be the tables, or the races or some rackety investment scheme where nobody ever made money but her father.

To be part of such a family was ... interesting.

Appalling.

Embarrassing.

And last but not least, terrifying. Because *rich one minute and poor the next*, was no way to live, and there was always the question of whether her parents were not just affable gamesters, but had delved into something more sordid. "Get me a dog and perhaps I will consider it. Perhaps." And icicles would drip from the chandeliers of hell's gaming room.

Mariah giggled. "You are like a dog with a bone yourself."

"Oh, very funny." Harriet made her way to the chair by the window, kicked off her slippers and sat down, tucking her legs under her. "To what do we owe this visit, Lady Scanlan?" Mariah enjoyed *anyone* using her title.

Her sister sat a little straighter, lifting her chin. "Charles and I are the fortunate recipients of an invitation to Lord and Lady Mandeville's ball."

Harriet took an apricot jam drop from the tray and took a bite, schooling her features so that Mariah would not realize that for once, Harriet truly *was* envious of her elder sister. A ball. The kind of ball she read about in *La Belle Assemblée*, with ladies wearing the most beautiful dresses and dancing until the wee hours of the morning. "I am excited for you. What will you wear?"

Mariah lived for any social crumbs that might be dropped from her betters, although her husband Charles seemed not to care one way or the other. But this *was* thrilling. To be invited to a proper ball, not some poor masquerade at the Pantheon where one never knew whose hand would land on your derriere.

Mariah ignored her question. "We thought to bring you with us."

Harriet coughed, and crumbs of biscuit flew in a majestic arc toward her sister and mother. They reared back. "Harriet!"

"I'm sorry. I was just surprised. Why ever would you want to bring *me* along?"

Mother and Mariah exchanged a glance. "So you can make connections and find yourself a husband," Mother said.

They turned to her and said in unison, "Of course".

29

"But …" Who would want the Truchard family as a connection? Sir Charles had married Mariah, but she'd always assumed blackmail was involved.

Mariah had obviously thought along the same lines. "Charles and I have spoken. Mother is going to travel up to Bristol to help Father with his canal project and it is the perfect opportunity to have you stay with us. You can then enter society from our household rather than this one. Mother agrees."

Harriet's eyes widened. She did? Why? How would this benefit her, other than the obvious 'one less mouth to feed' scenario? Or had she given up on her youngest daughter entirely?

It would leave Bertie alone with them, which was a sobering thought. Without Harriet in the way, they would steer him into their way of life. He'd be forever at the race-track, working the charm he had in spades to get inside information. What was worse, he'd love it.

It hurt to think badly of them, but history taught her naivety helped no one.

"If you will not use your talents for the family's better good, you should be married posthaste," Mother said.

Harriet took a sip of tea, her mind like a galloping horse as she weighed her options and the probabilities of success. "Apologies for being such a burden."

"This is your choice. You can either contribute to our family income or you can marry and start your own life and family. The same goes for Bertie. He has a decision to make, too. It's no use him spending every race day at Newmarket if his bets don't land. I did not have children for you to be a drain on our finances." She closed her eyes and took a breath that made her shoulders rise and fall. "There, now you have made me speak far too bluntly."

Au contraire, Mama. You have just confirmed my suspicions. "I prefer it. At least I know where I stand." The sly comments and exasperated sighs over the past three years had been much harder. To hear it spoken truthfully and without adornment was a blessing.

"You know I hold both you and Bertie in great affection." Mama blinked, her eyes misting over. "But we have our future to think of, and you have yours. Mariah's offer could not have come at a more fortuitous time."

Harriet took another bite of the jam drop and chewed thoughtfully, waiting a moment before replying. "I feel it incumbent upon me to point out I do not have a dowry."

Mariah pursed her mouth, inspecting Harriet like she was a dubious cut of meat. "Yes, and all that red hair. It will take a particular kind of man to overlook that."

Harriet clutched her breast and looked down in horror, as though Mariah had dealt her a mortal wound with a dagger. "Perhaps he will also overlook the woeful freckles across my nose and the way my bottom is a little too big. He must be a *paragon*, I tell you. Where shall we find such a man?" She sank into the chair as though in a decline. Teasing them was more fun than it ought to be, with her future thrown into the center of a card table like a pocket watch.

They would never find such a man. Especially when he discovered she was physically incapable of simpering and telling him how wonderful he was. Which was why it was lucky she had her writing.

"We are asking a lot," Mariah replied in all seriousness. Oh, how she must *love* this. "Mother, is there any chance you

31

could scrape together a thousand pounds? It would be better than nothing."

Mother shook her head and shrugged. "Harriet has the power to make that in a night if she so chooses. Leave it up to her. When is the ball?"

Oh, so she was to take to the gambling tables to provide her own dowry? But obviously, if it was to benefit herself, *surely* she wouldn't mind? Harriet sighed.

No. Absolutely not.

"If I must come up with that kind of money within a month, then I will not be forced to marry a man I do not wish to. If no man meets my approval, I shall take Bertie and we will set up our own establishment. That way, you are free of us both." *And I am free of your machinations, too.*

Mariah had been lucky she'd found Charles after a particularly flush time when they'd each had five thousand pounds allotted to them. Harriet had owned and lost dowries many times over the past ten years. Sometimes thousands of pounds, sometimes a few hundred. But last year, in what was generally known as the Truchard Family Disaster, not only was all available money spent, the funds set aside for both herself and Bertie were gone too.

"I hope you don't think to write that book you always spoke of, because I vow someone has stolen your very idea and it's all the rage!" Mariah crossed her hands over her lap, trying not to look pleased by the news.

"Oh dear, really?" Harriet replied as though her heart might break.

But Mariah really should know that when Harriet wanted to do something, she didn't *talk* about it for long. She just did it. They should be surprised she still didn't have a dog. But there was something about bringing an innocent creature into a house that didn't open its arms in love that made her hesitate.

"Only imagine, I was at Mrs. William's house just last week and she showed us a most diverting book called *Winning at Whist*. I flicked through the pages and saw immediately that a person with a great depth of knowledge of the game wrote it. Now that it has been done, you will have to think of another topic."

Harriet nodded as though Mariah had handed down sage advice when really all she wanted to do was spit jam drop at her again. "Perhaps it is just as well, since we are determined to marry me off. I would not like to add 'bluestocking authoress' to my red hair, freckles and large bottom." She couldn't keep the chuckle from escaping.

"I *do* wish you would stop talking about your behind," Mother said.

"True, it is the same as yours, so by insulting it, we also cast aspersions on your backside. Apologies." She hoisted herself up from the chair and took a macaroon off the tray. It was interesting that Mariah completely discounted the fact that perhaps Harriet had more than enough knowledge of the game to write a book like that. In fact, *had* written that book. The best thing about this information and the indignant look on Mother's face was that now it was obvious that Bertie could indeed keep a secret. Bless him.

"Well, that was our last chance that Harriet would create a windfall," Mother said, her mouth drooping.

As if Harriet would ever let Mother near her earnings, which she would use to finance their latest madcap scheme. No, the royalties were a freedom fund for her and for Bertie. She converted every bank draft into highly portable gems and her secret stash was growing quite nicely, thank you.

"You shall just have to think of something else," Mariah said cheerfully. "I'm sure there are many things you are knowledgeable about."

"Yes, of course. Although this does deal me quite a blow."

There was a tentative knock on the door and they all turned to see Anne, their maid while in London, standing in the doorway. "There's a Mr. Donovan asking if you're 'at home'." She said 'at home' like the joke it was since they were hardly of the aristocracy. But mother insisted on the niceties she had been raised with.

Mother instantly brightened. "Oh yes, do see him in." She turned to Mariah. "You were just going, I believe?"

Mariah blinked rapidly. Obviously, she had had no intention of leaving.

"He's not quite of your social strata. It might embarrass Charles if I introduced him to you."

Goodness, who was this scoundrel?

"I see." Mariah stood. "I'm off then, and perhaps through the servant's entrance. I'll see you soon, Harriet. If you don't have a ball gown, we can fix one of mine."

She swept out of the room, leaving Harriet to stare at her mother. "Can I go too?"

"No, no. Mr. Donovan is for you. Mariah might be working on your behalf, but your father and I have not been resting on our laurels. He is quite the catch. Not on Charles's level in society, but so wealthy, my dear, and when you meet him, you will see how ambitious he is."

A meal ticket for her and father, in other words. Where Charles had been so stingy.

She looked up as the door opened again, and her stomach dropped.

I very much think not, Mama.

CHAPTER 4

JUST BECAUSE A GENTLEMAN WANTS TO COURT A LADY ... DOESN'T MEAN HE CAN

To be fair, Harriet didn't care what social strata a man came from.

It was unlikely lightning would strike again, as it had for the beautiful Mariah, and a rich wonderful man would want to marry her. And yes, much as it hurt, Mariah was exquisite. Her black hair was glossy, her blue eyes were like pansies found deep in the forest, and her skin—well, it had, not ridiculously, been compared to moonlight. Charles never stood a chance.

Mr. Donovan bowed over her mother's hand, then brought it to his lips. "Mrs. Truchard. London air agrees with you."

Mother nodded, like such a compliment was her due. "Thank you." She turned to Harriet. "May I introduce Mr. Donovan to you, Harriet? He has recently become our friend."

When he turned to Harriet and nodded, there was a glitter in his eye that suggested calling him a 'friend' amused him. He was of medium height, his skin the color of someone who rarely saw the sun. His clothing was suitable for a gentleman, if not of the same exalted quality as Lord Beaufort's. His hessians were not nearly as shined, his coat not quite so well fitted, and something was off about the enormous size of the brass buttons on his sage-green waistcoat. But he had dressed carefully, that much was obvious.

"I will order us some more tea," Mother said, rising from her chair and going to the door. "Perhaps you would like to show Mr. Donovan the garden?"

Considering the garden was not theirs but belonged to their neighbor, this was quite brazen. Their rental was an unusual setup. From the street frontage, it looked like a normal town house, but they rented only the very front rooms on the first and second floors. The house next door had bought the property at some stage and taken the back end of the house and the entire third floor for its use, walling everything else off. It made the rent cheap.

Mr. Donovan watched her closely. There wasn't much humor in his obsidian dark eyes. "Or perhaps you would prefer just to stay here and wait for tea?"

"Thank you. I have just been for a walk and am quite fatigued." *And I would prefer not to be alone in the garden with you.*

His lips curled into a knowing smile. "Then rest we shall. It is lovely to make your acquaintance, Miss Truchard. Your parents have spoken highly of you, and I can see why." His expression was sincere. He obviously meant it.

Her brows furrowed. "How so?" Mother must have lied through her teeth. This should be entertaining.

"You don't want forced compliments, surely? Although I'm happy to give them to you, if you'll allow me to court you, as your mother thinks you will."

"I will?"

It was like listening to an Italian opera when you couldn't speak the language. You had a fair idea what was happening, but there were so many details missing.

"We should suit very well, I think."

"We should?" She couldn't think of a single way.

"Yes, of course. But let me tell you about myself. I am the son of a family in the butcher trade. My father worked all his life to leave me, his only son, a small legacy to continue on. But I dreamed of greater things and moved into banking at a young age. I was smart, smarter than the people I invested in, and now, even at eight-and-twenty, I am wealthy enough to buy my own property on Piccadilly. I've got big business plans and I would like an intelligent wife by my side to help me."

Harriet blinked. He was *very* forward. Horrifyingly so. "What have my parents told you to make you think I have any interest in business?"

But she knew the answer. *Harriet can do math in her head that took her father three sheets of paper to accomplish, she always knows which cards have been played.*

"They said you have an aptitude for games of chance." He smiled lazily. "I myself prefer a sure bet. That's what you are." This was delivered with the confidence of someone who imagined his suit was welcomed. "Together we will conquer London."

Suddenly Mariah and her ball looked very appealing. The only wonder was why Mother was letting her go when she had Mr. Donovan in her pocket. Likely hedging her bets, as she always did. "So, this courtship is a mercantile trade, then?"

He shrugged. "No need to take offense. Your noble relatives make these kinds of arrangements all the time. It's good for both parties."

Their *noble relatives* had cut them off with no contact before Harriet was born. "Pray tell, how is this good for me?"

His sidelong glance had enough heat in it to make her squirm. "It will be an excellent arrangement for you. You will have all the carriages and gowns you want, enough pin money to keep yourself in style. And me as your husband and protector."

He preened, suggesting that everything else paled into insignificance when compared to being owned by him.

And then it hit her what wasn't right about him. He might have the tailored clothing to make him look like a gentleman, he might have cultured his accent just enough to pass, but there was an air of violence about him that no amount of valet attention could erase. It coiled around his shoulders, making him seem ready to strike at any moment. What would she be marrying?

"Yes, I can quite believe it," she said, no falsehood uttered.

There must have been something amiss with her tone, for his eyes narrowed. "Don't you go thinking you're too good for the likes of me. I'll be ruling London in five years' time."

A king of the underworld, no doubt.

He gave her an assessing look. "And your parents owe me."

She looked at him squarely, unblinking. "Owe you what, exactly?"

"Let's just say I got them out of some trouble recently and they're suitably grateful, as I'm sure you would be if you knew the circumstances. Your father suggested our betrothal to even the score. Along with a hefty gold injection into your family coffers." He laughed to himself. "You're going to be an expensive wench. I can tell that already. But I'll treat you well."

The way he spoke was like their marriage was a foregone conclusion. It was not surprising. Men often thought women had no voice in their own future. This particular woman would run all the way to Land's End rather than marry a man like Mr. Donovan.

"Let's start with you visiting, shall we? My parents may not have told you, but I am considered an acquired taste." There was no way she would reject him outright. He was the kind of man who would get his revenge in every way he could.

He laughed out loud. "They told me you'd do as they bid."

She raised an eyebrow, giving him her best duchess-of-the-realm impression. "It would be the first time. I admire their confidence."

Rather than putting him off, this display of haughtiness seemed to impress him. A smile broke across his face. "There now. You'll suit me just fine."

And it would suit *her* just fine to send him on his way. But this time, she feared it wouldn't be so easy to escape the fate her parents planned for her.

CHAPTER 5

WHERE MISS TRUCHARD REVEALS HER SUPERIOR KNOWLEDGE

The next morning found Beau in his study, unable to concentrate.

He was looking forward to Miss Truchard's visit a little *too* much. The way his stomach jumped with nerves, one would think he had never been in the company of an intelligent woman before. He had, but perhaps not one as intelligent as he suspected Miss Truchard was. And beautiful. She took his breath away with her sparkling gray eyes and hair the color of a summer sunset. Not to mention the smattering of freckles across her nose that were entirely enchanting.

He shook his head. No. He must be remembering wrong. She could not possibly have been as alluring as he thought. It must have been a mixture of his excitement and the soft morning light in the bookstore. This second meeting should clear it up.

It wasn't as though he lacked female companionship, for there were many ladies, both widowed and married, who were happy to flirt with him at his parties. But that was different. For them he had to keep up the façade of the viscount who thought of little more than where his next glass of champagne was coming from, whereas with Miss Truchard he had the delicious indulgence of being totally honest. To her he was a businessman, first and foremost, which was how he thought of himself.

So perhaps that was why she felt like such a luxury.

Finally, here was somebody he could truly talk to about the things that mattered to him. Just mentioning money amongst other gentlemen would see them laugh uncomfortably and change the subject. But Miss Truchard had the gumption to publish her own book, secretly, and jumped at the chance to help him, showing she knew a good opportunity when she saw it.

He forced himself to drop the drape and took up pacing to his desk and back. *Damn it, Beau. Think about the bills piling up on the desk right there. The ones you can't seem to stem.*

Hundreds of pounds' worth.

The latest one from Monsieur Parmentier in Duke Street asked for ten pounds to cover what appeared to be nothing more than rout cakes. Certainly, twelve dozen of them, but nevertheless. He picked up another bill. How could sandwiches, tartlets, and champagne add up to such an exorbitant amount? And yet, their supper board was part of their success. No wafer-thin ham or watered-down wine at Beaufort's, and the Ton flocked to them because of it.

But it was sending him to an early grave trying to balance it all.

He imagined the scene at his funeral. "What did he die of?" they would ask, and some somber person would reply, "The high price of ham hock, I believe."

He smiled and glanced at the clock on the wall. It was almost eleven and she should arrive soon. He drew back the drapes again and looked out onto the square. There was a flutter of excitement in his stomach he couldn't quite explain. She was a mystery—speaking and looking like a lady, while it was obvious her family was not in society. He would not see her at Almack's. Many great family trees had small branches that worked for their living. He imagined her family fell into that category.

A tall man came into view, walking with a slightly shorter female companion. Her bonnet made it impossible to see the color of her hair, but by some magic, he knew it was her. The pair crossed the road, and he dropped the drape as they walked past his window.

Merrick opened the door before they could reach for the knocker and ushered them into the entry foyer, where he heard them chatting with his butler about the spring morning and what a lovely walk they'd had.

He came out, saving Merrick from fetching him, and walked toward his guests.

No, his eyes had not deceived him at the bookstore. She seemed to glow from within, her skin and eyes luminous.

He pulled his gaze away to the gentleman with her and held out his hand. He had the lanky frame of a young man not yet to reach his majority. But his shoulders were broad, and there was a power to him that suggested he liked to box. His hair was a few shades darker red than hers, his nose was aquiline and his eyes were a deep, sapphire blue as opposed to her gray. But the family resemblance was most certainly there.

He offered his hand to the young man. "You must be Mr. Truchard. I am pleased to make your acquaintance. I am Beaufort."

Mr. Truchard took his hand, a solid shake, not even slightly clammy. No nerves there. "The honor is mine, my lord. Please call me Bertie. I wouldn't want anyone confusing me for my father." He handed his coat to Merrick. "Harriet mentioned that your conversation is confidential, so I have brought along my book and will be happy in any distant corner you would like to place me."

It was all nicely said, and he had a roguish smile that would stand him in good stead with the ladies in years to come. "Yes, of course, unless you have similar skills to your sister and can add to the conversation?"

Mr. Truchard looked to his sister, as though seeking her approval. She smiled and nodded. "You can trust Bertie with your life. I know I trust him with mine. It would be useful to have him help us. He can deal."

Interesting that her brother had the same talents she did. What kind of family did they come from? One in which gambling was the primary source of income? He'd seen the desperation that engendered and did not envy her. No one's luck was ever in all the time.

He motioned for them to follow him. "Come through to the ballroom, which we have converted into our gaming room. There are a couple of smaller rooms toward the back where guests can partake of private games or supper, but the action happens here."

They followed him down the hall, their footfalls tentative. "You have a lovely home, my lord," Bertie ventured.

"Yes." He rarely thought about it, but he supposed seeing it for the first time, it would look magnificent. The entry foyer was large enough to have two cozy sofas underneath the area where the double staircase swept up to the upper levels. A large round mother-of-pearl-inlaid table graced the middle of the entry with a tall vase of roses that sweetened the air.

They followed him into the ballroom. Miss Truchard gasped behind him. "How beautiful!"

He smiled, trying to see it himself for the first time, too. It had been a beautiful ballroom before it was a gaming room. Four banks of floor-to-ceiling windows with straw-colored silk drapes, plaster friezes of country scenes, and two chandeliers that his father had brought home from Vienna as a young married man.

His heart squeezed at what he had turned it into.

Under each chandelier was a long table. One for Faro and the other for the dice game, Hazard. Smaller card tables and sofas were dotted around the room for relaxing or private games.

"Do you still use it as a ballroom?"

"Not since my elder sister's come-out six years ago." And he would have to stop this way of life before Emmeline was ready for her debut. She could not shine with the shadow of a gaming table behind her. "Mother decorated with the help of Mr. Hope. It had to be beautiful to entice the ladies of the Ton to attend with their husbands."

"Does having their wives in attendance lead to better behavior than one might find in a gentlemen's club?" Miss Truchard was still looking around in wonder.

He smiled. "Sometimes." He turned to Bertie. "To catch you up, in case your sister has not told you, my gaming tables have been severely challenged by what I believe to be—"

"Foul play?" Bertie finished with a raised eyebrow.

"She told you?" His gaze snapped to her, and she raised an incredulous eyebrow as though to say 'don't be silly'.

Bertie shook his head. "No. But why else would you ask her here? If anyone knows how to ferret out foul play, it's Harri."

Harri. It suited her. It was vibrant and slightly mischievous. Even without knowing her long, he knew it fit.

Would he ever get to call her that? Likely not.

She pursed her lips, looking annoyed. "I would like to make an important distinction that, while I *know* of these means, I never use them."

Bertie snorted. "Much to Father's disgust."

She threw her brother a warning glance that made his eyes widen. Very well, he was not to know who they were. But he would eventually. Knowing about people, after all, was *his* talent now, honed over the past five years of exposure to human behavior. He knew where the secrets were and who held them. "I'm sure no man would want his daughter to do such a thing."

She ignored the comment in a way that suggested it was so naive it was beneath her. "You are wrong, Bertie. Father does not want me to *cheat*, he just wants me to *win*."

Beau was intrigued. "And you refuse?"

"I have already told you how exhausting it is to play even people who deserve to be fleeced. Of course I refuse."

"So do I," Bertie added with quiet pride. "Although I'm not Harri with the cards."

"And what can Miss Harriet do with the cards?"

She waved her hand away. "Only what my grandfather could. In any given game of Whist, I will know how many of the trumps have been played, and which cards of each suit have been played. I may have to concentrate and be very still, but if I see the cards played, I remember them. A simple trick, really."

There was nothing simple about it.

Miss Truchard, although it was difficult not to call her Harri now in his mind, clapped her hands. "Well, that's enough of that. Let's get a fresh pack of cards and I can show you the ways people will win at all costs, whether or not they have a father pressuring them."

He led them to a table by the window where he had two sets of cards at the ready. He pulled the chair back for Miss Truchard and she sat and handed Bertie the pack of cards. "Let's talk about people tampering with your cards first."

"I check them after each party. I look for pinpricks, thickening, or any discoloration."

"Good. Have you ever found anything?"

"No."

She shrugged. "That's a good start." She pursed her mouth. "I must tell you that the most obvious cheating comes from the person dealing the cards or dice, especially since you have been losing money consistently. So, in your case, the person administering the Faro bank or the Hazard table."

He knew that, too. "That is not my problem."

She tilted her head to one side, brow furrowed. "Are you dealing, then?"

"No."

She blinked once, slowly. "Then they *are* a potential problem. I know they cannot win any money when they deal, but if they are in league with people playing at your tables—"

"Impossible." He bristled. "I employ men of the highest integrity. Each one of them was an officer of the Royal Navy, wounded at Trafalgar." *Each one of them beyond reproach.*

Her expression softened. "Your loyalty does you credit." *Even if it is imbecilic.* He was sure that was the rest of the sentence. He could read her expression clearly enough. "But you will understand if I come to my own conclusions." She looked at her brother. "Deal us for Vingt-et-un, so I can show Lord Beaufort how easy it is for a dealer to cheat."

"I assume he is going to deal underhandedly?" Bertie looked too young and fresh to have any idea how to go about it.

But, then again, so did Miss Truchard.

She nodded. "Bertie will deal the first time, and you can watch him as closely as you like. Then we will play again, and we'll show you what he did. Vingt-et-un is interesting in that all past play affects future play. If one has a good enough memory, it goes beyond being a game of chance to being a game of skill. I can memorize all the cards floating through until I know, just by the odds, when it's a good time to bet."

"And when is that?"

"Well, because we're aiming to reach twenty-one, it's when a large proportion of the lower cards have been played, leaving a higher proportion of high cards like kings, queens, knaves, and aces. Of course, Bertie is also going to work his magic to make sure all those high cards are nicely concentrated for me after a few rounds."

"Family card parties must be a riot at your house."

"Indeed," she said dryly. "Never a dull moment."

Bertie shuffled the cards like they were an extension of his hands. Smooth and professional, his eyes fixed on the windows. Then he dealt them both one card, face down, then another. Nothing seemed untoward. They played five games, using his betting tokens, and everything seemed legitimate. Then, on one particular hand, Miss Truchard bet all her buttons and smiled at him.

Against the usual rules, she put her cards down so he could see them. Just a ten of clubs. No real way she should be betting every last token.

Sure enough, the next card was an ace.

"Luck of the draw," he drawled and sat back in his chair.

He'd been watching closely. Bertie had dealt with perfect propriety.

She cocked her head to one side, considering him. "Are you sure?"

"Entirely. I watched him closely."

"Bertie, show his lordship just how it was less luck and more artifice."

This time Bertie slowed down to one hundredth of the speed he had previously used.

Miss Truchard leaned forward. "Bertie shuffled the initial deck correctly, but then, as we finished each hand, he picked up the high card first and low cards second. That way, he always knew exactly where in the deck the high cards were. When he had the order perfect for me, he touched his nose and I bet everything."

Beau watched closely. And it was true. The young man was only shuffling the middle part of the deck.

"You see, the high cards remain on the top. Then ..." she looked at her brother. "Deal for his lordship, my dear." She turned back to Beau. "He will deal you cards from the bottom of the deck only."

Beau watched in horror as Bertie did just that, although even going slowly, it still looked like he was dealing from the top. That would be an incredible skill if it wasn't so terrifying. Did his dealers know how to do that? They certainly seemed as adept as Bertie.

"While I will get the high cards he knows I need to win the hand."

Beau blinked back his confusion. He would expect such adroit cheating from a wizened old knave. *Who were these two?* He must find out and discover the web of people they associated with. But how to get her to talk, when she was being so guarded about her personal details?

While his mind was still reeling, she put down her cards and led him over to the Hazard table. "Come, that's enough." She fished into her reticule for a couple of sets of dice. "See these? Clever, no?"

He inspected them and couldn't see anything amiss. "Are they weighted strangely, so they roll in a certain way?"

"Oh no, nothing so industrious." She held them up for him. "It is just that every side has either a four, five, or six. But our eyes can only ever see three sides of a die from any angle we look at it, so nobody realizes. You play these when it is your turn, and palm them as soon as you can." She showed him how. Both of them could tuck the dice into their palm and a person would be none the wiser. "And if the dealer puts the dice in, he would put dice with only low numbers, so the house wins. In fact, it is much easier for a dealer to do this. I suppose he could do it on behalf of a certain player?"

Bertie nodded. "If they are in cahoots, anything is possible." He stroked his chin. "And don't forget that with enough practice, people can control the throw of the dice. They'll hold it in a very particular pattern in their palm, barely shake it, and throw instead of roll. I've seen Father foretell exactly what he's going to roll twenty times in a row.

And then on to the Faro table, where Harriet looked at the green baize mat with disgust. "There is a reason Faro is outlawed. Are you unaware?"

Because the bank almost always won, and if tended by an unscrupulous person, huge amounts could be lost in short periods of time. "If only it weren't so popular, perhaps I would do away with it."

She nodded. "It's an exciting game. Everyone betting at

once, throwing their money on the table. I've seen it descend into a kind of madness. But that's also the reason it's easy for whoever is controlling the Faro bank to cheat."

"I pay them a guinea a shift to avoid this very thing. I don't know anywhere else that pays so handsomely. Surely they wouldn't risk it?" He would have to introduce her to his men, so she knew she was wasting her breath.

Or was *he* being naive?

"What if they could gather enough to feed their families for five years in a few months? I don't know your men. But I am aware of dealers who can manipulate the Faro deck to result in more sets of pairs coming through."

"Is there a way for the players to cheat?"

She nodded. "In the hullabaloo, they could shift their bet on the table." She frowned. "But mostly I have heard about dealers having a card of choice in the palm of their hand and depositing it on top of the dealing box through a sleight of hand. Normally to favor the bank, but it could also favor any player. It's dark in gaming rooms, isn't it? Anything can happen by candlelight. And if your bank has been broken twice in ten days, well, that would be deuced unlucky, wouldn't it?"

"What else? Because so far I could not detect anything you've shown me. Especially when I cannot be at all the tables all night." So many ways for people to cheat. Whatever happened to honor among gentlemen? And which gentleman stole from him? Because these parties were by invitation only, which meant that he either employed the thief, or he had the thief's name on a list somewhere.

"Which is why I advise clearing your staff and starting again." She said it crisply and without emotion. Just a decision, like whether to have champagne or punch.

He shook his head. "Impossible. These men would never find employment elsewhere. Why get rid of everyone when maybe only one is guilty of any crime?"

She shrugged. "The choice is yours. Now you are armed with knowledge, at least."

It was becoming very clear that behind that lovely facade, a hardened gamester resided. If someone like her visited Beaufort's, he would be helpless to stop her robbing him of every penny he had. Which meant, of course, that she was the perfect person to help him.

She turned to him, a question in her gaze. "Is that all, my lord? Or is there some other way we can help you? Those are my best recommendations."

She glanced at the door, obviously eager to be gone without exposing herself or her brother any further. When he'd thought she would have insight, he'd had no idea the gold mine he'd landed on. He must find out more about her before she slipped through the door never to be seen again.

"Thank you, I appreciate your expertise." *Your astonishing and ill-gotten expertise.* "Could we have a few words in private?"

She nodded, and her brother picked his book up off the table. "I shall make good use of this book then. I'll be in the corner."

"Perhaps a rubber of Piquet while we talk?"

Piquet was a highly skilled game and took much concentration. If she slipped up, perhaps he'd find out more.

This was a game he could win.

CHAPTER 6

WHERE MISS TRUCHARD CAN'T DENY
HERSELF THE PLEASURE OF WINNING

B less Bertie for not batting an eyelid when Lord Beaufort had asked for a quiet word while they played Piquet. He would know she had things she needed to discover, which he could only hinder by being part of the conversation. He'd always been very good at picking up her cues.

The question was, what was Lord Beaufort trying to discover? She took a deep breath. Whatever it was, he wouldn't get it from her unless she wanted to give it. He would soon find out that her focus could not be broken. And wouldn't it be fun to turn the tables on him and discover things he'd rather keep hidden?

But if she could earn her way into his good graces, he might introduce her to some gentlemen of his acquaintance if he was at the Mandeville's ball. If he did, then she would sit on this gilded chair all afternoon. It was really no imposition.

She smiled to herself. "Did I tell you my next book is titled *Profiting from Piquet?*"

"What about *How Not To Be Cheated at Cards.*" He fetched a cribbage board to keep score, and a deck of cards.

"That's a good title. I might use it. Or maybe *Victory Over Vingt-et-un.*"

"*Play Me at Your Peril,* or, *How to Spot a Cheat.*"

"Ha! Perfect. Is that a Piquet deck, or do I need to split it?" Harriet held out her hand for the cards. A Piquet deck had only thirty-two cards from the ace down to the seven in each suit.

"It is." He handed it to her, watching her as she shuffled the deck.

She gracefully flipped the cards, then riffled them back together repeatedly. Every time the cards clicked against each other, she felt a sense of calm wash over her and her breathing deepened. The south-facing room was bathed in sunlight and radiated a happiness no gaming room should. Did she trust her instincts and therefore Lord Beaufort?

"Does shuffling cards help you think?" His voice interrupted the meditation.

"It always has." She shrugged a shoulder. "I played with decks of cards before I learned my letters."

"I thought so. You are not unlike my Uncle Horace. He shuffles cards like a master, and being nearly blind makes no difference to his skill." His expression softened as he spoke, his eyes alight with admiration.

"Did he help you establish your parties?"

"Indispensably. He hired my dealers from naval men he knew, and manages them daily for me. My cousin Thomas helps him. I would be lost without them, truth be told."

And there was the reason he refused to look at his staff. His uncle was likely the closest thing to a father he had and his cousin might be more like a brother.

Now she understood.

"I'm sure it honors him to be of help to his brother's son,

too," Harriet said softly. To have elders one could trust implicitly, knowing they always had your best interests at heart, must be such a comfort. There were many things to envy the viscount for, but for her this was the greatest and had nothing to do with his title.

He lounged back in his chair. "I suggest that with each rubber, the winner is allowed to ask the loser a question as a prize."

She laughed. "Why would I agree to that?" She should have run while the going was good, but the chance of further opportunity here had her riveted.

"Let's just say I want to know more about you."

"I am only giving you advice on how people can cheat on a gaming floor. You don't *need* to know anything else about me." But with her skill, it would definitely be a chance for her to learn more about *him*.

He stroked his chin. "I think I do."

"I like the way you assume it will be you asking the questions."

"I consider playing Piquet to be a personal strength."

She smiled to herself. How typical of a man to think that just because he was good at a game, it was most likely he would win. An excited tingle raced down her spine. Drat the man, he had triggered her competitive streak. Now she just wanted to have *fun*. "My family considers me a middling player, so perhaps you are right. I will deal."

"You will deal, even though it puts you at a disadvantage from the outset?"

She nodded her assent. "Let there be no excuses when you lose." Being the dealer, she had to give him first chance to improve his deck by discarding his cards and pulling from the remaining eight cards in the middle. She could only pick from the leftovers.

He laughed. "But you won't cheat?"

She let out an exasperated huff. "To think I thought you understood me." She needled him with her best glare. "No."

"Just checking." A smile tugged at the corners of his mouth.

She dealt them both twelve cards, placing the remaining eight between them.

He inspected his hand, his gaze darting along the length of it. She did the same, making mental notes of all the different combinations that would score her points during the rubber. He swapped five of his cards, leaving her only three. That was the disadvantage of dealing. She discarded a couple of sevens, happy with the way the rest of her hand looked.

They went through the sequence of play for the first rubber, winning points based on beating the other's combinations, with Beaufort meticulously marking down each score. Each time he did, he shot her a sparkling gaze she couldn't interpret. Was he flirting, or merely as excited by the stakes as she was?

She had never been one for flirtation during card play, but something about this felt new, exciting and a little nerve-racking.

His gaze held a challenge and a lightness that suggested this play was fun for him, too.

She shifted her weight in the chair, lifting her chin. What game were they playing here, exactly? Was it Piquet or something else entirely?

By the time they had moved on to the sequences part of the rubber, Beaufort was fifteen points in front.

It did not bother her. Although when they reached the end,

she was dismayed to see that with the extra ten points he would gain, he would win the rubber.

"Drat," she said. "Well played."

He smiled a lazy smile that she hoped Bertie didn't see from his reading corner. There was way too much heat in it.

"Ask me if you must," she said, rolling her eyes.

"I *do* like a good loser," he said.

"It was only the first rubber. I may yet win the other five."

"You may." But his expression suggested it was very unlikely.

Her blood boiled just a little, heating her cheeks.

"My question is this. How do your parents make their living?"

It was entirely expected, but still created a small stab of hurt. He didn't trust her, or her kin. Well, he should probably learn that was a wise choice. "My parents earn their living in varied ways. They gamble, place money on the horses, run investment schemes and, once, my father ran boxing matches from The Quick Fox in Scarborough."

"An industrious couple," he said with mild surprise. She'd bet anything it was impossible to move him from that mild kind of reaction. He was such an aristo.

But Harriet turned to stare out the window, thinking that this was possibly the kindest way to interpret what her parents did. "They would not know an honest day's work if it bit them on the behind. My elder sister Mariah had the blessing of growing up mostly when they were ripping through a big win. But for Bertie and me, it has been a mixed bag."

There now. Enough said. The question was answered.

"Lean times?"

Drat. How could she not answer a question nobody had

ever asked? She'd been carrying this burden for her and Bertie for so very long. "Times when we had to leave a house in the dead of night with nothing but the clothes on our back and whatever furniture we could fit on a wagon. Times when every trinket they gave me for birthdays was pawned. Grandfather's watch, gone, and all Mother's jewelry. When they were flush with funds, we lived in Mayfair for the season and Mother and I got dresses in the latest fashion. You just never know quite which kind of year it is going to be."

"And obviously there is *no question* of saving against these leaner years." He emphasized 'no question' as though he understood what it was like to have foolish parents.

Now she was telling him *far* too much. "But why would you when you believe your luck is about to sail in and nothing can hold you back?" She smiled ruefully. "A note from the future, luck never stays in the harbor for long."

"There is no such thing as luck."

She nodded in agreement. It was such an unpopular opinion that she never voiced it. Even Bertie hated her saying it. "There are only odds and probabilities."

He looked up at her as if much struck. "Precisely." He blinked, looking down at the deck he shuffled as though surprised and somewhat shaken. Perhaps it was to be expected. Sometimes it felt like their entire society—from the duke wagering a fat roll of guineas on the turn of a card, to a butcher backing a horse at Newmarket—was addicted to gambling their lives away. Everyone was waiting for their luck to turn.

They'd be waiting a long time.

"Far better to make your own luck," she said blandly, watching as he dealt her twelve cards for their second rubber.

"You are telling me far more than I asked for."

What could she say? He was ridiculously easy to talk to. And somehow, she wanted him to understand her. "I don't know why, but I feel it's important you know that Bertie and I are not cut from the same cloth as my parents. We work honestly and hard to make our way. They will never understand us, just as I can never understand them."

"What happened to make you this way?"

She smiled down at her cards. *No more, my lord.* "That is, perhaps, a story for another day."

They were evenly matched in the next rubber, although Harriet pulled away in the final phase, getting twelve tricks in a row. "That is my capot, I believe," she said and was pleased to see him add forty points to her score.

A few minutes later, the second rubber was concluded in her favor. She exhaled. Good. He wasn't her superior in the game. That would have been hard to take.

"My question," she said, leaning back in her chair, "is what on earth happened to make you open your family home as a gaming house?"

He grimaced, as though, like her, it was the most obvious first question, but also the one he wanted to answer least. "It's a story you could probably hear on any street corner. It's so well known."

"I'm not one for idle gossip, my lord."

"Call me Beaufort or Beau. Everyone does." He looked down at his fingernails. "I inherited debt, a mountain of it. My father didn't gamble, but he did speculate."

"They often amount to the same thing."

He nodded in agreement. "None of this might have happened if he hadn't made so much money off earlier American land schemes. That kind of windfall can make one feel like a god, like nothing could go wrong and that somehow your intelligence in picking it had something to do with its success. Nothing could be further from the truth. The next investment went middling well and then along came North American Land Company. He had the misfortune of believing in it so strongly that he mortgaged our assets to buy into it. Needless to say, he did not get out of that investment fast enough and lost everything when it collapsed. He continued on for a while, a shadow of himself, then suffered a massive seizure that had him linger for three days before shuffling off this mortal coil." He took a deep breath. "And I had to do something about the debt."

"So you did this?"

He paused for a moment as if to add more, but then changed his mind. "I did this."

"Do you want to keep doing it?"

"Now that's another question."

"I'm sure I know the answer. It needs to be of short duration and it already feels like too long. And now maybe someone is stealing from you. Pushing back that date when you can pack up these tables and turn it back into a ballroom. Before you lose yourself in its darkness. It is no way to live."

"I agree." She saw the sadness descend on his features and wondered what his gambling parties were doing to relations with his family. His mother lived there. He also had sisters to take care of. Having them debut from a house running gambling parties was not ideal. "How many sisters do you have?"

"Two. Beatrice is my elder sister and is happily married. Emmeline will be coming out next year. I also have a younger brother, Benedict, but he is at Eton."

Nobody knew better than her what it was like to be a young lady at the mercy of a house focused on gambling.

Certainly, the situation was different, but it was enough the same to make her heartstrings tug for the sisters she would likely never meet. And maybe there was the chance to make a difference to someone like her. To make up in some small way for all the times her parents had cheated people out of their hard-earned money. In the blink of an eye, she went from wondering if he was flirting and if this was the last time she would see him, to wanting to help him in any way she could.

This was no time to play games. "Well then. Fixing this becomes of vital importance. Enough Piquet. Let's make a plan."

He wiped his brow. "Thank goodness. I was about to expire under the weight of all that truth. I don't know what I would have done if you'd won another rubber."

"Squirmed and answered my question about why you have never married."

His cheeks reddened with a blush, even as he shook his head at her brashness. "Worse than my mother, I vow. What's the plan?" He took a deep breath and exhaled. He had been shouldering this burden just as she shouldered hers.

"Very tight surveillance. You need people we can trust on each table, looking for any signs of false shuffling, any signs of cards being tampered with. Checking the dice after every roll on the Hazard table, watching for any kind of communication between the dealer and the players on the Faro table. And take all the mirrors down from the walls."

"Oh?"

"They are a perfect communication tool that people seldom notice. I could signal to somebody on the opposite side of the room with my back turned to them."

He cursed softly and shook his head. "That tip alone was worth bringing you here. My thanks." His mouth twisted.

"The problem is that the people I trust would not know what to look for. I couldn't see Bertie doing it and he was going slowly."

"I've already suggested you stand down your entire staff. If you aren't willing to do that …"

He searched her face. "Will you come, and will you bring Bertie too? Would you do that for me?"

Could she? She was still a young lady whose mother tracked her every move. Going to the bookstore had been challenging enough. How would she escape a few nights a week without anyone noticing? "I … I don't know. It would not be good for a single lady to visit a gambling establishment. Even if Bertie escorted me, he is only just eighteen. And what would I tell my parents?"

"You are right. I forget myself. Please, let us not speak of it again. I will rope my friends into helping me. They've seen enough dirty card playing that watching closely should do the trick."

He was wrong. It took a person honed in the skill of card manipulation to notice another person's particular method. Bertie could, of course. Her parents could do it; better than she. But there was no way she would suggest her parents should enter his establishment. They were more likely to see a soft mark and fleece him for everything they could.

They were good like that. *Sans Merci was the family motto for a reason.*

Beaufort rose from the table. "Come, then. I have your payment in my study."

"But we haven't negotiated a payment."

"Yes, but I appreciate your help, and I hope that by paying you well, I might entice you to come and visit me again when I have more information."

Bertie closed his book and followed them out of the room at a discreet distance. Beaufort led her into a room at the front of the house, just off the entry foyer. The first thing she saw when she entered the study was not a bookcase or a desk, but a board with hand-drawn portraits plastered all over it.

Intrigued, she moved closer to inspect it.

"Not the usual gentlemen's study art, I know," Beau said, stopping beside her.

"Who are they?" She tried to sound innocent, but an idea of the board's purpose was already forming, very clearly, in her head.

"Suspect people banned from entry into gambling establishments. See? I have done *some* research. Each of the gambling dens and hells around town has a board, just like mine. I had an artist go in and copy them, with the owner's approval, of course."

She glanced at him. "But I thought your evenings were very select and by invitation only?"

"True, but you would be surprised by the number of forged invitations and, on occasion, real invitations, that people use to gain access. They assume, because I allow both ladies and gentlemen to play, that there will be many lambs to fleece."

She scanned the faces, not surprised to see more than a couple of her parents' friends in the line-up. "Are these people criminals?" She searched row by row for Mr. Donovan, almost hoping to find him so it would confirm her suspicions. But no.

"Bow Street are interested in questioning more than a few of them. If they do visit, I am instructed to let them in with no quibble and fetch the Runners."

"Oh."

"Take these two." He pointed to draw her gaze to a man and a woman in the very bottom row. "They have been blackballed, but now Bow Street want to talk to them about a canal project they are raising funds for. They call themselves Mr. and Mrs. Taylor, but I doubt any of the names are real."

A very familiar pair of faces stared back at Harriet. They were old renderings, but it was hard not to recognize one's own mother and father when they stared back at you.

Fear coursed through her veins, and an icy chill of dread rose in her chest.

For the first time, she was thankful for the skills instilled in her from a young age. To never show emotion on your face, or give your hand away. But that same hand shook, so she shoved it into the folds of her dress.

Pictures of Mother and Father in every gaming room in London, warning owners they were wanted for questioning by authorities. What on earth had they done? And how long ago? And the canal project was a sham too? She should have known it.

If she thought about it, their visits to gaming hells had stopped abruptly. Perhaps they almost got caught, resulting in their pictures being on the wall.

How mortifying. But her racing heart suggested she was closer to terrified. Her parents were a hair's breadth away from being thrown into Newgate. They weren't funning, and they didn't teach Harriet and Bertie about how to cheat so they would never get cheated. It was so that they could go to places off limits to their parents.

Rotten apples falling from a rotten tree.

"But now, enough of these villains. Your payment!" He went to his desk, opened a drawer, and pulled out a small black box. He tipped something glittery into his hand and looked up at her. "Take your pick."

She blinked at the colorful pile of emeralds, sapphires, rubies and diamonds. Was he in jest? Did he know she collected gems with her savings? "No, no. That's most inappropriate." Even if she would desperately love any one of them. *Be a Truchard for once in your life, Harriet.*

His face fell. "Is it? Would you prefer guineas? I can do guineas." He sounded so eager to please that her heart squeezed.

"It's really not necessary. Both Bertie and I have been much diverted this morning. I hope we have been of some small help to you." She paused. "Actually, there is something you *could* do for me that might cost you a little pride, but would mean the world to me."

His gaze shifted to her lips and then back to her eyes, and she could feel the curiosity radiating from him. "My pride? You have piqued my interest."

"My sister is taking me to the Mandeville's ball the week after next. Would you stand up with me?"

"I would have stood up with you without you asking. You know this, surely?"

A spark of embarrassment and pleasure zipped through her body.

He lifted her chin, his fingers gentle yet firm. The heat in his gaze was unmistakable as he looked into her eyes. "You will be the loveliest in the room. But I thought you did not mix in rarefied circles, as you said the other morning?"

"My sister Mariah married Sir Charles Scanlan. She would like me to 'make connections' as she says. She is wasting her time, of course, and I think even she knows it."

His lips curved in a half-smile. "Perhaps." It wasn't an insult. But that didn't mean she understood what he meant.

"Wh—" She was about to ask him to elaborate when Bertie knocked on the open door.

"Come now, Harriet. Time for us to be off."

"I was just trying to give your sister some gems in payment," Beaufort said, "but she would prefer a country dance."

"A waltz might be nicer," Harriet countered.

"Or the dance before supper. That's what I should have."

"I would like that," Harriet said. Her voice sounded soft and shy, even to her own ears.

What was happening to her?

Bertie was transfixed by the portraits, just as Harriet had been. A montage of people, thugs and adventurers, who had floated through their sitting room.

He looked at her, panic in his eyes that only she could read. A slight tightening around the eyes in an otherwise amiable expression.

I feel the same way. They had to get away from their parents before the entire house of cards fell down on top of them. Why, oh why, had she not taken the gem?

———

Long after they left, Beau stood in his study looking at the board and the dubious portraits displayed there. "So, my lovelies. Who is it here that you know?" They knew someone on that board, and he would find out who.

The mystery of Miss Truchard continued, but it was a mystery he very much intended to solve.

CHAPTER 7

WHERE RICHES ARE ONLY THERE TO BE SPENT

Bertie waited until they were a suitable distance down the street before saying, "What on earth were Mother and Father doing on the wall of Lord Beaufort's study like common criminals?"

They walked down Portman Square, toward home. The footpaths were so clean and cared for here. Elegant town houses lined the street, tall and imposing. They were houses for diplomats, politicians and aristocrats. Not for the likes of the Truchard siblings.

"Along with Monsignor De Pallier and Mr. Blackmore? Now, let me think …" She tapped her chin, though in truth, no thought was really needed.

"I'll tell you what *I* think! They've involved in shady dealings," Bertie shook his head. "Well, beyond winning money from unsuspecting striplings, which is bad enough."

Harriet nodded grimly. "Lord Beaufort said they were known as Mr. and Mrs. Taylor and were wanted by Bow Street for a canal project. Sound familiar?"

Bertie ran a hand through his tousled hair. "By Jove! And

Father has me telling everyone at Newmarket about it. I'll end up behind bars myself!"

Since that was Harriet's secret fear, she couldn't disagree. "Everyone on that wall is barred from the gaming halls. Now it makes sense why they stopped gaming, and why they're so keen for *us* to start. The whole 'passing the baton to the next generation' was because they've been blackballed."

Bertie looked up to the sky. "Remember when we were little, they always had us writing letters to far away uncles and aunts asking for money?"

Harriet nodded. "Relatives we had never met?"

"Yes, those ones. *Were* those people related to us, or was it just another of their schemes?" He clenched his fists. "We were fools."

Harriet sighed. "We were children who loved their parents and wanted to please them."

Bertie swung around, his usually placid expression twisted in anger. "That doesn't excuse us now. Why are we still living with them, now that we know this? I can't do it anymore, I just can't." Twin blotches of red bloomed high on his cheeks. "We must do something."

"Agreed. It's only a matter of time before we get dragged into their troubles. I have another idea for a book, which I've just decided to call *How to Spot a Cheat,* where I'm going to reveal every trick they ever taught us. I will set us up in an establishment."

Bertie huffed. "That will take too long. We have to do something now. But what am I going to do? I have no occupation. All I've been trained for is how to play cards and how to pick a winner at the track. Fat lot of good I am." It was said with all the bitterness his eighteen years could muster.

"What would you like to do, love? If there's a way I can

contrive it, I will. There must be some cit who'd like to be fleeced by me. No cheating of course, just my natural prowess." She smiled up at him, but he didn't smile back. She would never do it for herself, but for Bertie, she would run that gauntlet time and time again.

He bent his head. "If you must know, and you'll hate it, I'd like to join the army."

Surprise rippled through her. He'd never so much as *mentioned* the army. But now she thought about it, he liked to frequent chophouses and pubs where the soldiers gathered. What's more, his natural sporting aptitude and negotiation skills would stand him in good stead in a military career. She didn't want to lose him, but couldn't find it in her heart to object.

Instead, she allowed her face to light up, and bestowed her most approving smile on him. "That would be *just* the thing for you. You're so brave and strong. They would be lucky to have you, even if I would worry myself silly the entire time. Which regiment would you like to join?"

"Wherever I can, really. But there is little use me being a cavalry officer because, while I can pick a winning racehorse, I have had little opportunity to hone my riding skills."

"But you are a crack shot and fight well with a sword."

"Yes. So maybe an infantry regiment. The Foot Guards or the like."

"It would be a waste of your brain, though. Have you thought about the Royal Engineers?" That would keep him more out of harm's way if only he would consider it.

He turned to her, eyebrows raised. "Engineers! No, by Jove you have to study at the Royal Military Academy to get a commission with them. I would rather be a soldier."

"You certainly know a lot about this!" Which only proved he'd been thinking about it for some time. "Very well." How could she make it happen? "How much is it to purchase colors these days?"

"I think near four hundred pounds to be an ensign in a regiment of foot."

She coughed despite her best attempts not to appear surprised. "We can do that." Such a large figure, but if you said it quickly it didn't sound so bad. Her secret stash of gems could possibly amount to that after all these years of saving. She would have to find out.

"We can?" He looked at her with doubt in his eyes.

"Why yes, my darling boy. I can do that right now. I have been saving for our future, you see, even if Mama and Papa have not." And certainly, this would limit her own maneuverability for the short to middle term, but it would be worth it to see him established in a career.

"Harri," he said her name as a long groan. "I won't let you use what you've saved."

She shrugged. "Unfortunately, you will have no choice in the matter. With me going to stay with Mariah, I need to know you are taken care of and that those parents of ours don't embroil you in something that lands you in Newgate. You can fight for England instead."

"I would prefer that, if possible. But you must allow me to pay you back."

She looked at him sideways. "You are aware that is called 'cashing out'? You need only promise me you will live long enough to do that one day."

"I will be clever and brave."

"Less bravery, more caution."

"Agreed."

"Very well. I will make it happen."

Somehow. Lord Beaufort had intimated knowledge of the military. Perhaps this connection would yield different but more important fruit.

CHAPTER 8

WHERE A SISTER TRULY BECOMES A SISTER

Mariah led Harriet down a wide hallway, then opened a door into a large bedroom. "This is your bedroom. I hope it suits."

The room was a calming shade of light blue, with paintings of pastoral scenes hanging on the walls. The furniture was sparse, as you might expect from a rented town house, but tasteful, with a bed, dresser and nightstand. The windows were large and let in the morning sunlight, which highlighted a large patch of the thick Aubusson rug.

"It's beautiful," Harriet said, turning to Mariah with a smile. "Thank you."

Mariah nodded, pleased. "I'm glad." Her sister perched on the edge of the bed and patted the space next to her. "You must treat this as your home. I know I have not been the best of sisters, but if I can do you this small service, perhaps it will go some way to you forgiving me."

Harriet had never thought there would be a situation where she and Mariah would be on good terms, thinking it more likely they would carry on sniping and bickering until they were gray.

Even now, with her sister giving her the very best guest room in their Wimpole Street town house, Harriet still felt distrustful. But what if this were a turning over of a new leaf, and she could actually have a sister, someone she could trust?

The thought was so absurd.

She decided to test it out.

"I can't tell you how much I appreciate the invitation to the ball. And also getting me out from Mother's pressures, even if it is only for a couple of weeks."

"A couple of weeks to start with," Mariah said. "Mother wouldn't agree to anything more. But we shall see. If you are being courted, she will be happy to let you stay, I'm sure."

"Two weeks is not long to have someone fall in love with me."

Mariah shrugged. "Charles and I fell in love quickly. It happens. But more than anything," Mariah continued. "I want you to have the same chance I did. It isn't fair that she is asking you to gamble for your own dowry when one was provided to me. I am so lucky having Charles as my husband, and his family are considerate of me in a way Mother and Father are not capable." She shook her head ruefully. "Not that I mean to speak badly of them. They did the best they could, I'm sure."

"The good lord should not bless some people with children," Harriet said with a smile.

Mariah reached down and put a hand on her stomach. Looking back up at Harriet with a slight expression of wonder.

"Are you in a delicate way?"

Her sister nodded, a slow smile spreading across her face. "It is early days yet, but yes. Please don't tell anyone."

"Who would I tell?" Harriet said, placing her hand over Mariah's and squeezing. "I am so happy for you both. You will be a wonderful mother. And I will be a fabulous aunt."

It also explained her changed attitude. Everything was going right in Mariah's world and the joy was spilling over. Well, Harriet would be happy to catch it. This visit could be about so much more than whether she could find admirers. If she could leave in a few weeks with an actual sister? She would be entirely satisfied.

She hesitated, uncertain whether she could trust Mariah. "Do you know what Mother and Father plan for Bertie? I am concerned."

Mariah bit her lip. "I don't know a lot," she said after a long pause.

But she knew *something.*

"He is far too young to be embroiled in their plans."

"But this plan sounds legitimate. It could actually be a good opportunity for Bertie."

"Mother is being cagey and giving Father speaking glances to be quiet whenever I enter the room. I can't help but think they are trying to hide the details from me." *And Lord Beaufort said Bow Street is interested.* But she couldn't say that without admitting her new acquaintance.

"You must admit, you are always harsh on their ideas. And they know how protective you are of Bertie."

"I'm going to find out anyway, even if I have to ransack Father's office. So you might as well tell me and save me the trouble. For my curiosity is well and truly piqued."

Mariah briefly looked down at her toes. She was wearing a fetching pair of pink velvet slippers embroidered with white flowers. "Very well. Father just wants Bertie to sign people up at Newmarket, ones he's already been talking to."

Contracting people to, what was in all likelihood, a fraud. When it was over, he'd be on the run just as much as they were. "How is Father funding such a large undertaking?"

"He already has a few investors, soon including Charles."

Harriet drew in a shocked breath. "Never say you'll let Charles invest in one of Father's schemes."

"How could I stop him? I tried, believe me. I told him it would be best to keep family and investments separate, but Father sold him on it, and Charles believes he would never mistreat family." She sighed.

"I wouldn't put it past Father to fleece Charles as a way of recouping your dowry," Harriet said darkly.

"Don't be ridiculous, he would never. You see too much evil in people."

She did, it was true. If only she was not so often right. "Please trust me on this."

The dream of sisterhood faded away as Mariah's mouth settled into an unhappy pout. So Harriet let it drop. But if she could just get Mariah's help with Bertie, all would not be lost. "This is a juncture in both Bertie's life and mine. You have been kind enough to help me, and now we must both do the same for our brother. I am going to find him a career."

Her eyes widened. "We can't risk their wrath, Harri. They must use Bertie's network at Newmarket to sell the canal project. They are pinning all their hopes on him to help them in their old age."

"But what if he doesn't want to do it?"

Mariah put a hand up. "Just don't. Get yourself out and let Bertie take care of himself. He is smart enough and old enough now to do so. I'm sure this project is entirely legitimate."

And since the success of the plan depended on Bertie's contacts at Newmarket and elsewhere, and Charles and Mariah were about to be heavily invested in it, Mariah would likely tell their parents of any plans Harriet made. It would have to be in secret, then, even though she could dearly use the financial help to buy Bertie's colors.

Harriet closed her eyes and took a deep breath. "I am glad you think that they have turned over a more honest leaf."

Their parents taught her from an early age only to gamble with people who had deep pockets. Her instincts told her there was no canal project at all, just plans and an elaborate framework, drawn up to convince investors. Then, when the foundational money was in, the Truchards would skip town with the proceeds. It was the bleakest possibility, but it was also the most likely. The quicker she got Bertie into the army, the better.

Mariah opened the wardrobe and pulled out a soft pink dress. "I had Theresa lengthen this ball gown by attaching flounces to the hem. I'll have her come and help you try it on. Can you let me know if it fits? I am so pleased to have you here. This is a new beginning for us."

Mariah kissed Harriet on both cheeks and left the room with a smile on her face and her hand resting on her still-flat belly. Harriet lifted the gown. The new flounces were a different fabric, and it looked very much like a short dress made to look longer. They had tried, but the result was not attractive.

The maid arrived soon after, helping Harriet out of her simple blue muslin and dropping the new dress over her head. "This was tricky, as we didn't have your measurements." She stood back and surveyed her work. "I did my best, but it's not right."

Harriet inspected the stitchwork. "You are an accomplished seamstress. I have never seen such neat stitching." She looked up, giving the older lady a grateful smile. "But as you can see, I have a most unfortunate figure, being both taller and built on a different scale than my beautiful sister."

Theresa smiled and chuckled. "She is a nymph, and you're more of an Amazon."

"That's a lovely way to see it. I have always thought my sister looked like a fairy princess."

In the past, it had often been the evil fairy princess, but perhaps that was changing.

Theresa attempted to secure the back. "You are wider across the shoulders than we expected."

"My apologies."

The dress, despite concerted effort over the next few minutes, would not do up. It was high-waisted, which should have forgiven a multitude of sins, but it pulled in all the wrong directions and Harriet could feel a breeze hitting her back.

"This is not going to work," Theresa said with a sigh.

Harriet agreed. "Will you let Lady Scanlan know that I will take care of the ball gown and she need not worry?"

The thought of using any of the gems in her stash made her stomach queasy, but sometimes needs must, and wearing a stunning ball gown so that she would not feel like a pauper when dancing with Lord Beaufort was very high on her agenda.

An agenda that was getting more urgent by the day.

CHAPTER 9

DID SOMEONE SAY FAKE BETROTHAL?

The following week, Harriet, Mariah and Charles stood in a line to be introduced to their hosts, Lord and Lady Mandeville. Harriet peeked through to the ballroom itself and gasped in delight. Brightly colored Indian fabrics were draped down the walls and from each corner into the center, making the entire ballroom look like a giant gorgeous tent.

"This is different," Harriet whispered in Mariah's ear.

"I'm not surprised," Mariah replied. "She is the most exciting woman in London. I am in awe of her."

Everyone had heard of Daphne, Lady Mandeville, even if only from the newspapers. She somehow walked that tight line between lady and creator, with her custom-blended perfumes. It was the same line that Sarah, Lady Jersey, walked as a board member of her family's bank. Some ladies made society look the other way when they indulged in their business passions.

How would it be to have the adoring gaze of a man like Lord Mandeville and also be able to pursue one's dreams? Like finding a unicorn. Or perhaps *being* one.

And things were obviously going well for the Mandevilles, if the sheer number of wax candles lighting their Palladian mansion on Curzon Street was any indication.

Mariah leaned in to whisper, "I know I admonished you for the color of your gown. However, I think we can both agree that it is perfect for tonight's ball."

Harriet smiled. Mariah had spent an entire afternoon trying to convince her not to wear the exquisite gown Madame Le Favre had delivered. It was too bold, not demure, attention seeking and her favorite complaint … risqué. But now they were here, and it was obvious an emerald-green gown would blend in rather than stand out.

They reached the front of the line, and Lady Mandeville took Harriet's hands in hers. "Welcome, my dear. I believe you are Lady Scanlan's sister? I don't think I've seen you around London, have I?"

Harriet smiled and dipped her curtsy. "No, my lady. We live in the country for the most part." It wasn't entirely the truth, but she didn't want to say anything that would suggest that Mariah's family didn't move in the same circles as Charles.

Mariah smiled and nodded, so she had definitely said the right thing. Suddenly, she didn't want to let her sister down. They were *both* worthy of being here.

Inside the lively ballroom, the air buzzed with the chatter of a hundred voices, creating a hum of excitement. A spirited jig played, the floor bouncing a little beneath her satin slippers from the dancers' jumps.

Oh my. A real ball.

The dancing was well under way and Harriet took a glass of punch from a passing waiter, sipping to steady her nerves.

She coughed. It was laced with rum and something equally strong.

"Easy on the punch, sister," Charles said. "One never knows quite what's in it."

Mariah laughed. "I will be careful, too. We will be gauche and drink lemonade tonight."

People in the ballroom exchanged pleasantries and conversed in a cacophony of voices. They said hello to Charles, but did not stay long enough to let him introduce his wife or her sister.

She was not part of their cliques, not one of them. She might as well have been invisible, but for the ladies who inspected her dress. It was one thing to dream of dancing all night, but the reality of her situation struck her forcibly. She knew not a soul here.

She hoped Charles knew some of them, but she had a suspicion he moved in different circles to these highfliers.

Harriet walked behind Mariah and Charles, who walked with their arms linked. This might actually be a very tedious night if she could not make new friends. She *must* try to be friendly, for she so dearly wanted this to be a night to remember. If she had to stand by a potted palm all evening, her dratted memory would allow her to recall every spot on every leaf. She would rather remember every dance partner and trodden-on toe.

Her first proper ball.

She scanned the room, looking for Lord Beaufort. He should stand out amongst the crowd, having such an impressive physique. She couldn't wait to see what he wore and how he looked in his evening attire. He had been striking enough in his buff breeches and tailcoat. She only hoped she did not lose her breath entirely looking at him.

Perhaps she couldn't wait for *him* to see *her,* too.

Not in a three-year-old dress that had been worn over and over, but in a gown the height of fashion, made by one of London's finest modistes. Not that gentlemen cared about such things. They generally didn't know their silk from their satin. Perhaps it was the confidence such a gown endowed one with that attracted them more.

She searched in vain. He was nowhere to be seen. She took a sip of her punch and sank into the background as Mariah and Charles spoke to someone she didn't know. Then her brother-in-law called her to them.

"Miss Truchard, may I introduce my good friend Mr. Bartholomew to you? He has just retained his seat in the lower house."

Harriet dipped a curtsy. "Congratulations. It is a pleasure to meet you, sir."

After a couple of insipid questions about the weather and the shopping, and how she found London, Mr. Bartholomew turned his attention back to Charles and started talking politics.

Oh dear.

She would have danced with him, if he had asked. But as politicians often were, he was more interested in talking about the affairs of the day than a country dance.

Mariah reached out and squeezed her hand, and Harriet started in surprise. At what time had Mariah *ever* offered her any kind of consolation? It was truer to form for her to laugh at Harriet's misfortune. But Harriet squeezed back. *At least I am not alone.*

Harriet finished her glass of punch and was sorely tempted to get herself a second, despite the strength of it, when she spotted Lord Beaufort bowing to Lady Mandeville. Lord

Mandeville clapped him on the back and beckoned the nearest waiter over so that Beaufort entered the room with a glass of champagne in his hand. The easy rapport between them suggested they were fast friends. But then most of these gentlemen went to Eton or Harrow and had known each other since they were ten years old.

Beaufort walked across the ballroom. She had never seen him in his natural element, but his predatory stroll was a lesson in how to be admired by all. It made sense. He couldn't set himself up in competition with places like Brooks's or White's without a degree of social cachet to make it happen.

He looked up at the tented ceiling and his mouth dropped open, just as hers had. She smiled. He wasn't too sophisticated to be impressed.

Then he searched the crowd. For her perhaps? Her heart swelled as his chin lifted and his gaze swept across the crowded ballroom.

Closer ... closer.

I'm over here.

His gaze moved over to her like she had called him. It landed on her and their eyes locked. His eyes widened and a smile pulled at the sides of his mouth. He allowed it to win and grinned at her.

Her heart clutched. Deuce take it, his smile was devastating. It seemed to hollow her out until all that was left was the light of it banging around inside. *Who are you to make me feel thus?*

The people in the room whirled around her, a cascading sea of color and laughter, while she and Beaufort stayed stone-still, their eyes connected, her heart pounding.

Oh my.

He took one step and then another, now ignoring the

people reaching to greet him. At the last moment, just before arriving at her side, he changed direction and walked toward Sir Charles. But before he stopped, he … winked at her? It was so fast she might have mistaken it.

Ah, because someone had not formally introduced them. Of course. He would speak to Charles first and ask to be introduced. Otherwise, questions would be raised. How did the young Miss Truchard know Lord Beaufort?

Be still, heart. That's much too fast.

"Scanlan, good to see you." Beaufort bowed, then held out his hand for Charles to take.

They shook hands, Charles looking a little surprised. "Lord Beaufort. A pleasure." His neck flushed red, suggesting he was a little flustered by the moment, too. But he rallied, asking Beaufort about a particularly beautiful mare he'd seen him purchase at Tattersalls a few weeks ago.

Men and their horses. A perpetual conversation starter if ever there was one.

Eventually, there was a lull and Lord Beaufort said to Charles. "But you have not introduced me to your lovely wife."

Charles laughed. "My understanding is that it's never a good idea to introduce one's wife to Lord Beaufort."

Harriet shook her head slightly. It should not surprise her he had a reputation for wooing the ladies. He just had to stand in a room completely oblivious and ladies would swoon.

Mariah laughed and put her hand on Charles' arm. "Charles! You should have more confidence in your attractions. I have eyes for none but you."

Charles *was* handsome, with his unruly brown hair, strong jaw and sharp wit. The fact he followed a pugilistic lifestyle meant he was fit and strong.

But this was a side to Mariah that Harriet had never seen. She was happy and flirtatious, and the snide comments that always frustrated Harriet were nowhere to be seen. Even her mouth was no longer a puckered moue, but shone with an easy and relaxed smile.

You are truly beautiful, Mariah. Which was something that occurred to her precisely ... never. Marriage had changed her sister for the better. Or perhaps she just had nothing left to prove.

Charles then turned to her. "But I will happily introduce you to my beautiful sister-in-law, Miss Truchard. Harriet, may I introduce Lord Beaufort to you?"

Harriet dipped into a deep curtsy and came up, smiling into his eyes. "And may I in turn introduce you to my sister, Mariah, Lady Scanlan?"

They all laughed. A few people turned to see what the joke was, looking at their little group with curiosity. As though now she was *part* of the ball, rather than just an observer. He smiled back and the mischievous imp in her loved that they'd tricked everyone into thinking they were strangers to each other. A little secret between them that felt warm and sparkly.

"Lady Scanlan, Miss Truchard, I am charmed to meet you both," Lord Beaufort said seriously. "Perhaps I could interest you in the next dance, Miss Truchard? I don't know what it is, but I feel confident that we can conquer it together."

"That would be lovely," Harriet said, putting her gloved hand in his, ignoring the impulse to throw a triumphant glance at Mariah. A small thrill jolted up her arm from where their fingers met.

Surprise briefly crossed his expression, suggesting perhaps he too had felt that jolt. Or was she reading too much into it?

"In the meantime," he continued, "we could circle the

room and inspect the beautiful decorations Lady Mandeville has installed. I'm sure the last time I came to this ballroom, it was an insipid pink."

She nodded and happily allowed him to pull her away from her sister with just the smallest smile. *What strange land am I visiting where a handsome gentleman whisks me away?*

"There," he said, continuing to smile at those left and right as he parted the crowd. He knew everyone. "I have extracted you from all familial bonds."

And of course, being on his arm lent her part of that glow. "That sounds nefarious. To what end?"

He turned to look at her, his eyes twinkling with merriment. "Dancing. That is my only end."

"You lie," she said evenly. "I know you are dying to tell me about your investigations."

His face clouded over. Harriet tilted her head to one side, trying to read him. Perhaps he *did* just want to dance and forget his problems. *I wish I had never mentioned it.* "I found nothing and saw nothing." A little pulse ticked in his jaw.

She squeezed his arm lightly. "These things take time. Did your Faro bank lose a vast amount of money, or did anyone else?"

"There were a couple of lucky runs in Vingt-et-un, but nothing major."

"Could be someone counting the high-low ratios. It can be hard to tell."

"Or the whole thing could be in my head."

She shook her head. "Absolutely not. You must trust your instincts."

"Do you?" He glanced down at her and when their gaze connected, it was hard to look away, or even think.

"What?"

"Trust your instincts?"

"Always." Even when they led her astray.

"What are they telling you about me?" He led her away from the dancing and toward the doors to the veranda, which were thrown open to circulate air into the sad crush of a ball.

Too handsome. Too magnetic. Far above my touch. She stopped still. "Why do you want to know?"

"I want to know how well you read me."

"Ah. Do you mean using my preternatural gamester skills?" Little did he know they included precious little human insight.

He nodded and turned to look her in the eye. "Yes. Those. Tell me what you see."

"I see a man who came here to fulfill a promise to a friend." Was she making a presumption calling herself a friend? Too late, it was done, and it made her feel mischievous. "Who then saw that friend looking incredibly fine in her new ball gown and has been at a loss for words ever since?"

He whipped around, a grin breaking across his face. Even more devastating because it was matched with deep, appreciative laughter. "So very true." He picked up her hand where it rested on his arm and brought it to his lips. "But tonight has been a revelation in another way. Now that you have crossed into my world socially, I can court you, and a wicked plan has come into my mind."

A wicked plan? Nothing honorable in the courting, then. What could it be? "Ah …"

"You can guess?" He stroked his chin. "Of course you can."

No, she really couldn't.

But perhaps just her being at the ball signaled she was a socially appropriate match for him. Her mind riffled through a few ideas before landing on the one that felt like a homing pigeon flying in to roost. "Do you mean we should stage a courtship so that I can attend your card parties?" She tilted her head to one side, waiting for his acknowledgement.

He nodded, a satisfied smile breaking across his face. "We are in accord. Perhaps even a betrothal, if it allows us more freedom?"

Not a real betrothal, of course. Even though her heart beat harder just at the thought. "We are not in accord yet, my dear Lord Beaufort. After all, this would seem to have a great deal of benefit for you, and not a great deal for me."

"There is the cachet of being betrothed to me."

"And then losing you. Not quite so enhancing."

He nodded. "True. Your reputation will take damage. Although we will take care that it's obvious you were left with no choice."

The musicians struck up a waltz, and Beaufort turned to her. "Do you waltz? Are you allowed?"

"I hardly think any patroness of Almack's will care enough to be outraged, so why not?" She had practiced with Mariah earlier in the year, when the dance was new to London from Paris. Certainly, she had taken the male part in that practice, but how hard could it be?

He led her onto the floor and pulled her into position. "Must I introduce you to other gentlemen? Would it be so bad to keep you all to myself?" He was musing to himself as though he didn't expect her to answer.

"I must be introduced to others," she said firmly. "I have every intention of dancing into the wee hours of the morning, and unless you want to make a cake of yourself by dancing every one with me, you had best oblige."

He laughed and put his hand lightly on her waist where it felt hotter than a bed brick on a cold night. Her hand hovered over his shoulder. *Rest it down, don't be scared.* Scared of touching him? It seemed so intimate, but surely it was no different to clasping hands during a country dance. She let one hand rest on his shoulder, and he took her other hand in his.

And yes, it was very different to a country dance. Because they stayed clasped together as the music set them off in a glide across the ballroom floor. Much better for an intimate conversation. "So tell me, Miss Truchard. What can I do for you to make this ruse worthwhile? For I am sure that the moment you visit my card parties you will make short work of this."

"Perhaps." She bit her lip. "And if I don't?"

"Then I will know I tried everything." He swallowed hard.

She tilted her face up, regarding him with the coolest stare she could muster in the circumstances. "Everything except letting your dealers go, which, as you know, is my first suggestion."

His expression was calm, but he gripped her hand a little more tightly. "You will see why it is impossible when you meet them."

"Very well. Let me think."

She didn't have to think for long to know what she wanted. And that she wanted it to happen almost immediately. "I have some savings to buy Bertie a commission, but I don't know how to go about it. If I give you the money, could you organize it for me? I'd be so grateful."

Any damage to her reputation was well worth the cost.

"Infantry or Cavalry?"

"Infantry please, but the rest I leave up to you. I know different regiments can have vastly different costs. I think I may have five hundred pounds or so? But he is eighteen and at the upper age limit for an ensign. So you see, time is of the essence."

"Do you parents approve?"

"They will heartily disapprove. Does it matter?" She looked over his shoulder to where Mariah was dancing the waltz with a very handsome older man. Her energy and grace was catching the eye of others too. She would be thrilled.

He turned her to see what had snagged her attention, but his gaze came straight back to her. "No, not in the least. The army will accept men from sixteen onward whether parents approve or not."

"I would much rather this than him taking the King's Shilling, which is what he will do if I fail."

His eyes widened. "Agreed. I'll speak to an agent tomorrow. In the meantime, perhaps you could stop looking so worried and instead gaze wistfully into my eyes?"

"I'm not sure I will do a lovelorn look convincingly."

"You don't have to convince me. Just everyone around here. I will lead the way."

"And how will you do that?"

"I'll just tell you how the shade of your dress has turned your eyes from gray to something more like the silver of dew on a leaf in the early morning. That I find the freckles sprinkling your nose enchanting. If I could dance every dance with you, I would."

Harriet swallowed and after a quick look into his eyes, where his admiration did not seem in any way false, averted hers to the floor, abashed by the blush she could feel stealing up her cheeks.

"There, see? You are doing very well. That blush is perfect."

"That blush is because you are embarrassing me beyond belief!" And perhaps because the room was a trifle warm.

"You had best accustom yourself to it. I rarely court young ladies—"

"And you are not now." She did not mean that to sound quite so bitter.

"My dear Miss Truchard, let's agree to enjoy this. What's wrong with a little flirting? Bertie will get his colors and I will get help with my exceedingly boring problem."

Oh, so he thought he could just have some fun and nobody's feelings would get hurt? That hearing the most beautiful things said to you for the first time, knowing all the while not a single word was true, would not prey upon her feelings? The worst part of it was that he was by far the most magnetic man she had ever met. Every part of her wanted to know more about him and wished this might be true. Even if only for a few weeks.

How was she to know what was real and what was false? She was already confused, and they hadn't even started yet. No. It would not do. "I am concerned that I will not be able to tell the falsehood from your true intentions. How will I know?"

"That is a good rule to lay down. Because I could say the same thing to you. Let's make a pact. Whatever we say or do while in public is all a falsehood, but always with our underlying admiration for each other, meaning whatever we say must always have an element of truth to it."

"So, for example …" He whirled her to the edge of the ballroom where there was a fragrance on the air. It smelled like blown roses, but she could see none in sight.

"If I tell you that you are in fine looks tonight and that I am the luckiest man in the world, you are truly in fine looks even if I do not have the right to claim you as my own."

Oh. His words still struck and made her feel giddy. She

nodded. If there were rules, then perhaps she could navigate it without getting hurt. Or obsessed with him. "If this interlude means you are going to shower me with compliments and buy me flowers that my sister may or may not see, then I must admit, I am in favor."

"Does she give you trouble?"

"Not tonight. Tonight, she is the perfect sister and I can't imagine what has happened. But generally speaking, she loves to see me fail. At anything. It brings her a macabre joy."

"And yet you stay with her?"

"For the moment. I am biding my time until I have enough funds to set up my own establishment."

He misstepped and almost trod on her toes. "By yourself?"

"Of course. I planned to have Bertie join me, but if he is to join the army, I shall just have to do it on my own. I do not want to go back with Mother and Father and I can't live with Mariah long term. It is not fair to anyone."

"But surely they won't allow it!" He truly seemed shocked, which surprised her.

"Why ever not? They have been complaining long and bitterly that I do not earn them any blunt. They will be most happy to be rid of me."

"You can't mean that."

"In addition, they will not have to find me that pesky dowry they keep misplacing."

"Ah yes, the case of the missing dowry."

"Here one year, gone the next. Trebled the year after in the hope of landing someone as well-to-do as Charles, then gone when they remember no man in his right mind would marry a bluestocking."

"You are a bluestocking?"

"I am an intelligent woman who reads a great deal and

likes to have an opinion. That labels me beyond the pale in the eyes of society."

"So that's where I've been going wrong." His face had a wistful look to it.

"How so?"

"I have always wondered why the ladies of my acquaintance have never piqued my interest. Now I realize all I needed was a bluestocking."

A few people turned to look at them, because the music stopped just as he spoke and he almost shouted into the lull.

"I pique your interest?" Harriet felt another blush steal up her cheeks. *Drat my complexion.* "I have always been of the opinion that an intelligent man would soon become bored by an insipid lady who spends all day plucking her harp."

And why was she worried if she could not tell the truth from a lie, she, the person who had learned to call a bluff by her fifth birthday?

That part of her knew Lord Beaufort truly thought all those things about her. She knew it in her heart.

He was just afraid to own it.

The more frightening thought was what she thought of him. She wasn't stupid. If he honed his attention on her, whether he meant it or not, she would fall in love with him. And nothing could be more disastrous to her plans. Rules were not going to help her navigate this farce. Nothing would, because he was too tempting, too handsome. And she had too little experience to deal with it.

"Lord Beaufort?"

His eyes smiled as he looked down at her, crinkling around the edges. "Yes?"

"Perhaps you could just ask Charles and Mariah to your

card routs and I will attend." She swallowed hard. "I don't want to fake a betrothal to you."

For nothing good could come of it. He was a viscount, and while he might enter a fake courtship to help him meet his goal, any question of it transforming into the real thing was like blowing on a dandelion. Wishful, pretty, but ultimately blown to pieces.

Did she notice a look of relief cross his features? If she did, he schooled it quickly. "As you wish, my dear."

CHAPTER 10

WHERE A GENTLEMAN SHOULD NOT GET TOO ATTACHED TO HIS SUPPER PLATE

His only task at the ball was to ensure that Miss Truchard danced all evening, just as he had promised her she would. It was not to keep her all to himself, flirt, banter and dance every dance with her. Contrary to what his heart was telling him in no uncertain terms.

Dash it. Why did she have to be so beautiful? Her gown was emerald-green, and the fabric shimmered as she moved, making it look as though she floated across the ballroom. She was every bit as beautiful as her sister and he had an inkling she didn't know it.

The waltz finished, and Beau withdrew his hand from Miss Truchard's waist, fighting the urge to put it back where it was. It fit so very well.

"Who will you introduce to me now?" she asked, smiling up at him with a trust and openness he had in no way earned.

Very well. If I must. "Lord Templeton, I think. He's a very elegant dancer and a good friend of mine. I trust him not to whisk you off your feet, since he is newly married."

"You're the only one who could do that," she said lightly.

Did she mean she was just as entranced with him as he was with her? Dangerous times.

Beau introduced Lord Templeton to her, and the dratted man winked at him before sweeping her away. He would go and find Lady Templeton and see how he liked *that*.

Beau watched with equal parts jealousy and amusement as she took to her new partner with just as much enthusiasm as she'd given him. Even to the point of a blush creeping up her neck at something he said. She had literally stolen his breath when he'd first seen her. The candlelight, which he had never seen her by, making her skin glow like caught moonlight. *Listen to him, talking like he was in the throes of calf-love.*

Harriet held her head high when she danced, looking up into Lord Templeton's eyes and smiling. She looked like a young lady enjoying her first ball with none of the ennui that characterized ladies a few seasons hence. Happy to be there and happy to dance with whomever would ask her.

Which, he was not sure if it was fortunate or not, was a long line of gentlemen after Lord Templeton. They obviously saw her natural enjoyment and just wanted to be part of it. She would not ask sticky questions or look down her nose at one. Tall, short, handsome or plain, she danced with them all.

He would miss his supper dance if he did not claim her soon.

"Beau," a voice said at his side. He turned to see Lord Mandeville looking at him with an amused glint in his eye. "You might want to take your eyes off her for just a second."

Beau started at Mandeville's words. "Am I that obvious?"

"Oh, I'm not saying you're alone. Miss Truchard is garnering more than one admiring glance tonight. It's astonishing we have not seen her before now, but Scanlan has not really been in society. His election into the lower house might change all that."

"Yes, especially if his wife sets herself up as a political hostess. Men who can traverse both sides of the house can be dashed useful." And their sisters would be accepted into polite company.

"My thoughts exactly."

"And you have now taken your seat. Congratulations."

Mandeville groaned softly. "More like commiserations, I'm sure. But there is too much to do and I can be a voice of reason in the Lords, I think."

"Or a voice of mayhem. Goodness knows the Lords don't like to be challenged."

Mandeville laughed. "Take your pick."

The music of the Allemande wound down, and the supper dance was announced. "Best I secure this one before some other buffoon runs away with her," Beau said.

"May luck be with you." His friend clapped him on the back. "You'll need it."

Beau made his way back to Lady Scanlan, awaiting Harriet's return. "Your sister is having a splendid evening, I think."

"She has not missed a dance yet," Lady Scanlan replied, nodding with pride. "I am thrilled."

"You are an excellent sister."

He was surprised to see her face cloud over. "Thank you," she said quietly, as though she were not quite sure it was true.

Before he could think on it, Harriet returned, her cheeks flushed and a sheen of perspiration he should not have noticed on her forehead. "Shall I meet you in the supper room? I need to visit the ladies' retiring room for a moment. I trust you to make me up a plate."

He nodded. "You will have all my favorites."

He strolled to the supper room, and filled their plates with slices of ham, lobster cakes and small tins of negus ice. It was too much, but all the dancing made him hungry.

She returned a few moments later, searching the room for him. He raised a hand, but then left the seats he'd found and went to fetch her.

He held his arm out for her to take and ignored the small thrill of her looping her arm in his. "How are you enjoying your evening? Or is that a ridiculous question since you have not sat a single set out?"

"I have not, have I?" She blinked in surprise. "How astonishing." She patted her hair. Her strawberry tresses were styled with loose curls at the front, then neatly pulled back into a small cluster of curls, drawing his eye to her elegant neck. Most distracting.

"Not really," Beau said, picking up the ice and taking a scoop. Cool and caramel, what could be better?

Watching Harriet as she took a similar spoonful. Her eyes opened wide.

"Barely tolerable?"

She swallowed and then leaned forward to speak privately. "Divine. Who makes such a thing?"

"Mr. Gunter, if I'm not mistaken."

She picked up a lobster cake and ate it in three delicate bites. "This is the very best night of my life."

He could watch her all evening. Tiny bites, glancing around the room in awe. She was too entertaining.

Then she ate the fruit and the custard, and when he put his lobster cake on her plate, she ate that too, throwing him a sneaky glance. "You are a bad influence."

"I can't have you fainting with fatigue on the dance floor. We must keep up your strength."

"It's three in the morning. How could there possibly be more dancing?"

"A mere babe at her first ball," he said indulgently. "You have many more hours to go and shall leave here with the rays of dawn chasing you home."

"I will?" Her eyes lit up.

"Most certainly. So eat up." And with those prosaic words, it hit him: He could easily fall in love with her.

Which, under the circumstances, was a terrible idea. Besides not knowing anything of her family, apart from the fact they were hardened gamesters, he'd learned the hard way that he made a poor companion while running Beaufort's. It was all consuming and the lady tended to get consumed along with it. And yet she brought out every stupid over-protective instinct he had, and all he wanted to do was see the same joy and light in her eyes every day.

He wanted to be the one who put it there.

When supper was over, they rose from the table, and he bowed over her hand. It was time to get out of there and not dance with her over and over as he wanted to.

"I will see you tomorrow. I will have flowers in hand. Your sister will be most impressed. Perhaps we can talk business." There, that should get their acquaintance back on the right footing.

"With any luck, you will have to fight your way in from all my new admirers," she said, with a small laugh, as though she couldn't quite believe it.

CHAPTER 11

WHERE LADY BEAUFORT HAS A VERY SHARP EYE

Beaufort arrived at Sir Charles Scanlan's Wimpole Street town house to find Harriet's prediction had come true. The front sitting room overflowed with gentlemen young and old, flirting with both Miss Truchard and her beautiful sister. Harriet wore a simple white muslin gown, tied under her bust with a rose-pink ribbon. Her petticoats, hanging from the bottom of the gown, were much more embellished, with scallops of lace that had him staring at the pink slippers peeking out from underneath them.

Ladies were so pretty. Or perhaps just *Harriet* was so pretty.

Sir Charles stood near the door acting as host and looking somewhat bemused.

Beau shook his hand. "Regret bringing her to town for the season yet?"

Sir Charles smiled ruefully. "She never got a season at all, don't you see? She just wanted to experience it and, by Jove, I would do anything to make her happy." They both looked over to where Lady Scanlan was being entertained by Sir

Newington reciting poetry. She clapped when he finished with a pretty bow, and her tinkling laughter reached across to them. "She deserves the admiration."

"Just as long as it doesn't go any further than that. These young scamps can't be trusted."

Scanlan shook his head. "She has my complete trust."

Knowing how many ladies visited his establishment with gentlemen who were most definitely not their husband, Beau hoped he was right. "You're a lucky man."

"Are you visiting Miss Truchard or my wife, my lord?"

"Considering I foolishly danced three dances with your wife's sister, I think it's safe to say Miss Truchard."

Scanlan nodded. "I am happy to hear it."

He had brought her a small posy of peony and anemone blooms. She would never know how much thought had gone into it. Or how he hoped his mother wouldn't notice he had raided the flower delivery. And now it appeared he might not get the chance to give it to her. Luckily, predicting such an occurrence, he had left a card in the posy.

Their eyes met across the room, and a faint blush of pink appeared on her cheeks. She was not dressed in the height of fashion, but then, she needed no embellishment. It would just be surfeit. He crossed the room, and despite the fact men were literally crouched at her knees, she barely took her eyes off him.

He bowed. "Good morning, Miss Truchard and assembled sycophants."

"I say!" One gentleman said, but Beau merely shot him an amused look.

"Lord Beaufort, how lovely of you to come." She looked at the posy. "Are they for me?"

He glanced at the side table that had two other bouquets.

99

"But of course. Shall I place them on the table with the others?"

"This little table next to me would be better." She smiled and took them from him, putting them in pride of place. "They are beautiful. Thank you."

"A trifle." Like he hadn't spent half an hour choosing exactly the right blooms.

"I thought perhaps you came to remind me of your invitation to drive in the park tomorrow."

He what? He had offered no such thing. It must mean she wanted to talk to him. "Why, yes," he said, without skipping a beat. "Would eleven be acceptable? We never set a time."

"Perfect," she replied with an almost conspiratorial smile.

Minx. He bowed. "I bid you good day."

On the way out, he put his hand in his pocket, pulled out a brass filigree key, and offered it to Sir Charles. "I would be happy to see you, your lovely wife, and her sister at my establishment any time. This key will allow you entry. I have a well-earned reputation for fair play, and you can safely bring the ladies. If they don't feel like playing, they can dance or have a quiet coze away from the action. I think you'll find that the Thursday evening gathering has the most attendance by those in both the upper and lower house. Or so I've noticed."

Charles nodded. "I'm grateful to you, my lord. I am finding one of the largest challenges in taking my seat in the lower house is my lack of connections."

"Then, gambling or not, this is your best bet. I'll introduce you to get you started. And call me Beau." He had a feeling he and Scanlan would become firm friends no matter what happened.

He bowed to Charles and then caught Harriet's eye again, bowed to her, and left the room.

Objective achieved.

He returned home and found Mother busying herself in the gaming room, replacing the vases of flowers. Spires of foxglove, bunched with roses and tulips, brought the garden inside. She wore a gown he had not seen before, a very handsome cornflower blue silk with puffed sleeves and a lace fichu. And he could say nothing about the bill that would arrive in the mail, because he had not told her how tight their finances were.

"Funny, I do not have all the peonies I specially ordered from Mr. Cochran. They have only just come into season." She turned to him, a secretive smile on her face. "Have you been courting?"

How shrewd she was.

"I have been courting." *Although not somebody you would have me court.*

"Very good. I'm glad our chat helped you see the way forward. We can't rely on this enterprise as surely as we can the gold in a young lady's dowry. Not to mention the connections it will give you."

The Truchards would offer neither.

But Miss Truchard could perhaps help him see a way out of their troubles, and that alone made her a worthwhile connection.

CHAPTER 12

WHERE A JEWELER IS DESTINED FOR
DISAPPOINTMENT

The following morning Beau spirited Miss Truchard away from Lady Scanlan's house before her admirers descended.

She was dressed in a cream muslin walking dress covered with a dusty blue pelisse with buttons embroidered with delicate rosebuds. "Did you stitch those buttons? They are very pretty."

She nodded. "I did. Although I have stopped embellishing handkerchiefs because Mother keeps selling them."

He loved her brutal frankness. His tiger, Jim, jumped onto the back of the curricle, and Beau moved into the traffic. "Is Lady Scanlan thrilled with her first season?"

Harriet inspected the brass lantern on her side. "Mariah is acting like a debutante more than a matron, and Charles encourages her. He is trying to secure vouchers to Almack's."

Beau raised his voice over the clatter of the horses' hooves. "She is a very dashing matron. There is no harm, I'm sure."

"You wouldn't say that if you knew how complete her self-admiration is already."

He laughed. "Spoken like a true sibling." He brought the horses to a halt at the top of the street. "Hyde Park?"

She paused, her mouth puckering. So perhaps *not* Hyde Park. "Actually, I have a secret errand to run." She clutched at the handles of her reticule and if he didn't know better, he'd say she was nervous.

"I am happy to be of service," he said easily. "By the way, my secretary has contacted the agent that takes care of commissions, and all is in hand. I have also organized a letter of recommendation from a friend. Bertie will have his colors as soon as possible."

With her large-brimmed straw bonnet, he couldn't see her expression, but she made a small choking noise that alarmed him. "Thank you."

Simple words, but there was so much emotion behind them that either nobody ever helped her, or this was very important. "This errand relates to that. Could you drive to Mr. Proud, the jewelers on the Strand? I have a few gems I would like him to purchase from me."

"And this will go better with a peer of the realm in tow?"

She flashed him a mischievous smile, the blue ribbon on her bonnet fluttering under her chin. "If I come with you, they may assume that by treating me well, they will get more of your future custom."

He couldn't argue with her deduction, because being Lord Beaufort meant the longest credit, the fastest service, and only the very best goods from tradesmen and artisans. It was a position of privilege that he would have for the rest of his life, and it remained even when their fortunes were reversed. These days, of course, he paid his bills as they arrived, liking his bank account to be an accurate indication of where he stood.

"If that is the case, perhaps we can visit my family jeweler, Rundell and Bridge? It's on Ludgate Hill."

Her brows creased for a moment. "Very well. I admit to not knowing Mr. Proud and am happy to go where you are known."

"Ludgate Hill it is." It was such a beautiful day for a drive that he couldn't help feeling disappointed that Hyde Park was not their destination. Or perhaps even a little further out to Richmond or Kew. He would love to have her by his side with the wind flapping at her straw bonnet and a flush on her cheeks. He reached back and pulled the soft cream cashmere blanket from behind the seat and placed it on her lap.

"Thank you." She tucked the ends under her and put her reticule on top of her lap, still clutching it.

At a guess, it held the entire earnings from her book. All sacrificed to have her brother taken care of. Something her parents should have done, but either wouldn't or couldn't.

They arrived at the jewelers, a five-story building marked with a golden salmon hanging out front. A sales associate opened the door, then upon recognizing Beau, ushered them past the cabinets of glittering gold and gems, into the back room.

Mr. Philip Rundell was seated at his worktable. His hair was still a mess trying to escape his old-fashioned queue, but now it was fully gray. The buttons on his knee breeches were undone, and he hummed an indistinct tune. Beau shook his head. One would never guess from his appearance that he was one of the richest non-titled men in England.

He looked up and let the loupe fall into his hand, a grin breaking across his face. "Lord Beaufort, as I live and breathe. And bringing a young lady to my premises! To what wonderful occasion do I owe this honor?"

Ah, he thought they were betrothed. "No particular celebration … but when there is, you will be the first I visit."

"Perhaps another day," Mr. Rundell said, looking between the two of them and smiling a very knowing smile.

"You sound as though you're in league with my mother." Beau took a deep breath. "This is my dear friend, Miss Truchard. She requires you to assess some jewels she has in her possession, to see if they interest you."

Mr. Rundell's eyes widened and then narrowed. "Of course." He rubbed his hands together. "Rundell and Bridge are always on the lookout for fine gemstones."

Yes, and Beau had heard the stories of how hard Mr. Rundell negotiated for them. He was a businessman foremost. "You have a fine reputation for hard negotiating, but I would ask you to put this tendency aside as a favor to me."

Mr. Rundell barked out a laugh. "You have me there. I do like to get the best price. But very well. I will give your lady a very fair price and mutter about it later." He raised an eyebrow, implying Beau would be back very soon, perhaps, to buy that betrothal ring?

Miss Truchard exhaled. "Oh, thank you. My brother would like to trounce Napoleon and we are to buy him a commission. I hope the jewels are fine enough for you to help me." She reached into her reticule and took out a small crystal bottle, the kind ladies used to store smelling salts. She unscrewed the silver lid and carefully tipped the contents onto a black square of velvet on Mr. Rundell's workbench. They formed a tiny glittering pile. He tried to count the gems and assess their size. He was no expert, but Harriet had hundreds of pounds of jewels in her little bottle. *Where had she bought them?* Every time he was with her, he had more questions and less answers.

Mr. Rundell lifted his loupe to his right eye and picked up his tweezers, pushing the small mound of gemstones, then picking up one gem after another. "Excellent quality." He looked up at Miss Truchard, surprise in his eyes. "You have always purchased the very best you could, haven't you, my dear?"

Harriet nodded. "I always choose quality over size. So some gems are smaller than I would like."

"But all are of the first water, my dear. But tell me, how much do we need to send this young man off on his adventure? I'd say six to eight hundred pounds should suffice. Is that correct, Lord Beaufort?"

The jeweler looked from her to Beaufort and when he nodded, went back to inspecting the gems, separating three off to the side. "I will have to take all of them, but it will reach eight hundred. Which is a very generous price." He threw a glance at Beau that clearly said 'you and I will talk later.' "And I would be happy to have them. Now, a rather important question. Do you want me to hold off using them for as long as possible in case you would like to reclaim them?"

Harriet shook her head vigorously. "No need for that. It has taken years to save this many. Please use them as you feel fit."

He looked to Beau, who shook his head slightly, trying to tell Mr. Rundell to wait on making them up, until he could figure out how much they meant to her, and the jeweler nodded. "Very well. Let's do business, shall we?"

Harriet clapped her hands. "Oh, thank you. You can't know what this will mean to us. You are making his dream come true."

Mr. Rundell shook his head. "No, my dear, it is you who made this happen."

Beau looked at Harriet and could swear he saw a shimmer of tears in her eyes, but she looked away, and within a moment had composed herself.

They left the jewelry shop with a draft on the jeweler's bank account for eight hundred pounds.

Miss Truchard turned to him with a broad grin that brought out a dimple in her left cheek that was hitherto unseen. Matched with her sparkling eyes, she took his breath away.

It made a man want to make her this happy *all the time*. But he had a funny feeling Mr. Rundell had just paid eight hundred pounds for four hundred pounds of diamonds. Which he would never have done if he hadn't thought they truly were about to be betrothed and he could recoup the money on a betrothal ring.

Beau assessed his feelings on it. No, he did not feel in the least sorry. This was an important turning point for both Miss Truchard and her brother, and he was happy to be a small part of it. Especially when he knew she would fulfill her part of the bargain and find his cheats.

"That was incredibly easy! Much easier than I thought it would be. Who knew my gems would be worth so much? I vow I have spent nowhere near eight hundred pounds on them."

"Sometimes things *are* simple." Beau lifted her up into his waiting carriage then jumped up on the other side. "I have never met a young lady who carries diamonds in a smelling salts vial."

"Ah, I love my parents, but when things get hectic, they will search the entire house looking for every spare shilling. I don't think you could imagine how it feels to come home and find that they have sold your dresses, or the gold locket they gave you on your twelfth birthday has disappeared from your jewelry box. Anything they ever gave me, they still considered theirs. So when my book became popular, I decided what I gave them would be on *my* terms. They never know I often pay for our food at the market."

"Understandable. I would do the same. I had no control over my father's investments. Heirs never do. You earned those diamonds; you have every right to decide how they are spent."

To his surprise, she thrust the bank draft deep into his coat pocket. "I will give you this now before I forget."

"Before you change your mind, you mean?"

She looked down at her hands. "I don't cling to anything. What is the point when most everything I have cherished over the years has been lost to me? I'm not bitter, I'm just pragmatic. Now Bertie is going, too, and it is for the best. I know it is for the best. But I will miss him. Greatly."

She said the last, looking straight ahead, then turned to him with a bright smile as though the words weren't cutting her even as she spoke them. But he knew better, even on such short acquaintance. He hadn't watched losers at the gaming table for five years without gleaning some knowledge. With Miss Truchard, the brighter the smile, the more of a mask it was. Handing over the hard-earned diamonds had hurt. Letting go of Bertie cut even more.

"Did your parents move frequently?" He knew the answer before she said it, but wanted to see if he could discover more of her feelings on the matter.

"Oh yes, we couldn't become attached to a house, town, or friends. Soon enough, I'd be woken in the night and told to pack my cases. We moved at least once a year, but often two to three times. Whenever it was deemed prudent."

What a way to grow up. "I assume you mean whenever creditors were chasing your parents for money?"

"Yes. Because why pay tradesmen or grocers when you can gamble what you owe them? The worst part was, they *would* turn those small amounts into winnings. And every time it happened, it just reinforced their belief that luck was with them."

Which was why she found gambling abhorrent. "I suppose you must despise me, doing what I do."

She frowned. "Gambling itself is not the problem, so no, I do not despise you. You made the best choice you could with the strengths that you had. And, unlike my parents, I feel you could walk away from it."

"Why would I want to? Such a diverting way to earn money." It was casually said and a lie, but one he'd told so often he almost believed it. "But you are wrong, I have no particular strengths, just a position in society I have used woefully."

She shook her head. "I watched you at the ball. You couldn't make your way across the floor without being greeted, smiled at, clapped on the back or having a hand shaken. If I had the power of popularity, I would open a gambling house too, because I know everybody would come."

"I must admit that the thought of opening my Faro bank only came after I had thrown so many successful card parties it seemed silly not to rebuild our fortune from it."

"The Faro bank always wins."

He exhaled. "Except recently. It makes me wonder whether I should stop fighting and close. I only planned for this to be of short duration, but that drifts further away from me."

"I know the feeling," she said wistfully. "I am firmly back at square one."

"It sounds like somebody better get cracking on her next book." He lifted his whip and performed an excellent crack in the air to punctuate.

"Stop it," she said with a laugh, "or you'll startle your horses."

They arrived safely and without startled horses at Sir Charles Scanlan's house, and he halted the team in front. Jim jumped down and went to the horses' heads.

"And here we are, after a most excellent ride in the park," Harriet said.

"So invigorating!" he replied with a wink.

Instead of blushing, she winked back. "I believe I shall see you at your card rout later this week?"

"Excellent." He was about to guide her into the house, when Sir Terrance ambled up to his curricle.

"Ah, don't get up, my good chap. I'll take care of our dear Miss Truchard."

She smiled and took his hand, allowing herself to be guided up the steps.

The dratted impudence of the man.

Jim jumped back up and Beau drove back to Portman Square, far more annoyed than he should be.

As though he was the only one entitled to her company.

He'd best get over that.

CHAPTER 13

WHERE LADY BEAUFORT MAKES HER
FEELINGS KNOWN

A few hours later, Beau wandered to the kitchen to see what was on the evening's supper menu. Part of the reason for their success was Mother's ability to order the very best fare London had to offer, supplemented by what Cook produced in their own kitchen.

It was his favorite room in the house. Situated at the back of the ground floor, with long wooden benches and an old-fashioned range, which he was going to update for Mrs. Barrett just as soon as he could afford it. She kept the old cast-iron spotless, like the rest of her kitchen. Scullery maids dashed around him in the usual skittering-mouse fashion. They all did so much work so Beaufort's could be prosperous.

And then all of society gave him the credit.

But he knew better.

Mother looked up from where she was inspecting a box that had just been delivered. "My dear! Do come and try these strawberry tarts. They are a few shillings less than the Parmentier's, so I thought it might be a prudent swap."

He reached into the box where rows of tartlets looked up

at him, the strawberries suspended in clear jelly. He popped one into his mouth, his eyes widening as the underlying crème pâtissière popped. "They're delicious. I'll make sure Merrick serves champagne tonight. It will go perfectly. Do you have any friends coming this evening?"

It was good to know which of her acquaintances would be visiting so that he could make sure their favorite table was reserved. If they deigned to visit her, he liked to make it as special as possible.

Mother shook her head, her gray curls peeking from underneath her turban. She took a quick peek in each of the boxes. "I'm happy with the delivery, Mrs. Barrett."

"*Bon. Merci, madame.*" Mrs. Barrett said, speaking French with a bright cockney accent.

Mother turned and linked her arm through his. "Come, Beau, let's take tea."

"I'll send it up *á la* minute, madam," Mrs. Barrett called out after them.

They walked through to the front drawing room. "I have been out and about this week making morning calls."

"As per usual." She and Father had been an unstoppable social whirlwind. Until they weren't.

"I like to make sure that my friends visit, for I know every bit helps."

He closed his eyes against a wash of guilt. She should not have to go to her friends begging their attendance, which was surely how they must see it.

"In any case," she continued. "This week some of them have declined. Our reputation must be suffering. How are your investigations going?" Her silver eyebrows were drawn together and her gaze questioning.

This was the opportunity he'd been waiting for. He must

come fully clean and now, thanks to Miss Truchard, he could, because action was being taken.

He sat on the sofa, his gaze briefly caught by the Sevres vase sitting on a Doric column. It had been an anniversary present from Father. If only Father hadn't speculated away their fortune on 'sure' investments, Beau would not now be forced to gamble the family's standing. "They are not wrong to stay away. Someone is cheating at the Faro table, and perhaps even at Hazard. You know the bank has been broken twice in the past few weeks, but there have been many smaller instances that I can't quite put my finger on. It has become too big to ignore now, and our ability to pull ourselves out of our financial mire is being compromised."

He exhaled. There. Now it was all out in the open.

There was a shocked silence, in the heartbeat of which he regretted not keeping it to himself. But he knew what it was like to be kept in the dark. To know that something was wrong and that well-meaning people were protecting you from the truth. Not amusing.

"I see," she said slowly. "They are probably too kind to say it, but they must feel Beaufort's is not the safe place it was a few months ago. This is terrible. What are we to do?" She put her teacup down and wrung her hands in the skirts of her gown.

"I have been trying to find someone with the ability to spot the cheating, so we can root out the person responsible." This was where it got tricky.

"So, you think it is somebody working alone? Could it not be a group targeting us?" Beneath that turban there was a very sharp woman. And she wasn't asking for her vinaigrette, instead her gaze had taken on a militant look.

Only part of the reason I'd move heaven and earth for you.

"I have no idea. Only time will tell. However, I have found somebody who knows this kind of thing inside-out and she is going to be in attendance tonight."

Mother inhaled deeply and let the breath out slowly. "Good. As long as it is not Miss Truchard; I heard from two different sources that you danced three times with her at the Mandeville's ball."

The society grapevine certainly moved quickly. "I also took her to supper."

"And gave her all my peonies, I'd wager. You wretch," she said good-naturedly. She paused, as though weighing her words. "But I feel it incumbent on me to warn you, even though it pains me to do so, as you so seldom take interest in any young lady of your acquaintance …"

"Warn me of what, exactly?"

Her eyebrows drew together again. "It is not a good family, my dear. In fact, it is possibly the very worst branch of the Truchard family you could find. A very old name and connected to an earldom. However, the branch of which young Miss Truchard is a member is not at all the thing."

"Miss Truchard herself?

"An apple never falls very far from the tree, does it? And when I was a debutante myself, her father was the definition of the word scandal."

He put his teacup down and leaned back into the sofa. "Do tell?" Miss Truchard herself had, perhaps naturally, not mentioned anything about a specific past scandal, other than stories from her childhood of the family regularly having to move at a moment's notice.

"Mr. Truchard was young and handsome, and he played deep when gambling was a way of life for almost all young men. But he started winning a little too much and soon enough, everyone knew he was cheating. I remember watching him one night at a rout. He could shuffle cards like a magician. It was mesmerizing. Then it was duels over and over until he actually wounded Lord Lockley almost mortally, and nobody would sit down with him at all. At which point, he eloped with a beautiful young heiress and took her to the continent."

"With all her money?"

"Her family cut her off without a penny, so I suppose he cheated and lied his way across Europe."

Harriet's mother? "Was it a love match?"

She nodded. "Very much a love match. He was exceedingly charming, probably still is. That was the reason he got away with it for so long. Once the duels started and everybody knew what his game was, the jig was up, so he took the biggest prize he could find and left England. I had thought forever, because I have not heard that name in years. But it seems they are back."

"Miss Truchard speaks with perfectly accented English. I would not think she had been raised on the continent."

She shrugged. "A family of cheats is not who you want to associate with when we run a gaming establishment. Everyone of my generation will assume you are open to every kind of bad behavior there is."

"When in fact I am trying to stamp out that behavior as quickly as possible. You know the book *Winning at Whist?*"

His mother nodded. "Of course. It has been all the rage to use the tactics in it this past year."

"It also has a short section toward the back that deals with not being cheated while playing, if you recall. It piqued my interest, so I contacted the publisher and met with the author. She is coming to tonight's card party."

She clapped her hands. "Excellent work, Beaufort. We'll dig these thieves out."

"That author is Miss Truchard."

She blinked in astonishment. "Ah! Then you are not taken with her, you are just inducing her to help us with her knowledge."

"Precisely."

She exhaled. "Oh good. I hated to have to warn you away from her, but I see you are a few steps ahead."

"To be fair, I didn't know anything you just told me. Miss Truchard has been careful not to give too much away about her family situation."

"A smart young lady, then."

"Oh, yes. And from my first impressions, not cut from the same cloth as her parents."

"Careful now." Her tone was gentle, but underneath lay steel. "I don't want to be connected to that family. No, I *will* not. She will do whatever she can to increase her proximity to you. Pray, think on it."

Since she never warned him off anything, and usually trusted him to make his own decisions, he had to listen to her. For she was right: Harriet Truchard had to be nothing more than a beautiful and intriguing means to an end.

"I can admire her without falling in love and marrying her, you know. I just want you to know, since she will be in our home."

She nodded slowly. "Very well. Pray forgive me if I do not want to be introduced. It is not an acquaintance I would pursue."

He bowed. *Thank goodness.* The last thing he needed was his mother interrogating the only good fortune that had come his way.

CHAPTER 14

WHERE MISS TRUCHARD PLAYS THE PART OF FLUFFY INGENUE

The ballroom at Beaufort's was transformed from the bare room Harriet had visited earlier in the month.

The rolled-up carpets were unfurled to reveal plush Axminster. Silver urns overflowed with spring flowers, and the gilded plasterwork shone in the light of the chandeliers. It was elegant, magical, and promised a good time would be had by all.

Cheers rang out from the Hazard table as a young man won the round, with a lady clinging to him.

Wednesday evening would normally see Harriet curled up with a book by her bedside candle, but in this other world, people were carousing about, drinking and gambling.

This was Mother and Father's world, not hers. And yet, here she was.

"We visit all the most elegant places, I vow!" Mariah whispered to Charles. "I never dreamed my season would be so sophisticated."

"It is mesmerizing, is it not?" Harriet replied, even though nobody had spoken to her.

"Be careful," Mariah said. "I don't want Charles to have to pull you off a hot streak."

Harriet nodded. It was better not to gamble at all, than to let it get its hooks into her.

"If she has a hot streak, perhaps I will just give her my coin," Charles said with a laugh, which just showed how little he knew. She certainly did not want either him or Lord Beaufort to see *that* creature.

The reasons she did not gamble were many and varied. And each entirely legitimate. "I have one guinea in my purse and that is all I am allowing myself. Once it is gone, it is gone."

Mariah squeezed her hand. "Knowing you, you'll turn it into ten."

No, I will not. No matter how elegant the gaming room was, she would not succumb to it.

She spotted Lord Beaufort before he saw her. He was at the Faro table, talking to his dealer.

The dealer straightened, and Harriet understood Lord Beaufort's hesitation to suspect him. With an eye patch over one eye, and the other gazing at a fixed distance, he was likely blind. Her suspicion was confirmed when he felt for the cards in front of him, rather than look down for them. It would not be easy for such a man to cheat.

He had a younger man seated next to him who called the cards as he dealt them. She watched the blind dealer for a few moments. He knew exactly where each card was played, where the players were, and handled the cards to perfection. It was the skill a person developed only when they had a set of cards in their hand every waking minute over twenty years or more. Like Father, who would sit in his chair by the fire after dinner, shuffling and reshuffling the pack that he always had in his pocket.

A quick glance around the room told her that the other dealers were also military. They might not be wearing uniforms, but their posture was straight, they had short, sharp movements, and eyes that seemed to take in everything.

If she didn't know someone was stealing from Beaufort, she would have thought he'd picked the perfect team.

But Harriet didn't care who they were or what their background was. Just because a man wore a uniform, didn't mean he was above suspicion. She'd heard enough stories of soldiers' gaming habits to know they were just men, like any other. The hard part would be convincing Lord Beaufort.

Mariah leaned in to speak softly to Harriet. "I'm afraid the play may be too deep."

Harriet shook her head. "Lord Beaufort said there are no IOUs, so everybody plays within the bounds of what is in their pockets or reticule. So not too much deep play, I think?"

But wandering from table to table, Harriet discovered how very wrong she was. Enormous sums of money were changing hands at the private card tables; while at the Faro bank, people were staking rolls of guineas at a time. She supposed pounds were just slips of paper, and an entire fortune could be in the large pockets of a man's evening coat.

Mariah chose not to play, but rather to lend Charles her luck. And she truly meant it. Father always said she was his lucky charm and liked to have a small lock of her hair in his pocket at all times. Mariah had taken this quirk to her heart.

As if such a thing existed. However, she smiled to see Charles play Hazard and gain a small pile of coins within a half-hour. He had just won another round and Mariah was clapping her hands, when someone stood very close behind Harriet.

Beaufort.

She knew without turning.

He put a hand under her elbow—a silent plea for her to withdraw from the table. She accompanied him, and he took her to the supper room, where he strode to one of the vacant tables.

He bowed. "Welcome to Beaufort's. I'm happy you're here."

She curtsied, looking up at him from beneath her lashes, feeling just a *little* flirtatious. "Of course you are!" She smiled, so he knew she was joking with him. "Do you have something specific for me to do? Because if you don't, I will float from table to table and see if I can detect any strange happenings. I'm playing a bashful *ingenue*, so don't be alarmed by the way I act."

He nodded. "A good plan. Let them underestimate you."

"You'd be surprised what people say when they think you have feathers for brains."

"It is hard to believe anyone who conversed with you would think you lacked intellect." His gaze connected with hers and the room was suddenly a little heated and her thoughts disordered.

Tonight he wore an evening jacket made of velvet in the deepest of blues. His snowy white cravat had an emerald pinned to it, a shining thing that caught her eye.

He noticed her attention was snagged by the gem. "Do you like it?" His eyes were bright with mischief.

"Do I like it? It's flawless. I love it." It was bright green and clear as crystal.

"Yes, when you have a solitaire it needs to be. Would you like it? If you find my cheats, you are welcome to it."

Her heart skipped along a little as she envisaged herself unpinning it from his cravat, her fingers sliding close to the warmth of his body. Then she would lean into him slightly, her head tucked beneath his chin. He might wrap an arm around her and pull her closer. She would inhale the beautiful smell of him.

"Are you well?"

She snapped her eyes back to Beaufort to see him looking at her with concern. As well he might. She was being ridiculous.

"Very well indeed."

"Make sure you try the strawberry tartlets at supper. They are delicious. And I will see you afterward. These events go well into the night."

"I am quite used to being a night owl. Even if it is normally with a book."

"Nothing has happened here for the last two gatherings," he said. "It makes me wonder whether I've been imagining the whole thing."

She shook her head. "It is more likely our perpetrators have been visiting other establishments. I shall just keep attending until I see something."

He walked to the window, and she followed, looking at their reflection in the glass as she stood behind him. "I hope this doesn't take too long," he said, his shoulders slumping a little.

She pulled on his arm, to make him turn to look at her. "It will take as long as it takes. And we will keep coming back here, and Scanlan can win or lose his shillings at your Hazard table until it does."

He nodded and exhaled. "Thank you." He looked out to the gaming floor. She followed his gaze to where an older lady in a lavender gown and darker purple turban laughed with a small group of gamblers. "I will not introduce you to my mother, cousin, or uncle. The fewer people who know what you are doing, the better."

"Ah, of course." He wasn't wrong. Anyone could tip off the culprits. "I will stay out of their way and not do anything to draw attention to myself. Including speaking to you."

"Not because I don't *want* to introduce you. It's not that."

He would be a fool if he *did* want to. "Of course. Please, think nothing of it."

"They are not all in my confidence. I must be careful. Mother has already remembered your father's gambling history."

Oh, that was not good. Father's past was littered with duels, cheating, and generally making a nuisance of himself. It just proved that society had a very long memory. Lady Beaufort would be suspicious of her, if not repulsed. How disappointing.

"Well then, I would prefer not to be introduced to your mother too." She dipped into a curtsy. "I'll start right now, but in all likelihood nothing will happen."

Harriet was not wrong. Nothing happened that evening. Or the evening after that, or the following week.

It pleased Charles to keep visiting, as many of his Parliament peers frequented Beaufort's and he could make important connections. The brass key was entry to more than the just the parties, it seemed.

But she couldn't just wander from table to table all evening for weeks on end. Eventually she would have to sit down and gamble, which she did, playing Vingt-et-un with small amounts, so that by the end of the night she came out with roughly the same number of coins that she went in with. Maybe a few more.

When the play went too deep, she excused herself. She was careful not to win too much and played the lucky young miss to perfection. She was also careful to handle her cards the way a novice would, and ask just the right number of obvious questions.

Some nights, she'd stand at the Hazard table and Beau would stand beside her, ostensibly to cheer others on, but somehow his hand always brushed hers. Other nights, he'd saunter past her while she sat at supper, and place a tart on her plate. He never spoke, never greeted her unless he was greeting Charles and Mariah as well.

She would have thought he'd forgotten her, if you didn't take into account their constant game of *caught you staring*. Sometimes Beau would spy her looking wistfully at him as he leaned over a table, or laughed at someone's joke. Which was hardly her fault. He was never more handsome than when he laughed, with his head tipped back and the candlelight catching the golden streaks in his hair. She looked up whenever she heard it, because why wouldn't she?

Other times she would catch him staring at her, his gaze heated. Those times she would slowly wink at him, then look away as though he didn't interest her at all.

Which was such an enormous lie, but so much fun.

Three weeks, and many fruit tarts later—Harriet stood at the edge of the gaming room watching proceedings. She now recognized the regular guests and ruled them out for unfair play. This night, however, differed slightly from the others. Unfamiliar faces milled around the room, and a flicker of alarm made her body tense. Something was off, and she couldn't put her finger on what.

She contemplated the tables for a few more moments before she realized men seated at different tables were positioning themselves so that they were in communication with each other.

One at the card table would tap his foot, one at the Faro table would touch the left or right side of his nose, meanwhile, the one at the Vingt-et-un table was accepting all the communications.

She wandered over to the table, watching the dealer. He was a third of the way through his stack of five decks. The further he made his way into those decks, the higher the probability that someone counting the cards or watching the cards would know what was coming up.

The man at the Faro table had a clear view of the dealer, who was lifting his cards a degree too high. Was it on purpose? Was he unwittingly revealing a full view of the next card he was going to deal?

All she knew was that soon the man playing Vingt-et-un was going to bet everything he had. There would be a special communication to signal it and Beaufort would be taken for a great deal of money.

How had they gained admission to Beaufort's? Although it wasn't just the *crème de la crème* of society who made their way to Beaufort's. Indeed, it was quite an eclectic crowd. Bluestocking spinsters, society hostesses, MPs and even the clergy. People were allowed to bring a guest, just as she had come with Mariah and Charles, so perhaps they had gained entry that way.

She walked sedately toward Beaufort, who was in conversation by the fireplace. He saw her approach and interpreted her raised eyebrows as a request for his presence.

He shook the man's hand and left, coming to Harriet with two outstretched hands as if greeting a long-lost friend. "How can I help you, Miss Truchard? I hope you're having a lovely evening."

The touch of his hands sparked a thrill up her arms, and

she squeezed them back, ignoring his question. "There are three men, the one in the brown coat on Faro, the bearded one on Hazard, and they are both communicating with the man in the blue coat playing Vingt-et-un. The dealer is lifting his cards too high and the man at the Faro table is watching. You will lose a fortune any moment unless you swap that dealer and card deck out."

His hands clenched hers, and then he let go abruptly and walked over to the table, tapping the dealer on the shoulder. He murmured something in his ear and took over.

Although he knew the deck was compromised, he did not replace it. Instead, he dealt the games himself, making sure that the man behind him had no chance to see the cards he was dealing. The game cycled through to the end of the decks, without any large bets being placed, and Harriet breathed a sigh of relief. Perhaps she had saved him some money, but more importantly, perhaps this was the group of men who had caused him so many problems.

Beaufort closed the table down, then she watched as he went straight to his major-domo and had footmen stationed at the door. He went to each dealer and had a quiet word in their ear. Then his gaze searched the room, only stopping when he reached her. Their eyes met and when she nodded toward the ladies' retiring room, a flash of understanding passed between them.

She strolled out, waiting for him to catch up with her.

He did. He touched her elbow, stopping, and then turned her around to face him. There was a triumphant light in his golden-brown eyes, and it made her glow inside. "How did you know?"

She lightly rested her hand on his evening coat. The velvet was soft under her fingers. "Something didn't feel right, so I watched until I figured out what it was."

"They were looking at the dealer's cards?"

"Yes, he was indiscreet. I would have to watch him for another few sessions to see if it is habitual. Plenty of criminals take advantage of dealers who don't do their job well. They search for it. It doesn't explain your Faro bank breaking, but it might be the same gang."

"So not his fault, perhaps. I have asked my men to quietly remove them from the room and detain them."

"You should call Bow Street," she said. "Sometimes just the sighting of a Bow Street runner is enough to stop these people in their tracks. They like to operate below the notice of the authorities. Which is why you won't see them coming back to your establishment every single night. But there are only so many places they can go. Especially now that travel to the continent has been all but cut off."

"I have sent for my contact there. He'll arrive soon."

He didn't elaborate, just lifted her hand and brought it to his lips. She closed her eyes as he kissed her gloved fingertips. "I can't thank you enough."

Even through the silk, the brief touch of his lips sent shivers up her arm. Her breath hitched and her knees felt too weak to support her. *I must leave before he sees how he affects me.*

"It was nothing." She gently pulled her hand from his.

But he just took it again, leading her down the hallway. "Come, let's wait for Richard in my study. We won't be missed."

"We should not be alone. Your reputation—"

"My reputation—and yours—will be quite safe," he cut in. "There are none to see us. They are all too busy at the tables. He won't be long, and then you can go back to your sister."

She should not. But how could she not follow him when no one had ever intrigued her more?

CHAPTER 15

WHERE LORD BEAUFORT TRIES TO RESIST TROUBLE

Beau schooled his features into a calm mask, when all he wanted to do was pump his fist in the air in triumph. The cheats were being rounded up with the lure of an expensive shot of brandy and would then be taken to the cellar to await the arrival of Richard Wolfe, his contact at Bow Street. The only contact who would look the other way at his card parties. It was hard to say if any arrests would be made based on Harriet's testimony, but at the very least they would be questioned and would think twice before visiting Beaufort's again.

He led Harriet into the study and carefully left the door open.

She sank into the comfortable leather chair by the fire. "This chair is like a cloud," she said. "How do they make it so soft?"

"Feathers, I believe." He smiled that such a simple thing could make her happy.

Her slippers—poking out from underneath her satin gown —were faded and the ribbons a little frayed. She wore a saffron-colored gown that by rights should clash with her red hair, but instead turned it the color of rosé champagne. Her cheeks were flushed with their triumph, and a smile lingered on her lips.

She looked, in short, incredibly beautiful.

"Being a young lady," she said. "I would prefer not to be here when Bow Street arrives. I told you everything I saw, surely you can relay it? It would be more convincing coming from you."

It would also keep her out of Bow Street's crosshairs, and that had his eyes narrowing. Surely her name could not be known to them? But an innocent would not try to avoid the authorities.

She looked at him for an answer. He exhaled. *Any* young lady would not want to be subjected to the law enforcers.

"Certainly. After all, once you pointed it out, I saw what you saw."

But only *after* she'd pointed it out. He would have missed the whole exchange otherwise.

Three weeks.

That was all it had taken for her to find the culprits, for surely there could not be more than one group of cheats. He had been battling this for almost six months.

He must have stared at her for longer than he should have, because she shifted uncomfortably. "What?"

He shook his head. "Oh, nothing. I'm just happy to finally have this terrible time behind me."

Her eyebrows drew together. "I'm not sure you have. I managed to find one table, and one game, where a careless dealer created an opportunity to cheat. What about the losses at Faro and Hazard? We should continue our investigation for a few weeks more."

"But three men, working in tandem, surely we have caught them all? I am amazed you picked up the cheating at all. You cannot have frequented the gaming hells where this kind of ruse happens."

"I knew what to look for," she said, her tone holding the slightest edge of derisiveness. "And I can tell you that when a group of men band together with the object of stealing, three is not a large number. Mother and Father have spoken of groups of ten or more men intent on one goal and working together. Please, don't give this up too early because of one small win. I am here to help."

Mother's words drifted back to him. *She will do whatever she can to increase her proximity to you. Pray, think on it.* And what was worse, he wanted her around, perhaps a little *too* much.

She rose from the chair to stand in front of him and he took her hands in his. With him resting on the desk, they were at eye level. Her luminous gray eyes, almost silver in the candlelight, were framed by eyelashes that were a mix of red and gold, long and curled. Was she an innocent bystander, caught up in a web of bad people through no fault of her own? Would she lie to him if he asked? Was Mother right? Would she hide their past to stay close to him?

"I know you are. But you are closely related to people that would do me harm. Can you assure me your parents would not take advantage of this situation if they could? Who are they exactly?"

She dropped his hand and looked away from his gaze. "You have asked this before. They are just … my parents. I am not in possession of all the things they have done, but I can tell you neither of them has been before the Old Bailey. So they can't have done anything so terrible, can they?"

Message received. She would not tell him the entire truth, the history his mother had shared. He couldn't help feeling a drop of disappointment.

He pushed himself off the desk and took her hand again. "Well, this is the end, I suppose. Thank you for everything. I'm sure Bow Street will interrogate the men and we will get all the answers we need."

"Wanting it to be over doesn't mean it is." She lifted her free hand as though to touch his face and then let it drop to her side.

He was still holding her left hand, and he looked down, transfixed by the sight of her fingers woven with his. His arm lifted involuntarily and before he knew it, he'd tucked a wayward lock of hair behind her ear.

And just like that, he realized Mother was right. He didn't just admire her beauty; he wanted it for himself.

He must say goodbye to her this evening, because soon he wouldn't care who her parents were or what they had done. He would kiss her. And then perhaps he wouldn't be able to stop kissing her. Because those lips that she just moistened were delectable, and it was hard work to resist them.

A few moments of silence passed, and he was about to release her hand when she raised her gaze to his. "I know you don't want me here for a moment more than you must. A Truchard helping you? Unthinkable." Tears pooled in her eyes, and he had the inkling they rarely did. "But I am not them. Bertie and I never have been."

She was begging him to accept her, even though she knew her family walked a crooked line. And what could he say? He had trusted her from the moment they'd met. But that didn't change what her family was, and that aligning himself with them while running a gambling house spoke louder than any denials he could utter about fair play at Beaufort's.

"There now," he lifted a hand and used his thumb to wipe the tear that fell down her cheek. "No need to apologize. We cannot choose our family."

It was, apparently, the right thing to say. Her expression cleared, and she leaned in to kiss him on the cheek. He stilled, not wanting to move the wrong way, but the kiss landed at the very corner of his mouth anyway, as light as butterfly wings. It set goose bumps alight from his arms to the nape of his neck. He closed his eyes.

"Thank you," she murmured, still close to him. He so desperately wanted to turn a little to the left to capture her lips and find out if she tasted of the champagne he had seen her sipping earlier. But no, he couldn't take advantage of her in that way.

Then, as she started to pull away, her lips caught his, and he knew he was lost.

With a soft groan, he slid his arms around her waist and pulled her closer, until it felt like they were touching from their toes to their shoulders.

She felt so incredibly good.

So right.

He deepened the kiss and all awareness of the world beyond the two of them came to a sudden stop. All his attention, all his effort, just for her. She did taste of champagne and also the sweetness of the strawberry tart he put on her plate every party.

She relaxed into him and sighed, like everything she had ever wanted was happening right at this very moment. It was easy to guess it might have been her first kiss. Her heart hammered through her chest, but then, his was hammering just as hard. Her hands stole up past his neck and she ran her fingers through his hair, setting off a reaction he was sure she was unaware of.

Her touch ran through him like a wildfire, igniting smaller blazes wherever it went.

This was dangerous. He needed to step away, now, no matter how much he ached to do otherwise. He gently pulled away from her, his gaze sweeping her face, taking in everything—the freckles sprinkled across her nose, her delicately arched brows. "That's the kind of goodbye that makes me wish it were not a goodbye. But it must be. I will take you back to your sister before Bow Street arrives."

A pretty blush crept across her cheeks. "Yes, of course. But it's not far, I can reach it by myself." She let her hands drop to her sides and took one step back, and then another, before turning toward the door. When she reached it, she stopped.

"Goodbye for now. I truly hope this is the end of your problems. It has been a pleasure."

He undid the emerald pin from his cravat, to give it to her as payment.

Her hand came up as if to take it, but she hesitated, conflict evident in her expression. Her hand dropped back to her side. "You already paid me with Bertie's commission. I'm no fool, I know those diamonds weren't worth so much."

She curtsied, bowing her head, and went through the door, closing it softly behind her.

He sat in a daze, staring at the wall of offenders that had so caught her gaze the first time she visited his study. How many of those people did she know? Would she have told him if he asked?

It was best this way. His lips still tingled from her kiss, and he wanted more than anything to call her back. But this was what he needed to do for his family. His *duty* called him to repay all the debts and close these card parties down.

Deep in thought, he bit on his thumb and tasted her salty tears from when he had dashed them away earlier. Dear Harriet, so much softer than she would like him to believe. It would be all too easy to fall irrevocably in love with her.

———

Slightly shaky and with her head still reeling from the kiss and all the dangerous feelings it evoked, Harriet returned to the gaming room and found Mariah sitting on a settee, fanning herself. Her skin had taken on a pasty hue, and she looked anything but well. Harriet rushed to her side.

"What has happened? Have you taken ill?" Harriet said. Mother always complained about how sick she was while pregnant. Perhaps Mariah would be the same.

Mariah cradled her stomach. "I'm so glad you're here. I'm not feeling quite the thing, and Charles would like to take me home. He is calling for the carriage. I'm sure this is quite normal for my delicate state, but that doesn't help."

"Then let's go home and tuck you into bed, all cozy. These late nights might be a little much for both of us."

Harriet linked her arm through Mariah's and guided her sister down the stairs and toward the front door. They passed Beau's study, where he stood in front of the board with all the portraits on it.

Perhaps her leaving was for the best after all.

CHAPTER 16

WHERE A BROTHER STEALS THE FOOD FROM YOUR PLATE

Two weeks later, the secretary to the Commander-in-Chief requested Bertie's presence at his offices to sign paperwork for his commission. With the last of her royalty payment, Harriet took her brother to his favorite chophouse, Dolly's, to celebrate. It was a small establishment hunched in the shadow of St. Paul's Cathedral and so noisy she could barely hear him.

Ever-hungry Bertie ploughed through the enormous steak that covered his plate, with the appetite that only a gentleman not yet reached his majority could summon. He finished chewing a mouthful, swallowed, and took a gulp of ale. "I vow, Lord Beaufort is a good egg. I'm grateful beyond words to him. And to you." He reached across the table and squeezed her shoulder. "You are a capital sister."

The excitement and gratitude in his eyes were all the thanks she needed. She handed him the thick envelope that had been delivered to her at Mariah's, as she hadn't wanted it sent to her parents' address. "Present yourself at the Secretary to the Commander-in-Chief at the Horse Guards tomorrow with the signed paperwork."

And with that, she had done it. The faint dream of helping Bertie to be more than a Newmarket scourge was achieved. But the achievement could not have happened without the help of Lord Beaufort, and that connection had sadly ended before she'd really had the chance to make best use of it.

He had sent her away with a kiss and a thank you, and it was over. But not for her. She constantly thought about him. Or, to be more precise, about the desperate need to kiss him again. Which should have been a warning sign that her heart was engaged, but that first kiss had been abominably short. Did all gentlemen kiss that magically?

But if he was going to disappear out of her life, she should have taken that solitaire emerald. Her stupid honesty and sense of fair play had hobbled her again. She had miscalculated in the heat of the moment, and now she was down a perfectly good gem that would have come in very handy.

She took a deep breath. *Concentrate on the important things.* With Beaufort's help, Bertie would be an officer, fighting to defend England. Even if she would not have a good night's sleep until he was home again, at least one of them was free.

Using his butter knife, Bertie opened the envelope and scanned the letter. His eyes opened wide. "The 88th foot? Never did I think the 88th. Not that I wouldn't have been happy with anything, but this is a dream."

"The other letter is from Lord Beaufort's man of business, outlining all the shops he has placed credit to purchase your uniforms, boots and whatever other paraphernalia a new officer needs."

More useful than the emerald, perhaps. And unexpected. She'd hoped that Beaufort would visit Mariah's house in person as opposed to sending written confirmation of Bertie's acceptance into the army, because she'd wanted one last glimpse of him. When she asked herself why, there was no answer but a small stab of hurt.

"It was jolly good of him. But I suppose you solved his problem, so I will accept the help and say nothing more."

"We had best not, considering I don't think his problem is solved."

"No?" Bertie motioned to the attendant for more ale.

"One little band of three men responsible for so much loss? Hardly likely." She pushed her own ale over to him.

"He seemed to think it was over. Surely he knows."

"Stupid man wants it to be over, so thinks it is. Doesn't have the sense he was born with." Harriet cut her steak a little more violently than necessary.

He brother frowned and reached out, wrapping his hand around hers. "You care for him."

Harriet drew her hand away instantly. "What on earth makes you say that?"

"You call me stupid and you love me, too." He grinned and lifted his tankard in the air. "Only the stupidest men for you, Harriet Truchard!" A frown replaced Bertie's smile. "Although I think that Donovan chap is not the answer, no matter how often Father tells me he is."

"Did you meet him?" He had been blessedly absent from Mariah's drawing room and she'd hoped he was gone altogether.

"He visits every day, sauntering in with a walking cane that he obviously doesn't need. I think he likes to whack people with it." He took Harriet's roll and buttered it, then gave it back to her.

"I am ambivalent toward him, but I could grow to hate him

given half a chance," Harriet mused. "If you can, find out what he has over Father. It's something."

Bertie swallowed. "You think? Odds teeth, it would be too bad of them to sell you off to such a scoundrel. Run away if they try, won't you?"

Harriet smiled. To be eighteen and think one could just 'run away' with no thought to the funds needed to do so.

She might be trapped if she couldn't find a way out fast. The thought put her off the fine food that sat in front of her. She put her knife and fork together, and Bertie swooped, stealing the rest of her steak and depositing it on his plate. She was still laughing when a gentleman came to their table. He cleared his throat, bowed when they looked up, then said. "Excuse me, do I recognize you from my cousin's gaming parties?"

There was something about him that was familiar. His muttonchops? They were *spectacularly* bushy.

"Sorry to introduce myself. Not the done thing." He addressed this to Bertie. "I am Mr. Thomas Astley, cousin to Lord Beaufort."

Bertie looked over at Harriet. "Harriet, may I introduce Lord Beaufort's cousin, Mr. Astley to you?"

Ah, now she knew. He was the man who sat with the skillful blind dealer, who she now realized must be Beaufort's uncle Horace. There was something in Mr. Astley's arrogant expression that made her grateful Beau had not introduced her to his family.

The waiting maid assumed he had joined their table and plonked a tankard of ale in front of him, as well as a knife and fork. He didn't correct her.

Thomas leaned in. "Now what I want to know is, why my

bore of a cousin was obsessed with you every night you attended. He stared at you all night long. I noticed."

Harriet shifted uneasily in her chair. "I do not believe he did so unless he was keeping me in check."

Bertie laughed. "And if ever anyone needed to be kept in check, it's you, Trouble."

"I've not been called that for years, Bertie, and I'll not have you resurrecting that horrible name."

Thomas grinned, but there was something calculating in his cool gaze. "You are trouble, are you?"

"Oh, I have a veritable *talent* for trouble," Harriet replied. "But I am putting it behind me."

Mr. Astley was about to say something, but Bertie got in first. "I gather since you call your cousin a bore that you don't see eye to eye?" It was exactly the question she would have wanted to ask, but so much better coming from Bertie.

Mr. Astley crossed his arms over his chest and rocked back slightly on the chair. "He's the most prosy old thing ever. Doesn't let a man have any fun. I thought if he got into the petticoat line, he might mellow and increase my allowance. So when I spotted you here, I couldn't miss my chance to find out."

Ah, now she understood. He was the kind of gentleman who wanted someone to pay his way, instead of earning an honest living. He wouldn't find any sympathy with either her or Bertie. Harriet shrugged, her wariness mounting. "Surely you knew this was likely not the case when he did not introduce you to me."

"Oh, that's no surprise," Thomas said, waving the comment away with a hand on which rings glittered brightly. "I have a history of sweeping in and carrying away whatever lady he might have his eye on. You see, ladies don't want to dance with a man who puts them to sleep with stories about how many candles Beaufort's burns per night. They want to be told they are enchanting and dance like angels."

He kept talking, but Harriet stopped listening after he said the word 'enchanting'. Beaufort had said that to her. Had said, *I find the freckles sprinkling your nose enchanting, If I could dance every dance with you, I would*. Oh, to have that evening again.

"It's the way at our age, I think," Bertie was saying, "We don't have enough income of our own, but living here in London is deuced expensive. I have run up bills at fifteen shops around town. The quarter payments can't come quickly enough."

Since no shopkeeper would ever extend Bertie credit, this was not true. It meant Bertie was playing Thomas with practiced ease, making him relax to gain information. Which just proved there were some things their parents really had taught them well.

"Precisely. That's what I keep telling Beaufort. I can't live like this. I'm not a child, I'm a man trying to live on a pittance. Can't be done." He stopped abruptly, perhaps realizing he had said too much. And he had that desperate look that she'd often seen on her father's face after a particularly bad run of luck.

She glanced at Bertie. He met her gaze briefly, eyebrow arched. He'd seen it too.

"Surely if your cousin knew you were in truly straitened circumstances he would come to your rescue?" Bertie said.

He laughed bitterly. "He said I should live within my means, as he does."

Bertie's face lit up. Only she knew it was false comradery. "Come and be in the 88th foot with me!"

"You know, a set of colors might be just the thing." He

returned his attention to Harriet. "Anyway, I'm glad my cousin is not pursuing you. I can see you are a lively lady and don't deserve to be lumbered with someone like him for the rest of your life."

"That was never on the cards," Harriet said. "Bertie and I do not move in the same circles as you or he. I may be a gentleman's daughter, but sometimes the caliber of a gentleman truly does matter."

He shrugged and there was something in his expression that suggested she'd been dismissed. Harriet smiled. He had none of the polish of his cousin and it was truly hard to believe he'd ever stolen a march on him at all. It was probably all make believe.

To Bertie, he said, "I went to the mill in Cheltenham last week."

Bertie nodded and the two of them continued to talk of mills and the pugilistic science until Harriet's eyes glazed over. She looked around the room until her gaze landed on a familiar and unwelcome sight, sitting at a table alone, waiting for her to notice him.

Mr. Donovan.

He was alone, but there was an extra tankard at the table and the other chair was pushed back as though someone had just vacated it.

Her stomach dropped.

He lifted his jug of ale in salute to her. *Please don't come over here, please don't come over here.*

Perhaps she should leave posthaste.

"Gentlemen, I will leave you to this very interesting conversation. Bertie—" she put a few shillings on the table. "Thank you for dining with me today. I hope you will have news for me soon."

Once out on the street, Harriet took a deep breath and hailed a passing hackney. She was in the cab and away when she saw Mr. Donovan exit the chophouse, looking up and down the street for her.

Not today, Mr. Donovan.

CHAPTER 17

WHERE AN OLD SEADOG COMES CLEAN

Beau closed his eyes and swore softly under his breath. From any angle, the dice in play only had sides with fours, fives, and sixes. Exactly as Harriet had foretold. But just as he reached to stop play, the set was swapped for another that had all the proper markings. The game was moving fast and the opportunity to prove his suspicion was over in a second. But each time it happened, someone bet a large amount. Who profited? It was always an unknown gentleman and always someone different. His dealer was the one swapping out the dice, so that, at least, was a common denominator.

Harriet was right. Not just the Hazard dealer. All of them. The men he'd defended as brave and honorable. He watched each game the ex-sailors administered from vantage points around the room. It had taken a few weeks, but the evidence was there almost every night they operated. Dealing a card from the bottom of the pack, using bad dice, moving bets in Faro.

And he'd thought he was *helping* them by making them

croupiers. A guinea per shift so they could get back on their feet after the war. How they must have laughed at him. Anger burned beneath his skin, making him break out in a sweat. The only question was whether his uncle and cousin were in it with them.

That would be the ultimate betrayal, and one he'd never dreamed of.

But, devil take it, he was thinking about it now. If his uncle's blindness had taught him one thing, it was that an injury didn't stop a man from being skilled or perceptive. Quite the opposite.

While it wouldn't do to accuse his uncle without being utterly sure of his guilt—and indeed, Horace might well be more horrified than Beau, considering he had been the one to employ them—Beau still needed to discuss the matter with him.

But three o'clock in the morning, after a long shift on his feet, was not the best time to confront someone about theft. Especially when his anger was so high—it would lead to things being said in haste that he might well regret.

So, when his uncle arrived at his usual time Thursday morning to debrief his staff on the previous night's party, Beau had his temper under control. This was his father's brother; he did not want to sever the relationship without just reason.

Beau made for the small room off the kitchen that the staff used for all their meals. He stood in the doorway and Uncle Horace turned around. "Beau, my good lad." Horace said, with his uncanny way of recognizing footfall. He motioned to the men at the table with him—all of them dealers under suspicion. "Take tea with us?"

How often had he taken tea with them all, laughing and

listening to their stories when they'd been stealing from him? Too many to count. "Not today." Beau's gaze swept over the other four men. "Give us a few minutes in private?"

They left their meals without meeting his gaze and filed out. Beau closed the door behind them.

Uncle Horace took a sip of his tea and felt around the table in front of him for a biscuit. The staff always arranged his plate the same way, so he found it quickly. "I heard you've been watching the gaming tables closely. Is anything amiss?"

Beau took a seat and a deep breath. "There has been something amiss for quite some time, I'm afraid. Investigating has been hard because any cheating puts our dealers under suspicion."

Uncle Horace stiffened, and his teacup rattled in the saucer. "Now, not necessarily, my boy. There are many ways people can be underhanded in their play, without help from the dealer."

"Yes, I would expect you to take up your own men's cause. I felt the same way. Which was why I took it upon myself these last few weeks to do the unpalatable job."

Uncle Horace scowled. "And would you know a cheat if you saw one? You who have barely ever dealt on the tables? These people are so underhanded that their tricks go unnoticed even by the most experienced of players. There's little more to go on but a feeling that something's wrong." He shrugged. "It's why men so seldom get called out for cheating. Proof is difficult."

Beau leaned back in his chair. "I know what my eyes saw."

"And what was that?" Horace chewed on his biscuit as though Beau's answer was of no consequence.

"Well, on top of the dealer giving players a very good glance at his upcoming cards in Vingt-et-un, I also saw a set of dice on the Hazard table that sported sides with only fours, fives and sixes. Not to mention shady dealing on the Faro table and the fact that I'm sure money is being skimmed off the takings. The house won a great deal last night, and I kept a reckoning in my head. The takings were down from even the simple calculation I made. How do you explain that?"

"You saw all of that in *one* evening? My, you have been busy." Horace chuckled and planted his hand on his belly. "And fanciful. Ghosts, Beaufort, you're looking for ghosts to explain our run of bad luck."

"I'm looking for *reasons* for a fall in profit. I caught it over many evenings, not one night. However, when you put it all together, it's quite damning isn't it? The question is whether you trust my word or the word of the men we have working for us."

He didn't mention that Uncle Horace himself was under suspicion. He didn't have the stomach for it, even though he desperately wanted to know.

"It was that chit, wasn't it?"

"I don't know any *chits*, Uncle."

His tone was severe, and Uncle Horace closed his mouth. But only briefly. "I know who she is, you know, and you shouldn't trust her."

"I trusted only my own eyes and ears in this circumstance."

"Been trying to place her voice ever since I heard her on my Loo table," he said. "I finally got it last week. But when it seemed you dropped her, I decided not to mention it. Sounds just like her mother. Louisa Truchard."

"I'm sure I don't need to know. Old news." But what was interesting was how quick Uncle Horace was to point the finger elsewhere.

"Francis Truchard," Uncle Horace continued determinedly, "was a rotten apple at Eton and only progressed from there. Nobody likes to accuse a man of cheating, especially a gentleman only two steps removed from an earldom, but when it becomes blatant, there's no ignoring it. He was challenged to a duel but chose instead to take Louisa and run to the continent. It looks like they're back. More's the pity. I'm sure you can't trust his children further than you could throw them."

"I am fully apprised of Miss Truchard's parentage."

"And are you aware that her mother and father have portraits in your study?" Uncle Horace stilled, likely listening for Beau's response.

And he couldn't help a sharp intake of breath that his uncle's astute hearing would no doubt pick up.

"There, you didn't know *that* one, did you?" Horace said, triumphantly. "And you'll wonder how I know, but Thomas is a wily one. He met her at Dolly's and he made the connection."

He remembered back to the day when Harriet looked so intently at the wall of portraits. But what had she asked? *Are all these people criminals?* As though she couldn't bear the thought her parents were. In her mind, they were unreliable, but not criminal. Her opinion would be they had never outright stolen anything, if you didn't count cheating at cards. Which he most certainly did.

He mulled over the revelation, trying to decide if it changed his affection for Miss Truchard. The horrifyingly honest answer was that it didn't. "I am not concerned because, unlike my own employees, she was *not* trying to steal from me."

"Give it time."

Beau shook his head. "She hasn't been here for weeks—and in that time, the bank has lost multiple times."

He hadn't spent so many nights in her company without understanding her character. She wasn't writing *How to Spot a Cheat* so that she could run her own scam. No, she was fully aware of the kinds of swindlers that frequented gaming establishments, and she wanted to raise a warning flag for unsuspecting people.

Besides, when she *had* visited his nightly parties, she only ever gambled pennies or shillings at a time, maybe a crown. She only won a little, and never played to the extent of her abilities. Because he'd watched her do that when she played with him. There was an aura of focus to the exclusion of all else that was absent when she played at his tables.

"And you will be alarmed to hear that this does not change my opinion of Miss Truchard, no matter what her parents might be guilty of," Beau said, and then added in a firmer tone, "Tell me what you know, Uncle. I will discover it in any case."

"You don't take after your father much, but in stubbornness, I believe you do." Uncle's face was a mask, but his lips were tightly pressed. He put his hands in his lap, perhaps to stop Beau from seeing how they shook.

A long silence stretched out between them, until finally Uncle Horace nodded and lifted his unseeing gaze to his nephew. "If they took anything, it was only to benefit other veterans in dire straits who were not so lucky as to score such a wonderful job."

There was an element of pride to his pronouncement that sharpened Beau's suspicions.

"Oh, truly? I suppose that makes sense." Beau kept his voice impassive. "You've always been such a strong advocate of veteran's welfare. So you knew what they were up to?" *Did you put them up to it?*

He shrugged. "Of course! I assumed you did, too. You said yourself that you wanted to support veterans coming back from war because the government doesn't, but then when I do it, you get all upset about it!"

Then when I do it. Beau's sense of triumph was as sharp as the stab of betrayal. Uncle Horace believed he was robbing the rich to pay the poor. His own family notwithstanding. It was obvious from his puffed-out chest and straight shoulders that he considered himself a hero.

"I see," Beau said calmly, taking a steadying breath. It wouldn't do to just pick his uncle up by the collar and throw him out into the street. He had more to find out.

Encouraged by Beau's mild demeanor, Horace forged on. "Why yes, my boy. So many veterans in such distress. It's impossible not to want to help them."

"I never thought about it that way," Beau murmured, still friendly. "I suppose you conclude the result justifies the means. I only wish it didn't come at my expense."

Uncle Horace let out a bark of a laugh. "Fine for you with the weight of your title and hereditary lands behind you. These men have *nothing*, sometimes even less than the coat on their backs. These are men I fought with."

"And if only my father had a clutch of daughters, the title would be yours."

"I don't think about that." His frown suggested that perhaps he did.

"My question is, are you the mastermind who thought it all up, or did you just ignore it?" *Keep going, Uncle.* There was nothing he liked more than to be thought more intelligent than everyone around him. Most often, he was.

Uncle Horace sank into his chair. "I find I cannot lie to you, not now that you ask me directly." He exhaled. "There was nothing in this to hurt you, only the fatted calves you have at your routs."

Oh, well that's fine, then! There was the chance he didn't realize how serious the thieving had become. But what of Thomas?

"I can't believe you would willingly hurt Mother or myself. You are my father's brother and for that, and for the fact you are one of England's heroes, you will always have my esteem. I just need to get to the bottom of this."

Beau made it sound like it was investigative only, and for his edification. Not that everyone was about to lose their jobs. Uncle included. He seemed to have convinced himself that this form of cheating was honorable. The mind played funny tricks when it wanted something badly enough.

"I may have encouraged the boys a little. Perhaps let them know that if they did something slightly underhanded to help their brothers, I would do nothing to stop them. Indeed, how could I? I am blind."

Beau sat in silence for a few moments, not trusting himself to speak. This was it, then. The end of the mystery. But he couldn't be glad of it. Not when it meant a family already beleaguered by debt was to be further torn apart.

"Did you not think of us at all? I cannot afford to give away hundreds of pounds a night. I need it to pay this family's debts."

"Hundreds of pounds? Doing it too brown, my boy. They took the barest amount."

"No. They're getting greedier by the week. When the Faro bank broke twice, we lost closer to five thousand."

His sharp intake of breath told Beau he hadn't known. "Can't blame them for the Faro!"

"I can, and do. Give them an inch, and they'll take a mile. Isn't that the saying? Well, they took many miles, and it stops now."

"Thomas wouldn't let them," he retorted.

"Wouldn't he? Is this the same Thomas who is constantly at *point non plus* and begging for his wages early?" Beau pushed back from the table and stood. "It would be best if you and Thomas left. As much as it pains me."

"You would throw us out?" His mouth was a flat unhappy line. "After everything we've done for you?"

"Not just you, but your entire cohort of dealers. They will receive their quarterly wage early today and will not work here again. I would point out that you have encouraged young and impressionable men to commit fraud."

"You can't. This is all I have. All Thomas has."

"Then you should have been more respectful of it. Perhaps you should volunteer at an old soldiers' home or something of that sort if you feel so strongly about helping them."

"But what about my allowance?" His uncle had received an allowance from his brother since the time he signed up to the Navy as a fourteen-year-old.

"That remains unchanged," Beau said. It would be worth it to be rid of their poison. "But if there are rumors, Uncle, or this establishment is bad-mouthed, that allowance will stop. Consider it a consequence of stealing from your own family."

"I don't know what you think you're going to do, or how you're going to run and manage this place without us."

It was unpalatable to have to stop his routs while he sorted this out. But what alternative was there? In this highly competitive climate, he would lose customers, and his rivals wouldn't waste any time raising scurrilous gossip about the reasons he was closed.

Gossip that would only increase when the men left. No. It wasn't ideal. "I will find a way." Beau stood. "You should pack your things."

Uncle Horace gave him a smug little smile. "Your mother won't be happy with you throwing me out." He pushed the tea tray away. "Maybe you should let things settle."

Beau shot that smug smile straight back at him, not that he could see it. "I don't think so. And you're right, she won't be happy. But not for the reasons you think. Her friends refuse to come here because of the foul play. She's lost what little social standing she had left because of your actions. But knowing we never have to lay eyes on you again will make both of us feel better."

Beau left the room before he felt compelled to say more. Mother *would* be heartbroken. He took a deep breath. Perhaps it was time to start a family of his own to bring them all some joy.

If only his dratted heart hadn't immediately conjured up a vision of Harriet.

CHAPTER 18

WHERE THE ANSWER TO BEAU'S PROBLEM IS OBVIOUS FOR ANYONE WITH HALF A BRAIN

A gentlemen's club was supposed to be a refuge from the world, but White's was failing dismally today. Even ensconced in his favorite wingback chair in front of the fireplace, Beau flipped between his newspaper, a book, and staring blankly out the window.

Knowing his employees had been stealing from him didn't lessen the guilt when putting together their final wage envelopes and handing them over one by one. Indeed, he had to stop himself from thanking each and every one of them for their service. It was only when the second to final one had said "I told them it wasn't right" that he started to feel any vindication at all.

Now he had a real problem. No dealers, and when he did replace them, no one to manage them. Uncle Horace and his son, Thomas, had always taken care of the staff. And although he had all their paperwork on the administration of it, he needed help to source new staff. Mother would know where to get household staff, but not croupiers.

What about Harriet? If she could spot dishonest players,

surely she could just as accurately spot the honest ones for him to employ? He needed her help once again, and it seemed she had been right. It wasn't goodbye when they parted.

He really shouldn't feel so excited.

There was movement near him, and Beau looked up. A solid man, with brown curly hair that flopped in his face, stood next to the twin chair across from the fire.

Beau stood immediately and stretched out his hand. "Scanlan, good to see you."

His hand was clasped warmly, and they both sat down again.

Sir Charles crossed one leg over the other and picked up the newspaper Beau had put down. "Looking for calm? You won't find it here. Hot bed of intrigue, this place." He caught the eye of a server and ordered a bottle of Burgundy. "And I hear you've just ousted your entire floor staff."

Damnation, was the news of it out already? "Where did you hear that?"

Scanlan shrugged. "Mariah, who heard it from her mother. Harriet looked jubilant, can't think why."

"She guessed they were cheating me." He leaned forward to speak privately. "Profits have been falling, and it turns out the entire lot of them have been stealing."

Scanlan inhaled sharply, his gaze widening. "Thieves."

"Precisely. So they're all out. But now, of course, I have nobody to run the dratted thing except Mother and I." He laughed, because what a joke it all was. "And I was sitting here thinking I don't have the connections to restaff."

Scanlan glanced down at the newspaper. "Harri could help you. She can spot a dishonest cove at twenty paces. She's writing a book about it! Ten chapters in now, apparently."

"So you know she writes?" He liked the thought that she had confided in Scanlan and her sister.

"Couldn't be prouder. But we only just found out. Mariah almost fainted."

The server arrived with a drink tray and put the bottle and two glasses on the table. Scanlan offered a glass to Beau. "If she's good enough to spot the cheats, could she work for you? It's not unusual to have a hostess."

It had to be fate, Lord Charles coming up with the very same solution he had.

Beau took his glass and swirled the wine around, as though to find the answers in it. The thought of working with her every night made him feel ... excited, hopeful.

But would she do it? She had already shown that she was both entrepreneurial and ambitious. And he knew she needed money.

Scanlan took a sip. "You might even find it is an attraction considering her good looks. Takes after her sister."

"She is beautiful, isn't she?"

"Oh dear," Scanlan said, with a laugh.

"It's not like that."

"No, no, of course not. Only that it is *exactly* like that."

"It can't be like that, if I am to employ her."

"True. You will have to keep a hold on yourself." Scanlan's gaze hit his, sharp and assessing. "Or I will track you down."

"I think I like you," Beau said. An image of a future where he and Sir Charles created business enterprises together for the wealth of both of their families flitted across his mind unbidden. "Do you think she would do it?"

"Matters have come to pass recently. I think she will jump at the chance."

A pit opened up in Beau's stomach. Harriet was strong, but

it was her virtue that made her vulnerable to her parents. They weren't above using Bertie to secure her compliance.

"Her parents have taken her home. Apparently it was the height of betrayal both to put their only son in the army and, even worse, to have paid for it with savings they had no knowledge of." Scanlan eyed him with suspicion. "Did you facilitate Bertie's colors?"

Beau nodded. "It was the price for her help. Although I would happily have assisted in any case."

"I feel the same way. There was no plan for Bertie, other than to follow in his parents' dubious footsteps. I must admit to being hurt he did not apply to me."

"Miss Truchard said she did not want to put you in an awkward position with your in-laws. This way, at least, you could truthfully say you had no knowledge of the plans."

Scanlan nodded. "Which I did when they accused me, so I suppose she was right in that. Those two have a remarkable ability to garner the truth of any situation. There'd be no point lying to them, because they can sense it like rats sensing cheese in the larder."

They both laughed at the thought. "Did you just compare your in-laws to rats looking for cheese?"

"I notice you don't disagree. I fell in love with Mariah and married her *despite* her family. But then, I am in the unhappy position of having lost my own parents some years past now. There is nobody to gainsay me."

"My mother would gainsay me all the way to Christmas, if I tried to marry into that family. I would never hear the end of it and she'd likely cut me off from my brother and sisters. They are the most complete scoundrels, you are aware?"

Scanlan paused, as if thinking about his answer. "I've always been given to think that they were affable scoundrels, not outright criminals. The kind of people that live off their own wits, and over the years this has changed them. Do you have information I don't?"

"Let's just say their portraits have been on the wall of my study, along with other notorious gambling cheats and swindlers for the past few years. Bow Street want to question them over some canal project they're hatching. Other than that, I only know that other gambling houses have blackballed them."

Scanlan drew in a shocked breath. "Never say it." He threw the newspaper back on the table, his face stormy. "I have been giving them the benefit of the doubt. They *have* been pushing for Mariah and me to entertain more."

"So that Mr. Truchard can meet new and unsuspecting investors for his schemes."

Scanlan ran a hand through his messy mop. "I feel awful. That canal project he is currently running seems so good. I probably *would* have introduced my friends to him."

"And he would happily have fleeced them. Not that I know anything of his new business. But based on past performance, it is likely all a sham. Take people's money for the bonds and then miraculously no act of parliament for the canal is forthcoming and all the money is lost. What a surprise."

Charles choked. "Good lord, I am in the process of investing."

"Not finalized?"

"No."

"You'd be better to back a horse at Newmarket. Not that I suggest such a thing." Beau smiled, feeling a brotherly affection for the man that had no basis in fact. "Let's just say that running my gambling parties for the past five years has given me an insight into human behavior that I would not have otherwise received. None of it good. But if it helps you see the truth of people around you—not including Mariah, of course —then the time is well spent."

Scanlan nodded. "I am glad Bertie is away from them, and I only hope Miss Truchard may be successful as well. You'll find her at 14 Half Moon Street. I knew when they leased it that they must be trying to fire her off, for it is exactly where they were situated when I courted Mariah. But, before you call there, look in at Green Park. Mariah said she has been spending a lot of time there due to her mother giving her grief over a potential suitor they're trying to convince her to marry. He visits daily."

The thought of Harriet marrying against her will only fortified his decision to seek her out.

Harriet had already shown she was desperately trying to escape the future her parents had planned for her. If he could help her, he would. If he had paid his ex-seaman one guinea each shift then surely she was worth two. Not to mention the lure of having a beautiful young lady as a hostess and dealer.

He had a pang of guilt when thinking upon her reputation. He would have to make sure she knew the repercussions that taking up employment with him would bring. Mariah may have made a very eligible match, but if Harriet worked for him, it was unlikely she would.

"I still have to find at least four others."

"Find your favorite people from The Cocoa Tree or Brooks's and offer them double the wages."

"Genius." He'd been thinking along the same lines himself.

"A little underhand but needs must."

Beau stood, glad that meeting with Charles had clarified his nebulous ideas. "My thanks, friend. I'm glad providence put you my way today."

Scanlan smiled and laughed softly. "Providence had nothing to do with it. Mariah sent me. Go find Harriet, then. I'll see you soon."

Beau left White's and took a hack toward Green Park. If she wasn't there, he would wait until she was.

CHAPTER 19

WHERE A WINDOW OPENS AND MISS TRUCHARD LEAPS THROUGH

T he days slipped by, punctuated by visits from the dreadful Mr. Donovan.

At least they had not been left alone, because Father graced them with his presence. The two men talked of nothing but Mr. Donovan's new business venture. A gambling house, of course. Because apparently, gambling and *loaning coves money* went hand in hand. Their mutual laughter still rang in her ears like an overenthusiastic church bell.

He was gone now, but her throbbing head, and the lingering smell of his cologne, remained. Perhaps a walk in the park would clear her mind. It had proven an effective balm for the curse of Mr. Donovan over the past weeks. The fields of lush grass and chirping of birds would have her temper back to normal within minutes. She rose to find her pelisse and bonnet.

Father looked at her, a shrewd assessment in his eyes. "What do you think about that, then? A high society gambling house! He'll be richer than Croesus." He purred with satisfaction. "The perfect solution."

"Perfect solution to what?" *Say it, Father. Admit you want to force me into a marriage I don't want.*

"Why, your future," he frowned at her as though she were in her dotage. "Since you have taken Bertie from us, we plan to travel. The Americas hold a great deal of opportunity to mine for gold. Once my canal project is up and running, of course."

Once you fleece the money from the investors and have to make a run for it.

"Considering I do not believe you literally mean to take to the ground with a shovel and pan, I warn you that America has seen its fair share of unscrupulous money makers. They do not name it *the wild west* for nothing."

He laughed. "Oh, nothing so crass as the wild west. Can you imagine your mother in the dust? East Coast, m'dear! New York or Boston. The Americans love the French, and Louisa and I pass easily as French. Especially if I buy her a new Parisian wardrobe."

Nowhere in these plans was Harriet mentioned. "And I am to marry Mr. Donovan, thereby granting you your freedom from any parental obligations."

Mr. Truchard lifted one shoulder, unconcerned. "Our obligations may have slipped our mind in the shock of Bertie's enlistment. You will do your duty and marry. Mr. Donovan can give you a luxurious lifestyle with no dowry required. You may have saved enough to have your own establishment, but you've blown that now, haven't you?"

Harriet did not care for the pleasure at her failure she read in his eyes. "Indeed, I have."

"I would still like to know how you saved so much and where you hid it."

Bless Mariah for not telling her secret.

"Here and there," Harriet said. *There is no way I am sharing this with you.* Wanting to put an end to the conversation, she turned to the door. "I shall go for a walk in the park. We can have nothing further to say."

"Yes, do my dear. It will help you overcome your little tantrum. Marrying Mr. Donovan is not up for negotiation."

The battle lines had been drawn, but even so, it was apparent Father didn't know her at all. She was much more his daughter than she'd like to admit and was willing to go to any lengths not to lose this particular battle.

"Very well. I will be back soon."

Harriet collected her pelisse and headed out, walking briskly along Half Moon Street toward Piccadilly, which she would cross to reach Green Park. It might be a little crowded today, being such a sunny afternoon, but looking upon the fountain in the water reservoir always calmed her. She would sit on a bench and stare off into the distance until her blood stopped boiling.

What to do?

Life had reached a crossroads. One way would be easy and mean she would likely have money at the ready for the rest of her days.

But at what cost?

The other was hazy and unknown. It was poverty and trying to eke out a living with her writings. She reached the park and made her way to the reservoir in the north-east corner, walking around it instead of finding a bench as she'd initially planned. She loved the view here, the expanses of grass, trees, with Westminster Abbey presiding over it all in the distance.

Green Park was indeed crowded, but pleasantly so. Birds chirped in the trees and life in London continued despite her turbulent state of mind. Maids played with their little charges, a pet terrier jumping around, eager to get in on the fun. Ladies in groups of two and three promenaded in chip straw bonnets while an elegant greyhound was going on his daily walk with his owner. Other people had the warmth of friends, pets and children.

She envied them, deeply.

But at least she wasn't trading barbs with her parents in the cloying atmosphere of Half Moon Street. Perhaps she would stay in the park until dinner.

She would never regret giving Bertie the money for his colors, but goodness, it would have come in handy now. She could have told her parents in no uncertain terms; she would *not* marry Mr. Donovan and would leave as soon as she could find premises to lease.

Now? That was an impossibility.

Perhaps she could finish the next book and hand it over to her publisher for advance payment. She was halfway through. If she rose early every day and had three good sessions of writing, surely she could have it done, perhaps by the end of the month?

Would Mr. Donovan wait that long? She had the impression his patience was growing thin.

Having walked the circumference of the reservoir, Harriet found her favorite bench and sat, folding her hands in her lap. What was she to do? Her parents could be packed and gone to America at any moment, leaving her alone with Mr. Donovan, a man who appeared ready to do anything to get what he desired.

For the first time, she had no answer. No clever idea or solution to give her hope. Just a dull ache in her heart, as though she'd reached the end of the road and was staring at the ocean with no boat.

A squirrel darted from a tree and across the lawn. It zigzagged across the grass and into a hollow at the bottom of an oak tree.

Tears gathered in her eyes, and she blinked them away fiercely. They would do no good other than releasing a fraction of all the horrible tension. She wasn't overwrought. She *wouldn't* allow herself to be. She would think of something soon enough. A few errant tears spilled onto her cheeks and she brushed them away. She hadn't lost the fight yet. She'd just hit a momentary stumbling block.

A shadow fell across her, then a light hand touched her shoulder. She whirled around, expecting Mr. Donovan and preparing a sturdy set-down.

But it was Beaufort.

Her heart leaped and her gaze greedily took him in. Dressed in a slate-gray coat, buff breeches, and a cravat that was a work of art, he brushed a leaf off the bench and sat next to her. "So I gather the new fiancé is not to your taste?"

"He is *not* my fiancé."

He pushed a lock of his dark-honey-colored hair away from his face and looked out over the ornamental lake, but not before she caught a flash of relief. Or was she imagining that?

"I empathize. I was advised to marry for money myself. Horrid thought. Not to be borne."

His tone was blunt, reminding her of Bertie's reaction when she'd scraped her knees as a child and cried. In fact, she would not be surprised if Beaufort slapped her on the back and said *cheer up*. Tear-stained cheeks always scared the life out of gentlemen. Harriet closed her eyes, fighting the blush of mortification that he'd found her crying. "Do not tell me to cheer up, because I do not want to."

He stayed silent, but handed her a pristine white handkerchief that had a 'B' embroidered on the corner. She dabbed her cheeks with it, annoyed at the tumbling mix of emotions that such a simple action evoked. But just having him there, such a solid presence, helped calm her.

"They're angry with me."

"Bertie?" His tone was sympathetic.

She nodded. "And in punishment, I am to marry a man of their choosing. And they are going overseas. I cannot see a way out of this situation."

He drew in a shocked breath. "I'd like to say they can't do that, but realistically, they have your hands tied, for where would you go?"

"Precisely. He makes my skin crawl. He looks at me as though he picked a juicy apple from the fruit bowl and can't wait to take a bite. And I can't escape because I used my savings to buy Bertie's colors. I could never regret that, but it puts me in something of a fix."

"Perhaps I can help. I came to offer you something, not daring to hope you might accept."

"Now *that* sounds disreputable." Her laugh sounded more like a hiccup. "Do you need a new mistress? I am sure I would be awkward at such things, but I'm willing to give it a try." She accompanied the last words with a small salute. He wasn't offering her something so sordid. She knew that. He had too much honor. But she did love to tease him.

He spluttered, his expression shocked. "Harri, don't say such things."

The use of her pet name, especially after she had teased

him so, had warmth blooming in her heart. "My dear Lord Beaufort, what else could you possibly want me for?"

"Your brains and skill, obviously." There was a delicious furrow between his brows.

"So, not my luscious person?" She clenched her hands in her lap and looked down at them, intending to tease him a little longer because it was more fun than thinking about her predicament. "How lowering."

"And also very much untrue." He picked up her gloved hand and slowly tugged the glove off, placing it on his knee.

Her heart skittered. "What are you doing?"

He removed his riding glove and lifted her hand to his mouth, placing a gentle kiss on her knuckles. He looked up at her over the kiss. "Do not tempt me."

She blinked rapidly against the heat in his eyes. "Oh. I didn't mean to. I would not think it possible."

Beau kept hold of her hand. "It is more than possible, but for what I am about to offer you, it cannot be indulged." He picked up her glove and handed it back to her. "You have pretty fingers."

Her heart thudded. *Make him laugh so he doesn't see how he affects you.* "They are my pride and joy. Some ladies have elegance or accomplishments. I have my fingers."

It had the desired result, and his eyes twinkled with merriment. "Minx."

Harriet pulled her glove back on and folded her hands in her lap again, hoping he wouldn't notice how they shook now. "So tell me this offer before I expire from the anticipation."

Beau turned to her. "First, I must admit that I was wrong, and you were right."

Ah. There was only one thing she'd tried to convince him of, and she already knew he had sacked them. "Your dealers?"

"And worse." He rubbed his brow as though thinking about it gave him an instant headache.

"Worse?" How could it possibly be worse?

"My uncle was ring-leading them and making them all believe they had my full approval to influence the outcome of the gaming. He told them it was for a charity to redistribute the funds from the wealthy to the returned veterans the government was ignoring."

She drew in a breath, shocked. "Let me guess, most of those funds ended up lining his pockets."

"Probably my cousin's, or maybe both." Beaufort looked away, but she could see the anger in his gaze. "So, they made the dealers commit fraud and then took the proceeds. How could I do anything else but cut them all off?"

He wasn't looking for an answer, but Harriet felt obliged to give him one, her own troubles forgotten.

"No, you cannot reward theft and dishonesty with further support. I met your cousin, you know, last week. He was at the chophouse Bertie likes, Dolly's."

"Yes, he loves chophouses."

"He complained about not having enough allowance and how expensive life in London was for a gentleman without means. I suppose he took matters into his own hands."

She slid her hand over his, squeezing gently. "My heart breaks for you. I know how it feels to have a family member betray your trust for their own gain."

"I suppose you do." His smile was rueful.

"That moment when you realize what you thought was an unbreakable bond could, in fact, be broken by a few hundred pounds. It destroys your faith." And it meant you hid anything good, expecting to have it stolen from you. Because you were only loved for what you could do for them.

"More like thousands of pounds, but the lesson is the same." He took a deep breath, his gaze meeting hers. "Will you help? The job would come with board, food, and two guineas a shift. Two of my previous dealers lived in the attic room of our town house, and I would be happy to give that room to you. I came here thinking there was no way you would accept my offer, but after hearing about your impending marriage, I wonder if this could be the escape route you need."

Harriet mused over all the implications—and there were plenty, for them both. The worst was that Beaufort had no idea just how bad her family name was. "I think this is more of a risk to you than you realize. The name Truchard is synonymous with cheating."

He nodded. "Yes, and your parents are on my wall of honor, I know."

"Oh." He knew the worst of her family and still wanted her help. Warmth flooded her, the first she'd felt in weeks. "Then if this is only for a short duration, until we can source you a new team, it might work. It would also allow me the time to finish my book and submit it to my publisher. With the royalties that keep coming in from the first one, I should be able to rent myself some rooms by the time we fix your issues. Although certainly not in London. I will have to think farther afield."

"Then this could buy us both the time we need. Will you do it?" He hesitated, and then went on in a rush. "It will not be good for your reputation. In fact, many would say it would be unsalvageable after this foray."

"What little I had thanks to mother and father," she said, with a touch of bitterness she could not control.

"It did not stop Mariah. You should think carefully." He

gave her a delightfully lopsided smile. "I say this against my best interests."

"No, I will come. Thank you for the opportunity not to have to marry a beastly man." It felt like there should be a choir singing. The decision felt *that* momentous. It wasn't every day a young lady left her family without the safety of marriage. This could be the biggest mistake of her life.

Or the making of her.

"How soon can you come?"

It was Monday. He was supposed to have his next rout in two days. But she needed to be gone sooner than that.

"Can you send a carriage for me in a couple of hours?" That should give her enough time to walk home, pack and find a way out of the house undetected.

"Absolutely. What will you tell them?"

She laughed. "I have no intention of telling them anything. There is a desperation about them that means I can't rule out them locking me in my bedroom until I agree. Now, we both know nobody can *make* me marry. However, all he would have to do is threaten Bertie, and I would."

"Have you heard from your brother?"

"Yes. He is off to the barracks in Galway soon and is staying with friends until he leaves. I just have to keep everything quiet until then. I will leave a note so they don't worry."

"Very well. I trust your judgment in this, and my ability to protect you should the need arise." He stood and held out a hand to her.

She put her hand in his, letting him pull her off the seat. He tucked her hand into his arm and together they walked back to the gates of the park.

She smiled, and in meeting his gaze felt a tingle of excitement. *What is this?* It was a silly question, for she already knew the answer. Infatuation. A dangerous thing to feel when you were a Truchard. *Well, Harriet, you'd best be infatuated by this opportunity and not by the very fine pair of shoulders that fill out his coat.*

He bowed. "I'll send my carriage in two hours and will be waiting when you arrive."

She nodded. "Thank you." Such an understated thing to say when he was throwing her a rope over the side of the boat, just as she was about to be washed under. He gave her something nobody had in a very long time. Hope.

CHAPTER 20

WHERE MISS TRUCHARD FINDS THE VERY
BEST KIND OF NEW FRIEND

When Harriet got home, she found her mother waiting for her. Standing in the hall, one hand resting on the hall console, the other clenched by her side. "I must apologize for what your father said. This is not what I hoped for."

Her apologetic tone caught Harriet between surprise and suspicion. She allowed their maid, Anne, to help her out of her pelisse while she schooled her expression. "And what did you hope for?"

Mrs. Truchard drew Harriet further down the hall. She was putting on a fine act of being worried, her brows drawn, her mouth pursed. And perhaps she actually was, since Harriet was putting quite a strong spoke in their wheels.

"Only that you would look at Mr. Donovan and feel the same way I did when I first laid eyes on Francis. That he was handsome, that you might like to get to know him better. Truth be told, I almost immediately saw my future the moment I looked into your father's eyes."

Despite her best intentions, the tears gathering in Mother's eyes tugged at Harriet's heart. But they were more likely to be false than true. She shook her head. "None of that happened when I met Mr. Donovan. All I felt was a vague threat to my person. I am not comfortable in his company."

"He is very kind to his mother. I always think that is a good yardstick." Mother paused, then impulsively grabbed Harriet's hand, squeezing tightly. "Just give him a little more time, will you please? He's a powerful man, but there's nothing wrong with that, especially if that strength is directed toward protecting you and your children. I think Mr. Donovan is very loyal."

Mother had not shown this kind of interest in Harriet for years. It didn't feel loving, but more like a determination to get her own way. She would wheedle and cajole for a while, but eventually, it would end in threats. "And you truly will leave England without me settled?"

Mother pressed her lips together, something she did when she was feeling particularly stubborn. "I know I just said I hoped you would find love, but in all honesty, it's unnecessary. All that is required is that you are provided for and encouraged to use your intelligence. Mr. Donovan offers both. You must stop thinking we are doing the wrong thing by you. Your father and I believe this is the right path for our beloved daughter."

Beloved? They must *really* need to leave England unencumbered. Likely, they already had the journey booked for two.

It was a sad world when she automatically believed her own mother did not have her best interests at heart.

Harriet forced a bright smile that in no way reflected her inner turmoil. She just needed to lull any suspicions her mother might have. "You always have my best interests at heart. I know that, even if your methods are unusual. Perhaps

—for your sake, I will give Mr. Donovan another chance to impress me. He may have an air of violence, but he was also beautifully dressed and is definitely trying to better himself. One must admire that."

Mother beamed in response and opened her arms wide. When Harriet didn't step into her embrace, she grabbed her hand. "Exactly! And you can help him. You have the manners and the breeding and he has street cunning. You will make a formidable couple. Mr. Donovan thought so, too."

Her heart sank. Mr. Donovan was definitely just buying her skills and, with her qualms about using them, she was bound to disappoint a man prone to violence. Well, bickering about it wouldn't get her out.

Harriet allowed herself to be pulled into her mother's embrace. It was one of a handful of times her mother had shown such affection, and she forced herself to relax into it. This could be the last time she saw her if they left England for America.

Yet another rash decision.

Harriet gently pulled away. "I'm going upstairs to lie down. My head is aching." *More like I'm going upstairs to pack my bags.*

Mother frowned. "Oh, I had hoped you might come to Madame Le Favre. Father says I may visit a French modiste, but I think you should come too."

Harriet kissed her mother's cheek. "Leave my new wardrobe to Mr. Donovan. And use the extra funds on your own."

Besides, it would be a blessing to have her out of the house.

Her mother's face brightened. "A wonderful plan. You ever were the smart one. Very well, I will let you rest this afternoon and visit Madam myself. I cannot wait. It seems an age since I had a new dress."

She whirled around and immediately called for her reticule and pelisse. Harriet dragged herself up the stairs, pretending to be tired and weary, but once inside her room, she pulled her valise from the top of the wardrobe and opened it on the bed. If there was one thing the Truchard's had, it was a stock of good luggage. It was always easily accessible, just in case they had to leave a residence in the middle of the night. As had happened in Bath and in York.

She went through the wardrobe quietly, only putting in garments that were worthy of her new life at Beaufort's. All her evening gowns, her hairbrush and combs. Her toothbrush and tooth powder, and a few cosmetics, went into a smaller pouch. Then she lifted the floor of the wardrobe and found the most important thing—her latest manuscript.

A door slammed, and Harriet looked out the window to see Mrs. Truchard entering a hack. With any luck, the modiste would not tell Mother how Harriet had purchased her ball gown last month. Father was also out, but he could return at any moment, so she waited with bated breath, praying Beau's carriage would arrive first. She tucked a note to her parents under her pillow.

This was such a big step. Was it as rash as their move to America? Was she just as bad as they were?

Too late now, my heart won't allow me to do anything else.

The organ in question picked up its pace. The joy of deciding for herself was intoxicating. *Whether it's a mistake or a triumph, I chose it for myself.*

She would be closer in the drawing room, so she went one floor down, and stowed her valise behind the chair nearest the door. Then stood by the window, opening it a crack to let in more sound from the street.

Please come soon.

It seemed like forever before his carriage, with the Beaufort coat of arms painted on the side door, pulled up outside their home.

Harriet picked up her valise and ran as quietly as she could to the front of the house, hoping to reach it before the maid did. She opened the door and closed it behind her as Beaufort's groom jumped from his position next to the driver to take her bag.

Nobody followed, nobody asked where she was going. Hackneys went up and down Half Moon Street as they always did. The footman opened the carriage door, and she jumped inside, pushing herself down on the seat, out of view. The door slammed shut, and the carriage took off, the clatter of the horses' hooves soothing her racing pulse.

She was free of her parents and free of Mr. Donovan. Just free.

Beaufort waited in the guest bedroom that overlooked the back garden and mews of their mansion. If Harriet had been able to escape on time, her carriage would arrive shortly.

He owed a debt of gratitude to her unwanted suitor. If he ever met him, he might just shake his hand.

Now he just had to ensure she felt safe here. No more kissing of fingertips or anything equally foolish or tempting. He must not indulge himself, especially when she was in such a vulnerable position.

It was obviously just flirting, but still. She intrigued him, and there was a tantalizing air of the forbidden about her. She said exactly what she thought, and teased him mercilessly. Who could forget her arch expression when she'd asked if she was to become his mistress, as though it were the most commonplace question in the world.

At least he would be entertained.

"What *are* you doing standing in the guest bedroom, Beaufort?"

He jumped fractionally and then turned.

Lady Beaufort stood at the door, a quizzical look on her face. "I assure you, nothing interesting ever happens in our back garden," she continued, then her eyes widened. "Oh, you await Miss Truchard, don't you?"

She was far too insightful. She had disagreed most heartily with his decision to install Harriet as his new hostess, arguing that everyone would suspect that a young lady named Truchard was related to Francis Truchard. "They will not trust her to deal fairly," she had said.

"I would appreciate you welcoming her with me."

She sighed. "I suppose I must." She shook her head. "But please, for my sake, cure yourself of whatever infatuation you have for her."

He nodded, even as images of her sparkling gray eyes and mischievous smile flitted across his mind. "Though in truth, it will not be easy. I had thought myself over my infatuation until I found her in the park, looking like her heart would break. And did she seek comfort? Of course not. She was mortified, and dashed those tears away as angry as an alley cat. I can't help admiring that kind of backbone."

Lady Beaufort sniffed. "In that case, I had better get to know Miss Truchard. At least then I will not be judging her on the sins of her parents. I love and trust you, but you like nothing more than to save people."

He returned his gaze to the mews. "Whatever makes you say that?"

"Choosing your staff based on how destitute they were, perhaps?" She came to look out the window with him. The door to the mews opened, and a groom led Harriet into the back garden. "And here she is now."

Harriet walked slowly past the fountain and the bank of white camellias in full bloom. Then, as though drawn by something, she glanced up at the window and saw them. A smile played at the corner of her generous mouth, making her appear both mischievous and bashful, and she raised her hand to wave.

"I see," said Lady Beaufort. "Quite charming. You should have introduced me when she came to the card parties with her sister."

"You asked me not to." He returned the wave and let the curtain fall back. "Let's greet her, shall we?"

They went downstairs. By the time they reached the ground floor, Harriet had been led through to the foyer.

Mother stepped forward smiling, her expression showing little of the misgiving she'd voiced earlier. "Welcome, my dear. I hear you have come to be our savior."

Beau looked in surprise at his mother and sent her a silent *thank you*.

Harriet curtsied. "How kind you are, my lady. I am honored to lend my services and only hope we can install a group of gentlemen who are worthy of their positions."

Mrs. Pearce, the housekeeper—a stout woman with gray hair pulled into a severe bun—joined them. When Lady Beaufort introduced them, Harriet curtsied. Mrs. Pearce gave a nod of her head.

"Would you please show Miss Harriet to her room?" It seemed Mother was already trying to avoid the Truchard name.

Mrs. Pearce nodded. "The attic room is ready. We've cleaned it, but something was left behind by the old staff we could not remove, and we hope you don't mind too much."

"I am grateful for the room. All I need is a bed." She smiled at the housekeeper. "And maybe a desk. I hope I am not a bother."

Mother patted her on the arm. "I believe my son may be right about you."

He looked at Mother, unsure if her pleased expression was merely a facade to smooth things over, or if she was genuinely impressed by Harriet's kind manner.

All he knew was that things finally felt right.

Harriet followed the housekeeper up the stairs, while a footman trailed behind them with her bag. How incredible to be living in the house she had admired during the parties.

At the first landing, Harriet paused. "Where should I go for meals?"

"You are not a servant, but all the dealers take meals with us in the servants' hall. Come down to the kitchen. There is a room leading off that where we dine." The housekeeper stopped on the next landing to catch her breath before taking the last flight to the attic. "I don't get up here often. These stairs are deadly on the knees, and the slip I had coming down them early one morning puts me off. They get more uneven the further they go. Do be careful."

She reached the top of the stairs, opened the door, and stepped into the room. "It is only a small room, but I trust it will be comfortable."

The attic room was not small at all and had three casement windows through which Harriet could see the tops of trees and white clouds in a blue sky. There were two single beds with a bedside table between them. There was also a desk under the third window and a dresser on the far wall with a basin and jug on it. The room was warm, thanks to a small stove in the far corner that was cheerily lit, with blankets bundled up in front of it. "It's lovely."

"It's a little sparse," the housekeeper said apologetically. "But I will find some pretty things over the next few days to make it more homely. The officers used to make their morning coffee on the stove, and it does keep the room very warm. I will bring you tea supplies."

"Thank you. My tea would be cold by the time I got up here from the kitchen, and that's assuming I didn't drop the tray on the way!"

Something moved under the blankets next to the stove, then a fluffy black head poked up. Harriet stifled an unlady-like squeal. "A dog? Is that what you couldn't remove?"

Mrs. Pearce walked to the bundle of blankets and reached down. The dog rolled onto his back for a tummy rub. "Yes. He's sad, the poor dear. Haven't had a bark out of him since they left. Well, not until I tried to move him out this morning, that is. Then there was an uproar! He thinks Mr. Sefton is coming back, but I assure you he is *not*." She finished on a note of outrage that told Harriet the staff were aware of what had happened.

The little Scottish terrier took his tummy rub and then flipped over and yawned.

Harriet kneeled by the blanket, letting him sniff her hand, which he promptly licked. "He's beautiful. I am so glad he stayed." She gave him a scratch behind the ears. "There now. You're going to be just fine."

She looked up at the housekeeper. "What's his name?"

"It's none too original, but his name is Sooty. Make sure you keep your bonnets out of his reach. I am always finding him with a sock, hat or shoe in his mouth."

"Noted. Dear little Sooty. Can we be friends? I could use a friend and it seems you could, too."

He moved his head into her hand for more pats, and suddenly a day that had started with no hope at all broke into sunshine. She had a job, a roof over her head and, best of all, a sweet little black dog who needed all the love she had to give, and nobody to take him away from her.

"I'll leave you to unpack your things, Miss Harriet. Dinner is at five-thirty for the staff."

Harriet nodded and, once alone, quickly unpacked her clothes. There was no wardrobe, so she hung her gowns over the chair. Then she put her manuscript on the desk and arranged her ink and quill by its side.

Tired from all the excitement, Harriet sat on the bed and leaned against the wall, hoping Sooty might come and curl up next to her. Instead, he stared at her from his basket for a few moments, then, obviously deciding she was no threat, went back to sleep.

Just after she had unpacked her meagre belongings, there was the sound of a lot of groaning and scuffling on the stairs.

What in the world?

Harriet opened the door to the landing to see two footmen

carrying a large armchair up the staircase, being directed by Mr. Merrick. It looked very much like the armchair she had enjoyed in Lord Beaufort's study. Harriet stepped back as they made their way to the top, then maneuvered their way through the door.

"That's it, lads, you've made it. Place it over by the stove so Miss Harriet can enjoy her tea by the fire. His lordship thought you might like it."

"Thank you, gentlemen. I know how comfortable it is." They put the chair down and Sooty immediately jumped into it. "I'll put a blanket over it, because there's no way of stopping him sitting there if I'm out of the room."

The footmen left.

"I'd hide your bonnets and shoes too. He's a scamp," Mr. Merrick said. He was a tall and well-built man, likely in his late forties.

"Were you a pugilist, Mr. Merrick?" She'd watched the way he moved when they visited the club weeks ago and had been curious. He was calm, composed but powerful. The kind of man who didn't need to advertise his strength because it just radiated off him.

She'd never seen him so much as smile in all the weeks she'd visited and she wasn't sure if that was his personality, or his focus on his role as major-domo. Oversight of a business like Beaufort's was no small task.

He nodded. "I was indeed. I learned from the great Mendoza himself."

"What stories you must have." She didn't invite him to tell them; their acquaintance was much too short for such a demand.

"Not as many as I'd like. I was badly injured in a bout. I took to teaching at Gentleman Jackson's Boxing Salon, which was how I met Lord Beaufort." He frowned. "But I'm talking out of turn now."

"Just when things were getting interesting! Lord Beaufort must display to great advantage, I'm sure of it."

"He's got a bruising right, that's for certain," Mr. Merrick said. "But I shouldn't be telling you that, miss." He bowed his head. "Welcome to the household. We all know you're here to help, but how a slip like you could get us out of the suds we're in is beyond me."

"Watch and learn, Mr. Merrick," Harriet said with her sauciest smile.

He, of course, did not smile in return.

CHAPTER 21

WHERE HARRIET IS ENTRANCED BY MARMALADE

The next morning, with the smell of braising onion wafting in the air, Harriet took her place at the staff dining table.

The room was entirely empty.

She had slept in and missed breakfast after spending the night mulling over how to improve Beaufort's profit. She'd only hit upon the answer as she was drifting to sleep, and heavens knew what time that was. So now she was waiting on tea and toast, while everyone else was already hard at work.

The staff dining room was a homely affair, with mismatched chairs and a long table that looked like it had graced the Viscount's dining room last century. Three walls were whitewashed, but the fourth had a bucolic mural painted on it, with a majestic house in the distance.

Beau appeared in the doorway. "There you are!" He followed her gaze to the mural. "That's Huntingdon Abbey. Pretty, isn't she? One day we'll kick the tenants out and live there again ourselves."

He looked as though he had been awake for hours; dressed

for riding in gleaming black boots, breeches and a navy cutaway coat. His tawny hair was rumpled by the wind and he looked in high spirits, each step into the room bursting with coiled energy.

"It's very pretty," she replied, looking away to stop herself from gaping at him. *Delectable man.*

"I've just returned from visiting Lord Mandeville, who has gifted me two of his footmen who are keen to become croupiers. He himself will help us preside over tomorrow evening and, with the men I poached from White's, I think we may be set."

Relief ran through Harriet. "I also think you should employ someone to sit in a high chair to overlook proceedings. An inspector, if you will."

He sat at the head of the table and stretched his legs out, so they were pointing to her. There were blades of grass on his boots that his valet would hate. "I like it. Maybe the man from White's, who seems so sharp."

She pulled her gaze away from his boots. "It should pay more. He's guarding your business, after all, and should be loyal to only you."

He nodded. "How much do you think?"

It was flattering that he thought she would know the answer. "Eight pounds a week?"

"With us only open three nights?"

She nodded. "Start at six and tell him you'll increase based on his performance."

"You've been thinking about this."

"I missed sleep and *breakfast* thinking about it. It's unnatural." And perhaps thinking about him had taken up *some* of that time. But only because she felt the need to justify him employing her. To prove herself.

"I was awake a fair portion of the night, too."

Their gazes connected. So they were lying in their beds, awake and staring at the ceiling while the rest of the house slept? Joined by their insomnia?

They both stilled as a maid came into the room, put down a tray with a pot of tea, thick slices of toast, a pot of butter, and another of marmalade. Beau instantly reached forward, snagging a piece of toast, stealing her breakfast.

"Pardon *me*," Harriet said primly.

"You are pardoned." He grabbed a plate, slathered butter and marmalade on his toast, and smiled like an evil genius as he took a bite, watching for her reaction. So she gave him none. Merely picked up the second piece and did the same.

"I also suggest you concentrate on games where you have better odds. French Hazard, Faro and E.O."

"What you're suggesting moves Beaufort's away from select parties, and into the realm of a gaming hell."

He had a small amount of marmalade on the corner of his mouth, but she was not going to tell him, though her fingers did itch with the need to lean forward and remove it.

"Somewhat," Harriet said. "People who are used to carrying on their own private card games will be unhappy. Therefore, I would remove all but three of the private tables from the room and fill the space with more games where you can oppose everyone as the bank."

"But the odds are the same, are they not?" A crumb joined the marmalade, making it very hard not to look at.

"You have something on the corner of your mouth."

"Thanks." He wiped his mouth with the napkin, entirely missing it. Then he grinned, making her heart thud harder. "Better?"

Harriet rolled her eyes. "No. How could you miss it with a

napkin that big?" She took her own and gently brushed the corner of his mouth.

He stilled; his eye sparkling with laughter while he let her fix it. "I must eat toast with you every day."

She snapped her hand back. "Behave. Back to the topic at hand. The placing of odds is where we change things. When a person loses their stake, they lose one hundred percent of the wager. When they win, however, we decrease their payout by a small margin through the use of odds. Not enough to stop them betting, but enough to make sure we have a profit margin, whether our bank wins or loses."

"I am grudgingly appreciative." He poured himself a cup of tea, then topped up hers. Now it was too strong, having pulled from the bottom of the teapot.

"Why grudgingly? Trust me, if you don't want this idea, my would-be fiancé would be more than happy to take it." She took a sip and winced.

He obviously saw her reaction because he immediately asked, "Would you like more milk?"

She nodded, and he did that for her, too.

"Yes, but your would-be fiancé is a scoundrel," he continued. "I am not. My priority was to make the establishment a safe place where nobody lost their fortune. A fair place."

"It will still be fair. Make the odds clear to patrons by having it printed on the baize of the tables. But hopefully you will make a little more. Every game will have different odds and a different percentage of what you can win. Vingt-et-un, for example, will have a low margin. Hazard will have a higher one. But everyone that plays, plays against you."

He laughed. "Please don't write a new book titled *How to Set up a Gaming Hell*, or the secret will be all over town."

"I spoke to Mother and Father at length about this idea

years ago, but they never had the funds to set up an establishment. Whoever does this will grow piles of money. It can't lose." She hesitated as he frowned, and leaned forward, placing her hand over his. "What's amiss?"

"My honor. If you lose, you lose, and if you win, you lose." He looked out the barred window at the kitchen garden.

"It is a fair recompense for the equity you stake every night. And they only lose a little. You would be entirely transparent about the odds. "

"I know you're right. It's just ..."

"What?"

He rapped his fingers on the table. "Every step I take seems to be a step further away from the gentleman I'm supposed to be."

"And what does that gentleman do?"

"He runs his business and his estates honorably. He takes care of his dependents, from his closest family, to his smallest tenants. He is *honest*." Beau exhaled. "I'm being daft."

"You are not. But I would add more. He works hard to be worthy of that blessing. And if something threatens his family and his dependents, he does what it takes so that they can flourish once more. He is not afraid to do things that make him uncomfortable because he knows his character is strong. You did not get yourself into this mess, your father did. But you *will* get yourself out of it."

He raised an eyebrow, amusement briefly gleaming in his warm, caramel-colored eyes. "Because you are going to drag me out of it?"

"I am going to drag you by your coattails through the mud if I have to."

"Are you saying needs must?"

She shook her head. "Not entirely, for there is a line that

none of us should ever cross and we each know where that line is. I earned money my parents wanted, but I did not give it to them. Was that the act of an honest and generous person? No. But in doing so, I could help Bertie. You can punish yourself for your decisions, but there is no point in having a stiff moral backbone if the family is eating oatcakes for breakfast, lunch, and dinner. You are not doing anything illegal."

He winced. "Actually, yes I am."

"You mean the Faro table?" It had been outlawed for a very long time, and he was certainly running a risk by having one.

"*All* of it is illegal."

Her eyes widened. "Oh. I assumed you had a gaming license."

"I thought I'd only be doing it a few months. It's why I operate as select invitation routs rather than a subscription club."

"I assumed that was because you wanted to choose the attendees." Dash it, he was running this whole thing like her parents would. And there was no need. Being noble, the license would have been almost automatic. "You need to get one."

"You're right. I will." He frowned. "I should have applied for one, but when you have the Prime Minister and the Prince Regent attending, you assume everything will be fine."

"You're just lucky it has been so far."

"I have an agreement with the runners. Or at least with one of them, Richard Wolfe."

Harriet shook her head. His position was more precarious than he realized. "Yet another tarnishing of the gentlemanly patina."

"There are so many now, I've lost count. Mother says I should find a nice heiress to marry and then all of our problems would be solved. But how can I offer for anyone when this is my life?"

"Rubbish," Harriet said succinctly, because it was. "Do you see the way ladies watch you as you cross the room? They wouldn't care a button."

There was a rustling of fabric at the door, and they both turned to see a young lady dressed in a traveling ensemble standing in the doorway with a pug tucked under one arm. "Never say you're getting married, Beau!"

He broke into a smile, stood, and she put the pug unceremoniously down and rushed into his open arms.

"Emmeline, you cheeky minx. What are you doing here?"

"I refuse to stay moldering away in the country while there are so many diversions here in town. But if you're on the hunt for a bride, this might be the biggest distraction of all. I should like to see the lady who accepts all of this."

"That's precisely what I thought, but Miss Truchard here thinks I am very eligible."

Emmeline squinted at her. "Do you need spectacles?"

She was a foot shorter than her brother, with hair purer blonde than his mottled kind. Her eyes were the same soft brown, but sparkled with mischief. Despite complaining about country life, she was dressed in high fashion, a white muslin dress topped by a pale pink spencer that had elaborate cording and embroidery.

Harriet laughed, liking Emmeline's vibrant sense of humor. "No, I think I see him well enough."

Emmeline collapsed into a chair, and the pug promptly jumped on her lap. "Then perhaps *you* should marry him."

"I'm afraid I don't have the requisite fortune attached to me to make that worthwhile. I am actually an employee here."

"But you're a lady!" It was said with all the naivety of

youth. Then she looked around her in disgust at the room. "Although that explains why you're sitting in the staff dining room."

"Looks can be deceiving. I am no more a lady than your little dog there."

"Well, that's easy, for Rose is very much the lady. I have never seen anyone so particular about her dignity, what she eats and who she converses with. She's the most finicky creature you can imagine." She picked the dog up and received a growl for her efforts. Lady Emmeline kissed Rose on the top of the head. "There, see what I mean?"

"Seriously, Em, Mother is not going to be happy you are here."

"I don't care. I know you run gambling parties, but I will stay well out of the way. I'm not yet out, so I can't go to evening entertainments, and I don't want to go to the theater. I just want to visit the galleries and go shopping."

"Our funds are not so great that you can replenish your wardrobe," Beau said, a little stiffly. It had obviously cost him to admit such a thing to his sister.

"Pish posh. Your card parties rake in the guineas. Not that we should talk about such things. What matters is that you are doing tremendously well, no matter how inappropriate Mother thinks it is."

"We had a little rough patch lately, which is why Miss Truchard is here to help us. She is something of an expert."

"Ah, now I see why you don't consider yourself a lady. But surely you are the daughter of a gentleman?"

"I am both the daughter of a gentleman and the great-niece of an earl. But that doesn't mean I'm suitable. Every family has branches it would prefer ceased to exist altogether."

"If you say so." Emmeline rose and dipped a curtsy at her brother. "I am going to unpack. Don't tell Mother I am here. I plan to surprise her."

"Oh, she'll be surprised." After she'd gone, he turned back to Harriet and shook his head, his expression a mix of concern and loving amusement. "That's it. I will be flat broke by the end of the week. She is a menace when she shops."

"Then we will have to make sure there is enough money in the coffers to cover it, won't we?"

"I don't know if I'm horrified or relieved to talk so frankly with you."

"Relieved, trust me. This is a burden no person should carry alone."

He reached across the table and put his hand over hers. "I did not realize how alone I felt until I had you to talk to."

A comment that made her all the more determined to help him fix this.

A few hours later, Harriet took her manuscript to the garden to read over the chapter she'd just written. There were chairs and an old card table positioned to take advantage of the afternoon sun, but all that accomplished was to make her feel sleepy. She had convinced Sooty to come down by dangling a bone from the kitchen in front of him, and he was now happily gnawing on it at her feet.

The door to the kitchen opened, and Lady Emmeline strode through it, smiling when she saw Harriet. She had taken off her pelisse and now wore her muslin gown with a paisley shawl draped around her shoulders.

"Hello." Harriet put her quill on its stand and rose from her chair.

Sooty roused himself from his bone and sniffed the hem of Lady Emmeline's skirts.

"Is this your dog? How dear he is." She picked Sooty up and settled him in her lap. "I'm sure my little Rose would love to meet him—if she has time in her busy calendar."

Harriet echoed Emmeline's smile. "Did Lady Beaufort discover your arrival?"

Lady Emmeline grimaced. "She was mortified. She said this was now a house of ill repute, and my reputation would be tarnished if it became known I was here. I am to return home tomorrow."

"Probably for the best."

She frowned. "So the gambling parties really do put us in a bad position? I wonder at Beau doing it, if that's the case."

"I'm sure he will stop as soon as he is able." Harriet couldn't help the slight edge in her voice.

Lady Emmeline sighed and sat on the chair opposite Harriet, after first brushing it off with a handkerchief she pulled from her sleeve. "It is all very annoying. I thought it was a bit of fun, but Mother has certainly set me straight."

"I rather think that you should be proud of what your brother has achieved."

She laughed. "What has he achieved? Ruined the family's standing and turned Mother into a bundle of nerves? *And* he has done it just before I come out, jeopardizing *my* future. Who will want to marry me when people whisper we're no longer good ton? I'm not sure I can forgive him."

Her comment only proved how young and sheltered Emmeline really was.

"You have no idea what he has suffered for the sake of the

family," Harriet said, as evenly as she could. "And what he does over the next few months will mean the difference between you having a dowry and not having a dowry."

"Don't be ridiculous. Things aren't *that* bad."

"It's not my place to tell you how bad things are," Harriet said, aware she'd just done so. "But for your brother's sake, do not make complaints about lack of spending money, as he has enough worries already."

Lady Emmeline bristled. "Who are you to advise me on what I say to my brother?"

"I will tell anyone about to make a cake of themselves what I think. Beau needs the support of everyone around him."

Lady Emmeline rose from her chair, surprising Sooty who leaped to the ground with a disgruntled groan. "I take it back. I don't want my brother to marry you, no matter how pretty you are."

"And now *you* are the one needing spectacles." She smiled at the young lady, who was scowling. "There now, no need to get into a pet. I mean well, I truly do. If nobody tells you the truth of the matter, at least I have done that." Harriet looked back down at her manuscript, hoping their meeting was over.

"Good day to you," Emmeline said stiffly.

Harriet watched the young lady flounce away and chewed on her lip, worried that in defending Beau's action she'd just sacrificed her own standing in the house. They needed her help, true, but would that take priority over the whims of a sister?

As the kitchen door slammed behind Emmeline, the gate to the mews creaked open to her left. She turned to see Beau stroll into the garden. Harriet groaned softly.

CHAPTER 22

WHERE HARRIET PROVES TO BE A MOST
EXCELLENT ASSET

If Beau's expression was anything to go by, he'd heard some—if not all—of her conversation with his sister.

He sat down across from her and flicked an imaginary bit of lint from his breeches. "You don't have to defend me, you know. She was right."

"Deluded nonsense. If she can't see how you are single-handedly saving this family, then someone should tell her."

"Only you could see me in such a noble light." He picked up a white camellia that had fallen to the ground intact, and placed it on the table next to her manuscript. The grass was littered with them.

"I see you exactly as you are. Not the Lord, not the son or the brother. Just a man doing his best to overcome a terrible hand."

"I'm not a saint."

"Then join my unsaintly salon. We meet Thursdays to discuss our nefarious ways."

He smiled, which was at least something.

"What could you possibly have done differently?" Beau

asked. "You refuse to fleece people as your parents want you to. You've found a way to be free of them to avoid being tangled in their schemes. You *are* virtuous. Your hand was as bad as mine, and yet you made the *right* choices."

She looked down at her fingernails. "I do now, but that was not always the case."

He remained silent, so she forged on. "It's not a story I'm proud of. In fact, most of the time I bury it so deep I forget it's there. But it comes back swift and fast if I sit down at a table and look into an opponent's eyes."

There must have been something bitter in her voice, for he reached across the table and put his hand over hers. His touch was warm, comforting. Dangerous. "You don't have to tell me."

Oh, but she did. If she was going to work for him, he needed to know.

"When I came of age and was allowed to explore the full extent of my talents, I did. Without conscience or qualm. Mother would have you think they never saw a penny from my ability with cards, but that would be a lie. In the first six months I graced the tables in Vienna, I netted them close to ten thousand pounds. Father called me his goose."

"Golden goose?" Beau asked softly.

"Precisely. I had no thought for the people I won money from. I just swallowed my parents' teachings whole, and my marks were just wigeons, not worthy of care." She took a deep breath. "Until one day on the French Riviera, when I was playing a brilliant older lady. I had watched her the previous day and knew she had deep pockets. I also knew she desperately needed a reversal of fortune."

She paused as the face of the older woman swam before

her. Sharp, dark eyes, hair the color of a well-honed blade, and an energetic air about her.

"Go on." Beau squeezed her hand.

"We played, and I sank thousands of pounds into letting her believe she was on a hot streak. Then, when she truly believed her luck was in, I turned the tables. Within an hour, I had reversed my losses and come out ahead and in possession of a small French chateau. I can't explain what happened to me that night, but my mind counted the cards with a clarity and accuracy that should have scared me. I was a creature lost to the second deadly sin, thinking of nothing more than the carriages and the jewels I would buy." Tears glimmered in her eyes, tears she just couldn't blink away. "There were celebrations in the Truchard household that evening. Champagne flowed, and the party went into the early hours of the morning. But not for her. She died by her own hand later that night, rather than face the losses. I am responsible for that. I am a monster."

The words rang true as they always did, settling into her bones and reminding her who she really was. She looked up through wet lashes, expecting to see disgust. But he just looked thoughtful. "You are *not* a monster. She was probably already deep in debt and that night's gambling was the last straw."

"Precisely my point. When you sit across from someone, you never know exactly what they have at stake. For her, that night, it was her life. I will never forgive myself."

He looked set to argue, so she continued sharply, changing the subject. "In more encouraging news, there is no reason to hide my identity as an author now. Spread word around town that Miss Townsend, the author of *Winning at Whist,* will take all challengers at the Whist table, while giving them tips on their game. Let's get some people in and at the same time lose my Truchard surname."

"Are you sure you want to lose your anonymity?"

"It has served its purpose. Now let it serve yours."

He frowned, but she could see the excitement in his eyes. He obviously knew this could save the entire situation.

He paused only briefly. "If you are sure ..."

Harriet was proved right. Word had spread around town like wildfire that Miss Townsend would play Whist with one and all. It seemed every person in London with the key to Beaufort's presented themselves to Portman Square the following evening.

The rooms were full all night with a constant stream of carriages dropping off noblemen, politicians, clergymen, and gentry.

Beaufort's new crew just had to keep up with them. Beau had tasked himself with oversight on the green baize Faro table, Mandeville presided over Hazard, Harriet and one of Mandeville's footmen were the team that took on all comers at Whist, while Lord Mandeville's other footman dealt Vingt-et-un.

Harriet was playing with his money. She and her partner rarely lost a rubber, but always gave her opponents generous feedback. It was the perfect solution—she didn't feel like she was fleecing them, and they became better players. He had set his Faro table up so he could see the entire floor, but she drew his gaze like a magnet. He could watch her deal, shuffle, or pick up cards with her graceful, easy movement all evening.

But she kept catching him watching her. Over and over. It

didn't stop him, even when he vowed he would. He couldn't stop, as if a subconscious part of him would only be happy when his gaze rested on her.

Once, she tilted her head to one side, clearly asking if anything was wrong. Of *course* something was wrong. He wasn't seated next to her, listening to her banter, or flirting with her. He shook his head and forced his gaze on, scanning the room.

The new team worked together brilliantly. It had been a smashing night. There was no air of tension as he had felt on other nights, and he hadn't seen any sign of criminal behavior.

There was a long way to go, but maybe everything was on the up. Finally.

His gaze found Harriet's table again. He could see by the pile of markers on her side that she was winning quite handsomely. She'd said yesterday that her family had called her their golden goose, but she would never be that for him. He would never want her to be.

Two men left her table and approached him.

"Good evening, Beaufort," Lord Lennox said. "Just had wonderful instruction from Miss Townsend on the Whist table. We'll have to come here more often, eh?"

"Too right," his companion, Sir Anthony Brocklehurst, said. "That was dashed fun. I'm even over my initial shock that Harry Townsend is a lady."

"And she flirts like an angel," Lennox added.

Beau inwardly rolled his eyes. How did an angel flirt? Did it bat its wings and shine its halo? The man's name should be lummox, not Lennox.

"Have you considered that the flirting is the way she gets an edge on you?" Beau asked blandly.

"She's welcome to!" Sir Anthony said. "She's magnificent. I've a mind to make her an offer."

"Of the most disreputable kind, I'm sure," Lennox said, voice dry.

"You know me so well," his friend replied with a laugh.

Beau went from amiable chatting to bristling anger in the flip of a card. "Don't make me call you out, Anthony. It is such an archaic practice, but if you insult her virtue, I'll have no choice."

He slapped Beau on the back. "That's the way it is, is it? You're to be congratulated."

"That's not the way it is. She is just under my protection, as all my employees are."

"Indeed," Sir Anthony mused, stroking his chin. "Well, clean your guns and sharpen your sword, Beaufort. You're about to be inundated."

Beau glanced over to Harriet, who was in the midst of bestowing a saucy smile on her current opponent. This was an unforeseen problem. He'd been worried about customers discovering Harriet's family name and reputation, but not that she would be hunted by an altogether different threat. He would have to warn her.

The night ended, as it usually did, around four in the morning, with all the champagne drunk, lonely sandwiches left on the banquet table, and a few stragglers still attempting to recoup their losses before being moved on by Merrick.

Mandeville gathered the last of his takings and placed them on Beau's desk where Beau sat with all the night's winnings. His footman did the same and then Harriet came up behind them both and put a veritable mountain of guineas in front of him.

His eyes widened at the accumulated treasure. "I haven't seen a night like this for six months," Beau said. "What a fabulous job you all did. I know this is strictly short-term, but I can't tell you how much I appreciate your support."

He'd already decided to gift Mandeville a bottle of his father's best brandy from the cellar, knowing there was no way his friend would take payment. He'd brought it up earlier and placed it under his desk, so he reached down and handed the bottle to his best friend. "My thanks."

Mandeville's eyes widened. "You're most welcome. You'll have to come over later in the week and help me enjoy it."

Joshua and Mandeville, along with his other footman said their goodbyes, leaving him alone with Harriet. Well, almost alone. The door was open and footmen traipsed up and down the hall, cleaning and ferrying the last customers out.

Harriet collapsed on to a chair next to him, her gaze briefly searching his. "I think that went well?"

"If I wanted to prove I was losing profit, tonight has done that. Notwithstanding that we have never played Whist as the bank like you did, we've never had returns like this before."

"And I reined myself in," she said. "My competitive streak always wants to run riot. But I had to mentor them and leave them with confidence."

"You balanced it beautifully. There was a line of people waiting for you the entire night."

She laughed. "If I'd known there was such a demand for private lessons, I would have put my shingle out months ago!"

Beau remembered his conversation with Sir Anthony, and his desire to 'make her an offer'. "With regard to that, perhaps private lessons would not be advisable unless you are in a very public place."

A blush appeared on her cheeks. "Yes, I encountered some less than honorable offers tonight." She waved it away. "But let's not dwell on it. Rather, we should toast to our success."

He wanted to take her in his arms and hold her close. Maybe kiss her cheek.

But would he stop at just her cheek?

Of course not. He'd no sooner look into her eyes, see the heat there, and be snared once again.

He had a promise to uphold.

"I must dwell on it, because you are under my protection."

Her face clouded over. "Yes, yes, of course."

He resisted the urge to reach out and erase that cloud. "Go and get some sleep. You have a book to finish."

She curtsied to him, quite unnecessarily, but he had a feeling it was to stop herself saying more. "As you wish. Goodnight, Lord Beaufort."

So formal for someone who was becoming as important to him as air to breathe.

CHAPTER 23

WHERE THE DECK THROWS UP A JOKER

Beau stood next to Harriet as her opponent scooped up his winnings.

"I won against Miss Townsend and her partner!" he said in a booming voice, a flush of red running up his thick neck. "It's possible, my friends, she can be beaten!"

Harriet curtsied. "You were a worthy opponent, Lord Breckenridge."

A burst of applause rose from the assembled group. As Breckenridge swaggered away, Harriet glanced mischievously at Beau. "My, they do like to see me lose, don't they?"

"A few a night seems to be a good ratio," Beau replied. "After all, nobody wins *all* the time."

"Not even me," Harriet replied. The room had a vibrancy and joviality about it even greater than when she'd first visited with Charles and Mariah.

She wasn't convinced gambling was ever a suitable form of entertainment, but as always, it was not her place to judge what others enjoyed when they were harming no one. And *hundreds* of people had enjoyed Beaufort's over the past week.

For her part, hosting Whist games while tutoring her opponent was going *so* well, that Harriet wondered why she had never thought of it before. The money she could make would eclipse the royalties from the book itself. But then, she would not have the establishment or connections to do what she was doing without Beau.

Three card parties each week and by the end of the week, she had an envelope filled with six guineas. It was an outrageous amount for doing something she loved. Bantering with his guests, flirting a little, losing to them, but of course, more often than not, winning money for Beau.

His was a cause she could support. Because it was not a way of life with him. He was clambering to escape, just as surely as she was. Maybe they could escape it together.

It was that time of the evening, when the people who had been playing for a few hours decided they could use a break, and traveled to the banquet table, piling their plates with tarts, sandwiches and tiny cakes with fondant on top. They ate and drank at the tables in the dining room, and then made their way back to the gaming, refreshed and ready to win more money.

Harriet's stomach grumbled.

"My goodness, Miss Townsend! I know I shouldn't comment, but please get some food."

Beau's voice was so sincere that she broke into a smile. "Breakfast was a *very* long time ago."

"I saw your breakfast. It should have been enough to fortify you into next week."

"Certainly, it was large, but I did not mean it to be my *only* meal."

He leaned closer and whispered. "I have already arranged for a plate of the most delectable morsels from the evening to be saved for you, along with a bone for that little scamp of yours."

His breath caressed her ear, setting off a trail of goose bumps.

"I think he is becoming attached to me," she said, perhaps a little too keen.

"Truly? I thought it was the bones cook gives you and the blanket you have on the bed." He looked over to the Faro table, where his footman was valiantly trying to keep the peace over the riotous game. "I'd best get back to my Faro table."

He walked across the ballroom, his strides long and confident. When he got to the table, he said, in a manner that left no one in doubt as to who was in charge, "Right, you pack of rascals, behave."

Harriet smiled and took her next clients, playing on without a break. Stifling a yawn, something made her look toward the door. A familiar gentleman strode on to the gaming floor as though he owned it.

Her heart stuttered. *Thomas.*

The very man who had led Beau's employees to steal from him and who knew where the proceeds had gone. Perhaps some of it reached the returned veterans, but her intuition told her that most of it had lined Mr. Thomas Astley's pockets.

Her opponents looked around, too, and then back to her with a question in their gazes.

"His lordship's cousin and ne'er-do-well."

"Ah," Lord Breckenridge, now a regular client, said. "I can see it has discomforted you, which can only be good for my game."

She smiled. "How quickly you learn, my lord. I am indeed distracted and completely missed your last play."

"Voila," Breckenridge laid his cards on the table with a flourish.

With one eye on Thomas, who roamed from table to table, Harriet clapped and curtsied to his lordship. "Excellent game." She pushed his winnings across the table with a smile, then rose. "And now, if you will excuse me, gentlemen, it is time for me to take my overdue supper."

But as the men left, Harriet was dismayed to see Mr. Astley ambling toward her.

And Beau was busy with the Faro table, which was a riot of bets being made and laid, complete with shouts of triumph and despair.

Astley lifted a hand in greeting, but the smile on his face was anything but friendly. "Ah, I see the rumors are true, you are the author of *Winning at Whist*. How droll."

He stopped in front of the table and looked her up and down, his insolent gaze admiring.

"I have decided I don't like you, Mr. Astley," she said, primly.

He raised an eyebrow and sat in the seat vacated by Breckenridge. "It is of no consequence. I find myself somewhat short on funds. Let's play for high stakes, shall we?"

"No, thank you. As I said to the other gentlemen, it is time for me to take my well-earned supper."

He picked up the stack of cards and carelessly shuffled them. "It seems my brother likes *you* very much. Got your eye on the title? It's worth more than it was a few years ago, thanks to this place."

"My only focus is being able to take care of myself." She resisted the urge to look over at Beau. "And if you told yourself your cousin had more than enough to justify stealing from him, then you're more a fool than I."

"This is my family's business, and my ancestral house. I stole nothing."

"Oh, so anything here is *actually* yours? I thought the first son, not a distant cousin, inherited through primogeniture laws, but what would I know?"

"Beaufort never gave me enough."

"He gave himself less." She gave him a sweet smile. "And he *never* could give you enough, because you'd *always* want more. I learned that about you the first time we met."

"You'll be bad for him. I know who your family are now. If word got out that old Francis Truchard's daughter was dealing here, the crowds would flee. People have long memories."

A sudden coldness raised goose bumps on her arms. She fought the instinct to rub them away. "I do so love it when people blame me for something that happened before I was born."

He shrugged. "If my dear cousin had listened to me, we wouldn't be here right now."

"And where exactly are we?" Was there any chance she could get rid of him before Beau spotted him?

"Point non plus, my dear. Point non plus." He threw a pack of cards on the table. "I hope you don't mind if we use my fresh packet. You being a Truchard and all."

"I don't remember agreeing to play." Harriet kept her gaze steady on him. "But perhaps I will. You amuse me."

His brows drew together. Good. He should underestimate her.

She picked up his deck of cards, and he tried to snatch them back. "I'll deal, if you please."

He was providing his own cards, *and* he was going to deal. Did he think she was a greenhorn?

"I think not. Only dealers deal at Beaufort's, and we use fresh packets each evening." She kept hold of his pack, opened the box, and tipped the cards into her hand. She fanned them out on the table, noticing that they were *not* new cards, and had been arranged very deliberately with all the high numbers of each suit stacked toward the middle. Then she flipped the deck over, looking and feeling.

"Oh, poor Mr. Astley. I hope you haven't been using these cards for very long, for they are *quite* damaged. It feels like someone has pricked these with a pin." She put a set of five cards face down on the table.

"While these are fluffed on the edges." She put down another four cards.

Then she inspected another group, squinting her eyes at the reverse side. "It must've been a terrible batch by the manufacturer, for there are some color problems, too."

She pushed the cards back across at him. "No, I don't think we will use your cards tonight. In fact, I would prefer not to play you at all."

Heat crept into his cheeks, and his eyes glittered. "Are you calling me a cheat?" His voice rose and Harriet felt the gaze of everyone around them on her table.

"Merely pointing out that someone has tampered with your cards." She shrugged, even though inwardly she cringed. This was *not* what Beaufort's needed right now. She sensed a presence behind her. She didn't have to look around to know who it was. She felt it with every inch of her being.

Mr. Astley looked over her shoulder. "Hello, dear cuz. Come to defend my honor? I think your fair author is calling me a cheat."

Harriet kept her gaze on Thomas. "I have made no accusation. You may not know your cards are marked."

She was giving him an out, and the flicker in his eyes suggested he was aware of it. His next words told her she was wasting her time.

"My own cousin cuts me off without a penny, no allowance, and no way to make my living. Of course I'm going to turn to gambling, and where better than here?"

"*Anywhere else* would be a better choice, Thomas, and you well know why. Please leave."

There was a hardness in Beau's voice that made Harriet shudder. He was a man who would move heaven and earth to protect his own, but woe betide any who betrayed that trust. Family or not.

The gall of Thomas, coming here after all he had done, with the expectation of being welcomed. Beau angrily motioned to nearby footmen to remove him. This betrayal would sting until the end of his days.

Thomas looked around as they approached. "Really? I'm to be escorted out? Is there no end to your parsimony?"

"Years ago I paid for your colors—you cashed out," Beau growled, somehow resisting the urge to reach across the table. "I offered to pay your university fees—you declined. If you're beggared, it's your own fault. My loyalty to you is at an end."

It was hard to reconcile the man that stood before him, expecting handout after handout, and the cousin he had played tin soldiers with.

Thomas bristled. "You'll be sorry for this."

There was movement at the door, Thomas whipped his

head around and turned back, smirking. "I believe you already know my friend?"

It was Jinx. Flanked by his usual ruffians. He hadn't visited the gaming floor in the five years of the loan. That he was here now—and in Thomas's company—boded them all no good.

But Jinx wasn't looking at him. His intense gaze was focused on Harriet.

"What's *he* doing here?" Harriet said, in a fearful, breathy whisper.

She wrung her hands in uncharacteristic panic, and Beau's stomach sank. She knew him, too? Was Jinx another bad family connection?

"Nothing good, that much I know," Beau replied.

"He's going to destroy us." Harriet searched his face, alarm in her eyes.

He didn't try to calm her panic. He couldn't when he felt the same way.

Thomas sauntered over to Jinx and shook the black-guard's hand. Was his connection to Jinx a recent one? Or was Jinx involved in the cheating ring? Was this all much bigger than he had thought? Was Thomas working with Jinx to bring about his downfall, so Jinx could sweep in and take over?

The sad thing was that while he would happily be rid of Jinx and the debt that had hung over his head these past years, he would always grieve the loss of his cousin. Thomas was making decisions that could not be undone.

"Devil take it," Beau muttered. "What next?"

"I wish the devil *would* take him," Harriet muttered. "It would save us all some bother. How do *you* know him, or should I assume you're one of the *coves* he loaned money to?"

Beau was saved from answering as Thomas led his disreputable friend to the Whist table.

There were only two ways to go about this. Welcome him, or have Merrick throw him out on his ear. Only one of those choices did not disrupt the night's gaming. So he forced himself to smile, even though it was nauseating. "Welcome to Beaufort's. We are pleased to have you here."

"We most certainly are *not*," Harriet said under her breath.

Beau stepped around the table. "Can I get you a drink? Champagne perhaps?"

Jinx just kept walking toward him, his gaze focused on Harriet, as though he wasn't there for Beau at all. He stopped in front of the table and reached out, lightly putting his finger under her chin and lifting it. "Just my betrothed. It is beneath her to work a table when she will soon be married to me."

CHAPTER 24

IT WAS ALL GOING SO WELL ... UNTIL IT WASN'T

Harriet's world shuddered to a halt. She had not agreed to a betrothal. She had not even agreed to be left alone in a room with him. Drat it, she should have run further and faster to get away.

"Over my dead body," Beau said. *So much for not making a scene.*

Mr. Donovan spared him a glance. "If you like."

Harriet's eyes widened, and she pulled away from his grasp. "I don't remember accepting your offer. I am of age and make my own choices."

That only made Donovan smile, his golden tooth winking at her. "You will accept the inevitable." He looked around. "Do you like it here, at Beaufort's? You'll have to tell me the secret to running such an elegant establishment."

Stomach a quiver of nerves, she straightened, lifted her chin and made sure her eyes spat fire. "The secret is actually *being* elegant, which gives you *no* hope. Stick with what you're good at."

"You'll soon find what I'm good at," he said, looking at his cronies to laugh at his crass joke.

She very much did not want to know what the joke meant. He was leering at her like he already owned her, and she'd never felt more powerless. It was a horrible feeling, like a mouse being cornered by a hungry tom cat.

"My dear Miss Truchard, I am only going to tell you once. This will be your last night at Beaufort's. You will return to your parents' house, accept my generous offer, and your father will dance a jig over the settlement."

She raised her chin defiantly. "And if I refuse?"

Jinx smiled, but if a smile could be a threat, then Jinx had a knife at her throat. "Lord Beaufort will find out what happens, if you refuse."

Beau would pay if she didn't return. Lovely.

Beau mock bowed to the thug. "As you wish, Jinx. I'm glad you drew the line at actually threatening a lady."

Donovan took a glass of champagne from the tray of a server, who had the temerity to pass by, and drank the entire glass in one gulp. "We shall see. Will I get a wife, or will Beaufort get tipped out of his shiny London town house? Why not both?"

He laughed, too loud, too long, while Beaufort motioned to the footman to call Merrick. In a few moments, his staff flanked Jinx and walked him from the room. He laughed the whole way.

Beau looked at Harriet. She'd grabbed a deck of cards and was shuffling them from one hand to the other, the liquid movement obviously aimed at calming her nerves. But her hands shook.

"I am proud of you," he said.

She looked up, brows furrowed. "Why?"

"If he's the suitor you've been dealing with, that was no simple task. Most ladies would crumble under the assault." That spirit and backbone he'd boasted about to his mother was all too real. Even if it now put her in jeopardy. All he wanted to do was spirit her away, so Jinx's grubby hands could never touch her.

"Trust me, I was at my wits' end."

Laughter and play continued on around them. Shouts still came from the Faro table, and the lilies in the vases dotted around the room still smelled sweet. The turmoil was only inside the two of them. A guest wandered over with his wife to engage her in Whist. "Is this table open for play?"

"My apologies, but I'm closing this table for the evening." He grabbed a handful of tokens from the pile Harriet had accrued and held them out to the gentleman's wife. "Enjoy these on Vingt-et-un or one of the other tables. I wish you luck."

The wife smiled and bobbed a curtsy. "Thank you, my lord. I am hopeless at Whist in any case."

As the couple moved away, he tucked a hand under Harriet's elbow. "Come, my dear, we have much to discuss if we are to escape this tangle."

She disengaged herself, but followed him across the ballroom. "It has never been 'we', Beaufort, only your problems as distinct from mine. Although I am happy to help with yours in any way I can."

"Likewise, my dear. But I now think that our problems are woven together, and we might do well to pool our efforts." He led her up the stairs, all the way to the attic, where he stood outside her door, allowing her the choice to invite him in.

She studied him, her head tilted to one side. "You want to talk in *here*? It's not the most comfortable room in the house."

"We can leave the door open if you like, but I think having Sooty to pat might be more calming than a deck of cards."

"True." Her smile didn't quite reach her eyes as she led the way into the attic room.

The fire burned in the stove, casting a warm light across the room. Sooty let out a happy yip and jumped off the bed to greet them. She picked him up and gave him a cuddle he immediately struggled out of. Putting him down, she sat on the bed, whereupon the dog jumped up and rolled onto his back.

"No hug, but I can rub your belly, is that it?" she asked. She kicked off her slippers and tucked her feet under her gown. But not before he'd seen her stockinged feet and a pretty ankle. He concentrated on his own shoes, ignoring the quick stab of attraction.

Beau sank into the armchair that used to be in his study. "I know you said they had arranged a marriage, but they can't make you."

Her smile was sad. "And I know you said you'd borrowed money from a less-than-honest man, but I had no idea it was Mr. Donovan. He is never going to let you go, you know that, right?"

"I'm beginning to understand. I thought I was over being naive, but it seems not."

"It's not a sin to think people will behave honorably. He has forced my parents' hands, too. The betrothal was some kind of payment and they may well have borrowed more from him." Tears touched her eyes, and he fought the urge to go over and brush them away. To hold her and comfort her. Perhaps he'd made a mistake coming up here. It was entirely too intimate.

"God bless Mariah for wanting something better for me," she continued. "But, of course, that would never happen without a dowry, or Mariah's good looks. Although, never let her know I said that." She laughed, but it was a bitter sound.

It was not the time to tell her she was more beautiful than her sister. That even at this sad moment, with unshed tears in her eyes and a red nose, she was still the most beautiful creature he had ever beheld.

Harriet paused, her eyes narrowed in thought. "He will find a way to call in your loan tomorrow if I don't return home. Perhaps even if I do."

"But I am up to date on my payments. How can he?"

She kept her gaze on Sooty, who pawed the air for more pats. "I'll bet you a guinea your contract has traps for the unwary. There will be a payment you were a day late on that he documented for just such an occasion. Tomorrow you must have all your paperwork and the complete amount you owe ready, along with a Bow Street runner. Then maybe we can be rid of him. But we must act now."

"Oh yes, the entire amount. I have it laying by." He couldn't keep the sarcasm from his voice.

"Maybe you will ..."

Letting the thought hang in the air, she lifted her legs on to the bed and hugged her knees.

"Maybe I will what? I don't like the unhinged look in your eyes." But he did. He liked it very much. It meant she was hatching a plan with that brilliant mind of hers.

"Maybe you will find me some nice male attire and take me to a gambling hell."

He reared back in surprise. "What? I will do no such thing. You could never win enough in one night. And, anyway, I won't let you." He would not be just like all the others, using her talents for his own gain. Just the thought made him feel ill.

She stood and strode across the room to the window, looking out into the black night, her gaze alight with excitement. "Yes, you will. And I'll play like I've never played before, with stakes higher than I ever have before, and we will win the entire amount you owe." She turned, frowning. "How much is that again?"

"Twelve thousand." It may have been over a hundred thousand to start with, but that was still a fortune.

"I can do that." From across the room, she nailed him with a triumphant stare. "Do not underestimate my abilities."

He crossed his arms over his chest. "I don't. But I won't let you."

She shrugged a shoulder, unconcerned. "If you don't come with me, I'll just go back home, raid Bertie's wardrobe and go on my own."

"I could lock you in here for the night."

"Or we could try this." She crossed the room and kneeled before him. "Come, let me help you. I never do this for anyone, but I would do it for you. Let me be your golden goose. Take what I offer so that we can both move on with our lives. You can end these parties, and I can lease a cottage in the country and write my books. All I ask is that you give me whatever is over what you need."

Such a lonely dream. "Is that what you *really* want?"

"More than anything."

She dreamed of a future that didn't involve him. He should be relieved. It was his duty to make a match that brought wealth and prestige, while a family connection with the

Truchards would be cataclysmic. But every moment he was with her only reinforced the idea that he owed it to his heart to pursue her.

She was the first person in years to light a flicker of hope in him. The first person to make him feel like life could be fun again, *enjoyed* again.

Kneeling before him like some sacrifice, willing to trade her ideals and her honor to help him. And worse, every fiber of his being wanted to cup her face and kiss her. Not gently, but fiercely. "You humble me with such an offer."

"Don't be humbled. Go downstairs and get me some clothes. Stop wasting my time. That horrible man is going to come back tomorrow, and I want to see the look on his face when you pay him back completely and the Bow Street runners shoo him away."

"I don't deserve you."

That stopped her, and she grinned mischievously. "I *am* rather fabulous. But you can't keep me. I'm for a short time only." She looked away, but when he reached down and took her hand, she looked back, her gaze soft and her expression shy.

"If you are to leave me," he said softly, "then I must kiss you as often as I can before you go."

Her gaze widened, but she said nothing. He brushed his lips over hers, allowing her the choice to pull back while praying she wouldn't. She did the opposite, moving from her kneeling position to sit on his lap, barely breaking the kiss.

Her scent was intoxicating. Giddying.

"Minx," he said softly, smiling.

"Needs must," she replied, snaking her arms around his neck. "And I need and must do this. Who knows what tomorrow will bring? Now shush."

After a few long and delicious minutes, she pulled back and rested her head on his shoulder, tucking herself in as though she belonged.

Because she *did*.

But that was a thought that could go nowhere.

"This chair is so comfortable." She nestled in further and sighed.

"That's because the chair is me." He inhaled the lemony smell of her hair. "Well, if we're going to put this plan into action, the man you've just made a cushion of had better get moving, however much he might not wish to."

He gently deposited her back on her feet, then rose and quickly left, before his control gave way to the fire that still burned between them.

CHAPTER 25

WHEN A LADY NEEDS ALL THE LUCK SHE CAN GET

Beau's kiss lingered on her lips, making her feel clumsy and weak. What a crazy thing she had done, but if this all led to their doom, at least she had been well and properly kissed.

No regret.

Beau returned from raiding his wardrobe with beautiful garments that would make her look like a veritable dandy. He handed her the bundle and raised his eyebrows. "I hope they fit well enough."

"Why have I never seen you in these?" The frock coat was the color of a summer sky, the pantaloons dove-gray silk, and the waistcoat white silk embroidered with gray and silver flowers.

He leaned on the doorjamb. "Because we gentlemen dress in a more restrained manner these days. I was younger and smaller back then."

"I bet you miss strutting around like a peacock in this." She held up the waistcoat.

"I must admit that waistcoat was a favorite of mine." He

smiled, not his normal smile, but something gentler, then pushed himself off the door. "See you below."

Harriet took a deep breath and placed the bundle of clothing on the bed. What had she gotten herself into? It was heady, the way he looked at her, the way he kissed her. He made her want things she really shouldn't. Made her think she had the chance tonight to reach for the moon, and if she could grab it for him, surely he would be hers.

She sighed and started the long process of dressing. It was not as easy as it sounded, getting dressed in men's attire. The pantaloons were baggy on her, but the cut was tight in places she hoped would be covered by the frock coat. She lifted the soft linen shirt and let it fall over her like a cloud. Was this his, too? Had it been warmed by his body over countless days and nights? She hugged it to herself. It was way too big. How on earth was she going to scrunch all of that fabric into her pantaloons without creating bulges? Although, perhaps bulges weren't entirely out of the question.

Small blessing that he had not brought one of the cutaway evening coats that would make it all too obvious that she was not endowed with the usual male equipage. She might be tall, but she had a slightly curvaceous figure, so the bigger the frock coat, the better.

They had it easy, these gentlemen. No pinning pieces into place, no lacing of stays. As it was, she was sure she must look like a veritable stripling. But then, that could go in her favor if she had a shiny roll of guineas and a fresh youthful face. Nobody would know what she was capable of.

Please, my stupid talent, don't fail me now.

It would be just her luck that the one time she needed to win would be the one time the cards would not deal in her favor. Vingt-et-un was the only game she could trust her skill to bring the desired result. She couldn't bear to fail him.

She would free them both, dashed if she wouldn't.

She tied her cravat in front of the looking-glass and then used the hair cream Beaufort had supplied to slick her hair into masculine waves. It wasn't quite enough, so she took her mending scissors and cut her front locks into a poetic wave. There now. That looked almost Byronic.

The cravat would hide any number of secrets and by the time she placed the beaver hat on her head and swaggered toward the door, she was bubbling with excitement. Or was that nerves? It was hard to tell.

Oh, to have this kind of freedom. To walk anywhere in London with nothing but a cane for protection. To know that when you spoke, people listened. And that you owned all the property, and all the money in the land. You even owned women. All you had to do was marry one, and she became your chattel. Such a strange notion.

The first thing she would have done, if she were a married man, was place a great deal of money in the lady's own personal bank account, so she knew that love bound them together, not some horrible legal contract.

Imagine being owned by Mr. Donovan. She shuddered. More relied on tonight than she dared think.

If she could win enough, she would ensure all their futures. But she *must* not lose her nerve.

Don't fail me now. She wanted her talent, but none of the trouble that usually went with it. The inner dragon that took hold and led to disaster. *Stay quiet tonight, dragon.*

She opened the door and went down the stairs, holding the banister with one hand, and gently swinging her walking stick with the other.

Beau waited for her at the bottom. "There you are, Mr. Townsend."

"If you call me that, perhaps no one will play with me."

"Very well. We will just call you Harri." He looked at her with his head tilted to one side.

Oh, to know what he was thinking. "Do I make a magnificent male specimen?"

"You, my friend, make a magnificent anything."

He ushered her down the hall. Merrick's eyes twinkled as he opened the door for them, suggesting he was in on the secret. "Have a good evening, gentlemen."

The carriage waited for them out front, and Beau directed the driver to St. James, where the gambling hells congregated.

She spent the rest of the trip in silence, although it wasn't silent in her head. The words of one prayer after another ran through her mind. *Please Lord, help get us out of this mess. Please, please.*

She had to stop thinking this way. She needed a clear head, free of emotion, if this was going to work. Last-minute pleas to heaven wouldn't make a whit of difference. The good lord turned a deaf ear to prayers for a favorable roll of the dice.

Beau reached out and took her hands in his. "Everything alright?" She nodded, but he didn't look convinced. "I just want this to work."

He shook his head, the carriage lamps illuminating his small smile. "Don't put so much on it. This may work, or it may not. If it doesn't, we'll find another way. And if we run through the guineas in my pocket, we'll come back another night. I don't want us getting in deep."

She nodded. "You don't want us to be just like all those other fools."

He nodded. "Precisely. Desperation is never good. I can

afford to lose this money, so test your talent to the depth and breadth of it. Have fun. But not a penny beyond. Are we understood?" He lifted his hand and put his finger under her chin in a way that was not dissimilar to Mr. Donovan's action earlier that evening, but it felt entirely different. Instead of jerking away, she leaned her cheek into his hand, allowing him to cup her face. Soon, his other hand reached up, and he leaned forward. "A small kiss for luck."

His lips met hers, so soft, so sweet, sending shivers down her arms. Her eyes closed of their own volition, while her heart raced in her chest. *Again.* Could she ever be kissed by him and not react like a lit bonfire? He pulled away. *No.* She leaned forward, claiming his lips again. He smiled, something she felt with her lips rather than saw.

"You need *more* luck?" he said, his voice husky and amused.

"I need all the luck I can get."

He rolled his eyes, but he was smiling. "Look at us, suddenly believing in luck."

It must be wearing breeches that made her feel so bold. She pressed closer, until she was all but in his lap, and claimed his lips again. The strike of the horses' hooves on the cobblestones, and noises of St. James faded into the background. Beau became the world. She felt the hint of brandy on his lips and the roughness of his unshaven skin against hers.

They kissed for what seemed like forever, until the need to take a deep breath made her pull away. He watched her with a deeply lazy smile that made him look entirely too happy with himself.

"Why are you smiling?"

"I knew it would be this good. I just *knew* it."

"I am astonished you thought about it at all." She was about to add that she hadn't, but that would be a lie.

"It is *all* I have thought about." His gaze wandered down to her mouth again. "Much to my chagrin."

So, he thought about her and then admonished himself for it. Well, it might not be gentlemanly, but it was certainly flattering.

"Did you …?" He left the question hanging, looking deeply into her eyes as if he would find his answer there.

She shook her head. "Think about it? No, never." *Definitely. Every night, before I fall asleep, as though imagining kissing you was some kind of prayer.*

His smile suggested he'd seen right through her lies. "I know this is a crazy idea, but when this is all over, would you like to stay with me? In this case, forever?"

She laughed. "Oh, Beaufort, don't be ridiculous! You cannot be aligned to a Truchard. No matter how upstanding the Truchard in question is."

He smiled, like he was holding on to a secret. "Can't I?"

She was left feeling confused by his answer and the lazy smile he gave her along with it. "My parents would use you shamelessly."

"I should like to see them try."

She paused with a moment of mortification that she may have mistaken his meaning. "I assume you mean marriage and not something entirely different."

"Oh? What else might I mean?"

He was teasing her. But he really should know better. She *always* called a bluff. "You may have been offering me *carte blanche*. To keep me in high style in some quaint apartment, only visiting me when the mood moved you. You would buy me jewels and I would spend my days writing my books and my nights being entirely entertained." She paused, as though a thought had just struck her. "It is too bad that the idea is deplorable, because it also sounds enticing."

"Ha! See, you do adore me and you'd marry me in a heart-beat. Kisses don't lie, my lady."

"No, they don't." She sat back in her own seat, suddenly struck by the way he was sitting. He was entirely at ease, one long leg stretched out across the carriage. Like he was with the closest of friends that he had no need to behave for.

"I do adore you," she said impulsively, blood rushing to her cheeks at her unintended declaration.

He sat a little straighter, eyebrows raised. "Of course you do."

"As a friend."

Beau winked, actually *winked*, at her. "Of course, only as a friend." He coughed into his hand, masking what he said. "Liar."

CHAPTER 26

WHERE FAILURE CLOSES IN

The carriage stopped on St. James Street in front of the Berry Brothers wine merchant. But that was not their destination. To the left of the shop was a narrow oak-paneled alley, dark and ominous.

Beau took a deep breath. One last roll of the dice before everything came crashing down.

His debt called in by Jinx, bankruptcy looming, losing their Portman Square house and selling whatever they had left.

His sisters having no prospects at all.

Harriet married to Jinx, because she'd spent all her hard-earned diamonds buying Bertie a way out.

Failure on every front.

He was glad Harriet's nerves were made of steel because, without that fortifying kiss, his would be frayed.

He went to offer her his arm so she could step out of the carriage, then remembered she was dressed as a young buck ready for a night of gambling, so he took the hand he'd raised and rubbed his jaw instead.

Beau led the way down the alley, with Harriet following, the heels of her boots clicking on the cobblestones.

"I know this place," she said. "I'm not sure this is a good idea."

They reached the end of the alley, which opened onto the smallest square in London—Pickering Place. It was surrounded on all sides by tall buildings, each of which was a gaming hell. Cobblestones were set in circles around a large oak tree, and groups of drunk men talked loudly.

It was secluded, secret, and the kind of place that gentlemen conducted duels with their seconds standing guard at the entrance to the alley.

"But anyone can gamble here, no membership required."

Her mouth was a flat, unimpressed line. "No, Beau. Anyone can get *fleeced* here. And if you're not fleeced then you can be sure someone will pick your money and watch out of your pocket while you play."

"Are you sure?" It had been some time since he'd been out on the town, but now he thought about it, the times he had played at Pickering Place *had* felt dangerous. It had been part of the thrill at the time. But with Harriet in tow? It was not something he wanted to risk.

"Completely certain. What about The Cocoa Tree? I always fancy winning money off a Tory."

He laughed. "I didn't know you were political."

She shrugged. "They are more stupid than most."

"I believe I still have a membership there and could squeeze you in as my guest. But," he pulled a card out of his pocket and showed her. It was heavy cream card stock, embossed with a picture of a gaming table and playing cards of each suit. "How about The Club House?" It was a small gambling establishment where the guests were elite and play was deep.

"On Bennet Street?"

He nodded. She certainly knew all the gaming hells, even if she had not frequented them. "Yes, that would be acceptable. I have not heard of foul play there."

Which suggested she *had* heard of foul play at Pickering Place enough times to make her wary of entering. He would be stupid not to listen.

They turned and walked back through the narrow alley and then down St. James Street, toward the club on the corner with the shiny red door. "I hope you brought your luck with you tonight."

Harriet sauntered up the steps of The Club House. "My kind of luck is always in play. Proof of that is you bringing me here." She leaned toward him in a teasing way. "Instead of your *own* establishment." She had deepened her voice, so she sounded a little more masculine, but not decidedly so.

She was certainly no man, but perhaps she would pass for a stripling in the dim light. And if not, so what? What was the worst that could happen?

Actually, he didn't want to think about the worst thing that could happen—adding their social ruin on top of everything else—so instead he turned to her with a curt nod. "True. I hardly think my bank needs breaking again." He leaned in to whisper in her ear. "While the gamesters of this establishment can well afford it. They play Whist for high stakes here."

The edges of her mouth turned up. "Then you must find us a pigeon I won't mind plucking."

"I will have no problem there."

They entered the establishment, much smaller than Beaufort's, but still plush. Red velvet curtains and green felt tabletops, along with ample candlelight, meant the room had a warm glow but heavy shadows. Maybe, away from the harsh light of day, Harriet would get away with it. He ignored the nerves fluttering in his stomach.

He still couldn't believe she had offered to do this. Or that he had accepted. He saw people win money like this every week at Beaufort's, but always thought them fools because they came back the very next day and lost it.

If they won tonight, he would gladly never gamble again.

They took a position in the corner where they could view the entire room. She crossed her arms across her chest. "When playing Whist, communication is difficult. But if I am slow in playing my card, that means I want you to take control. If I am decisive, then I feel I have the superior hand and I would expect you to follow my lead. But these will only be minute hesitations."

"Understood. But what if I feel *I* have a superior hand?"

"Then play just as decisively and I will follow. We do not want to communicate to our opponents, after all. I think we know each other well enough to detect slight changes." She shot a glance at him.

"Yes, we do." But to be fair, he'd been able to read her from that first morning at the bookstore when the arch look of disdain on her face told him he was indeed facing the author of *Winning at Whist*. He didn't even know why he trusted her so implicitly. Perhaps it was no one thing, but a chain of times she had proven herself.

He looked down at her boots—his boots, making her feet look enormous. Beau pulled a wad of notes from his pocket and handed it to her. "Here's our stake tonight."

She took it and buried it deep in her pocket. "One question."

Her steely gaze took in the gaming room before her as though preparing herself for battle. "Yes?"

"This is something I have never done and would not normally offer. But would you like me to, shall we say, tilt the playing odds in our favor?" She turned her head, her gaze meeting his, as though the answer was hugely important.

He gave a swift shake of his head. "Absolutely not." He didn't know what to make of the fact that she offered. Was it because she thought he would expect it of her? Or because she so dearly wanted them to win that she would do it at any cost?

Well, that cost was too high. "You have never done that, and I would never forgive myself if I were the reason you crossed that line. No. Either we do this with natural aptitude and the numbers falling our way, or we leave here with enough to buy ourselves a midnight coffee at The Palace."

She inhaled and exhaled deeply. "Good, good." She looked back at the gaming floor and frowned. "You know, I think I have been here before. Father took me all over town when I came of age, seeing if he could find a place I would feel comfortable playing."

"But how? The only ladies here are hostesses." Which was a polite term for how these ladies earned their living.

"As I am now." She reached up and pulled her hat down. "They were forever dressing me up in different disguises to suit their needs of the day."

The very thought made him bristle. They'd used her abominably. "I may plant your father a facer if I am ever in his dubious company."

"He is a master at dodging them." She looked around the room. "Shall we warm up with some Vingt-et-un? I will pretend to learn from you."

They went to the table, where Beau played a few rounds

with Harriet asking the kind of questions only a fresh young man would ask at his first gaming hell. She spoke in a hushed tone about the hand he held, so the entire table could hear.

Beau let out a dramatic and frustrated breath. "I suggest, my dear cousin, that you hold your tongue before you tell our good dealer all my secrets. Just watch silently tonight."

She bowed and took a few steps back. "I'm sorry, Beau. I will await you at the refreshment table."

She did so, and he returned to her an hour later with a doubled stake. "Well played back there. Now everyone in the room knows you are a greenhorn." He took the glass of lemonade she offered and took a sip. "Nursery drinks?"

"Better than water, although the champagne is flowing freely."

"But of course. I do the same. I want happy and carefree clients."

"And I want a clear head."

"It's hard to imagine you without one."

She looked at him sheepishly. "A thimble-full of champagne would do it."

"Being intoxicated while gambling is a fool's game." He watched her gaze as it brushed past each of the gaming tables, landing on the Whist table. "That is Lord Chester and next to him Mr. Wosley. Both are fine gamesters. They are at Beaufort's once a month and never fail to either win or lose over twenty between them."

"Twenty *thousand* pounds?" Harriet said, her eyes widening. "In one evening?"

"Yes." He had to admit, he always gave a shudder when they arrived, although they always settled their debts. If Harriet were to play them, they might not be the horrible men she usually liked to play, but they were worthy opponents.

Her gaze snapped to his. "Oh. Fair play or foul?"

"Always fair. But beware, they are what I would call professional players. Not the pigeons you asked for."

She shook her head. "They are less pigeons and more falcons, I would say. But I don't mind being challenged. I would prefer not to fleece, as you know. Shall we try? We can always back out if things are not going our way."

"Let's not look too keen. Play around a little, and if they approach us, then we'll play them."

"A little risky. What if they don't? And won't they know you?"

"I'm sure everybody knows me. But I never play at Beaufort's. The joke I offer is that I don't play because the moment I sit down, Lady Luck leaves the table."

She threw him an amused glance. "But we both know what you really mean."

He took a sip of lemonade and grimaced. "What's that?"

"That Lady Luck stalked off in a huff because you said her services weren't required, because you could win on your own."

"Ha!" He laughed louder than he meant to, and men at the closest tables turned to look at them. Although not Lord Chester's table, because Whist was the kind of game where one never looked away from the play, no matter what inducement.

They wandered from table to table, Harriet a jovial bumbler who made him laugh more than the situation should have him do. He'd never seen this side of her. She was like a country cousin, landed in the big city and finding wonder wherever she looked.

"Look at the counters, Beau. They're capital!" She examined the gambling chip of The Club House with its engraved mother-of-pearl shimmering in the candlelight. "It's so handsome, I want to keep it."

"Some people collect them. Beaufort's loses a few hundred a year. And considering it takes a year to get them made in China, it's quite annoying."

"Father once had his own set made on a visit to Kantong." She turned the counter over in her hand. "He's since sold them, of course. But I used to love playing with them."

Then they played Hazard, but not for large stakes. They left it a little under the weather and were restocking on sandwiches when a gentleman approached with his plate filled. "Beaufort, good to see you out of your native environment."

He bowed. "Lord Chester, how do you do? May I introduce my cousin, Mr. Harry Bertram to you? He has had enough of my genteel gaming room and has asked to be introduced to London more broadly."

Harriet bowed.

"Is that the Bertrams of Northumberland?"

"Yes!" Harriet smiled as though cheered by his notice. "But we are the younger branch. The current earl is my cousin five times removed. A very remote connection. My father runs the bank in Hexham. It's small, but we are happy to be part of the community."

His eyes widened as he took in Harriet's dated ensemble, and a smile he was obviously battling to control twisted his lips. "What do you like to play, lad? Don't let the good Beau lead you anywhere near the Faro table."

"I do like Faro," Harriet said earnestly. "It's so exciting."

"Much better to play something more considered, like Whist. Mr. Wosley and I would be happy to play a few rubbers with you both. We have just finished up our game with Curruthers and his friend."

Beau shrugged. "It will do him good to play with seasoned gamers. But I reserve the right to exit the game if my young cousin puts me to shame." Beau turned to Harriet. "Do you think you will, pup?"

"I will hold my own, I'm sure. Mother and I played Whist many a time over the years."

Lord Chester again tried to hide his smile, no doubt amused by a young man thinking playing with his mother would be enough to make him a good opponent.

"Very well! Bring your glasses over to the table." He inspected their contents. "Good old lemonade. I didn't realize they served it here." The look he threw Beau was amusement sprinkled with a good amount of distaste.

They followed the gentlemen to the table and sat, Harriet with her legs spread in a manly way.

Beau looked away, not sure whether to be amused or embarrassed. Their knees knocked together and embarrassment won.

"Ponies good for everyone?" Lord Chester asked.

Beau nodded, but Harriet looked at him like she had no idea what a pony was. "Twenty-five pounds per game," he said casually.

She made a swift intake of breath and swallowed hard. "Very well."

He was sure that it was not nerves but excitement on her face.

It was a good thing he had brought enough blunt. If you're going to win a lot, most of the time you had to stake a lot. And the ponies would only be the beginning. "Actually, gentlemen, since my cousin is new to London, we might try one pound per game to start with."

"Certainly, we can start there." The rest of the sentence—that they would finish considerably higher—was left unsaid.

The play was even for the first rubber. They were well matched, aside from Harriet, who often played higher cards when a lower one would have sufficed.

Wosley and Chester noticed every mistake gleefully. But when they spied the thick wad of notes she had in her evening coat pocket, bound by a black velvet ribbon, they couldn't contain themselves.

"Will that ribbon be mourning your money?" Mr. Wosley said, producing a guffaw from his partner.

"If I have had fun, there will be no mourning," Harriet replied. "I must get used to city life at some stage. All I ask for is fair play and the opportunity to learn."

"Learn in a drawing room, lad. Come here when you feel surer of your skills," Lord Chester said.

"But I've done that! Now I fear the only way to learn is to play people better than me. It's no fun winning against your mother and aunts."

"Lucky to get your money out of them, too," Lord Chester laughed.

Harriet frowned. "Oh no, we only ever played for pennies. Nothing to lose, really. I like the thrill of staking *actual* money."

"Your father's money, you mean," Mr. Wosley looked to Beau, silently asking if this was the case. Beau nodded. Let them think she was spending her banker father's money.

Harriet looked down at her hands, then cleared her throat. "Perhaps you are right. I shouldn't play." She moved to push her chair back and the other men held up their hands in horror.

Beau laughed inwardly. She was already taking them for the ride of their lives, and they didn't even know it.

"No, no, young man. Do sit down. You have nothing to fear here. All play is above board. We will not let you lose more than you want to."

She searched their faces, nodded and sat back down. "If you say so."

They played on.

Harriet varied her style, sometimes attacking with clear intent, only to swap to a defensive game on the turn of a card. Always making it seem like any wins were a surprise.

To watch her, you'd think she was a complete novice. She was slow to play her card, as if overthinking it when he was sure she was not. She toyed with her cravat and before she won her first trick, started tapping her foot in an excited way.

Their opponents shared an amused look that turned into smug smiles.

"We were all young once, gentlemen," Beau said gently, and they smiled more indulgently.

They were five hundred pounds down, a huge amount of money, and Harriet was tapping her feet and frowning. Between rubbers, she looked at him. "Surely our luck must come in soon? You told me luck flows around, coming and going. We've had an awful lot of going."

Since he had never even *thought* that, much less said it, he realized with not a little relief that she was still acting, still working up to something.

Lord Chester exchanged a glance with Mr. Wosley, one Beau had seen many times before. It said 'get ready, we've got ourselves a pigeon.'

They had taken the bait.

The stakes grew, and before long they were staking

hundreds of pounds per rubber. He would love to know the trick on how she made her cheeks blush on demand. Only he knew that by doing so, and by them reading her expressions, she was schooling them.

As time wore on, her game became more consistent. He didn't know if their opponents noticed. If he played a high card to lead the trick, she played a low one, always supporting his game. He did the same for her and between them, within the space of an hour, they were almost a thousand pounds ahead.

He remembered what she had told him in those first heady days of their acquaintance. *In any given game, I will know how many of the trumps have been played, I will know which cards of each suit have been played. I may have to concentrate and be very still, but if I see the cards, I remember them.*

When you put that together with her masterful knowledge of the game she'd written a book about, it was astonishing to watch in action. Worse was that, if he'd thought himself half in love with her before, each time they won another rubber, he fell a little bit more.

He'd never felt this kind of connection with a lady. Never even known it was possible to feel like you were a small army that would take on the world together. She wasn't just his love, she was an ally he would fight for. Die for.

"Right, that's enough of the small stakes. Let's make this a little more interesting, shall we?" Lord Chester said, rubbing his hands together. "As a final hurrah. Come, Beaufort, you've got deep pockets, lend the boy some blunt."

"He doesn't need me to lend it to him."

Harriet lifted her chin. "So you think you can fleece me? Very well, do your best!" It was youthful swagger in all its glory. "We stake five thousand for the first pair to reach eight games."

What was she doing? That was double what they had in their kitty. Everything they'd won so far—gone. If they lost—he would be leaving a promissory note with Lord Chester. The idea of playing everything on the next few games was crazy ... and yet, he had to trust that she knew what she was doing. Had to ...

But it was nevertheless a big risk.

"Perhaps not such a wonderful idea, scamp." He said it with a touch of warning in his voice. She ignored him, staring down at her cards in concentration.

"You wanted me to play, I'm playing," she said, with an obstinate set to her mouth.

Like a surly youth.

"No, Harri, think on this."

Her reply was to throw all her money on the table.

He sat back in confusion. What was she doing? She'd understood him and had not listened. How could she risk it all in one possibly foolish move?

He kept a lid on the spurt of anger and tried to think rationally. She'd warned him they were playing for high stakes; she'd assured him she wouldn't risk anything he didn't want her to. But this position she was putting them in, he hadn't banked on it feeling so perilous. Like walking on a pond that had only just iced over.

What if she had been lost to the lure of the cards, like her fateful days on the continent? What if not even he could bring her back and had to just sit there and watch her lose everything? Every part of his body capable of breaking out in a sweat did so at that moment, prickling and cold all over.

Perhaps his implicit trust had been premature. Sweet lord, he hoped not.

Mr. Wosley and Lord Chester exchanged loaded glances, but Wosley merely shrugged. "If you wish. You must learn, my dear boy, to keep your emotions away from the playing table. I'm surprised your cousin hasn't taught you that."

"You can't teach a hothead," Beau replied with a mildness he did not feel. "Do you like that stake, cousin?"

Please say no.

Harriet shrugged. "I could double it and still like it. Shall we?"

Double it. *Double it.* He closed his eyes. "This is not brave. It is foolhardy. We don't need to play like this."

"I want to. If I lose all my money here tonight, then so be it. I will spend the rest of my trip counting my pennies and hoping Father doesn't find out."

"Oh, I'll tell him," Beau said through gritted teeth.

"You wouldn't!"

"I won't join your stake, and we both know that to cover an IOU for ten thousand pounds you would have to write home." It felt like all the blood had drained from him and was pooling around his ankles.

"Let him stake, Beau. He's a grown man."

Her eyebrows drew together. "Yes, exactly. Will you still play with me, Beau?" She shot him an annoyed look, and he didn't see any gaming fever in her eyes. No suggestion she was out of control. But she did look excited. Her cheeks were flushed and that could not be feigned.

"Of course I will." There was a hardness in his reply that was entirely real. She shrugged, like his opinion mattered not. He took a deep breath to control the surge of anger, knowing he was frowning but unable to stop himself.

Harriet looked at their opponents with barely concealed excitement. "Very well, twenty thousand to whomsoever wins the best of eight games."

He clenched his jaw. May God have mercy on their souls.

Harriet did her best to ignore Beaufort, who radiated so much anger she could almost taste it.

And well might he be furious, given she had just staked so much more than they had. Foolhardy any other time. But she had an understanding of the men they were playing with now.

It was time to give the game her entire mind. Beau had stopped watching her and had his concentration back on the game.

I hope he forgives me for this risk.

Pray I am right about what's left in this deck.

She remembered the anecdote of the man who'd bet his entire fortune on the fact that the seven in the trump suit was still in the deck. But it was not.

Fortune lost.

Nobody ever heard from him again.

She'd be lucky if Beau didn't drag her down St. James Street behind his horse if she was wrong.

He exhaled deeply, and she sensed that he had put to rest the internal fight she had seen in him. The moment when he looked at her as though she were crazy, and questioned his decision to trust her entirely. She saw it as clear as day.

Please, please let me be right.

But the part of her brain that recorded every minute detail knew she was. Lord Chester was showy, often leading with high cards, discarding with a flourish. Mr. Wosley was calmer and took his partner's foibles with equanimity. He was shrewd, though. He watched Harriet with a sharp eye that probably didn't miss much. Perhaps even seeing past her male attire to the young lady beneath.

Instinct told her this was the perfect time to strike.

But she had never trusted her instinct with someone else's money, or indeed with their entire future.

Hold steady, girl, hold steady.

The jovial nature she had employed until now vanished, and she kept her eyes firmly on the table and never on her cards, even when it was her turn to play. Where previously her hand was organized by suit—now it was not. Nobody could guess how many of each suit she had by where she pulled a card from. She watched everyone else carefully, quietly, as they organized their cards into order. Wosley has three of one suit, four of another and a smaller mix for the rest of his thirteen cards.

Soon she would know exactly what those suits were, rather than the guessing. These were not tricks she had shared in *Winning at Whist*, because very few had her memory to accomplish it. They were exposing their hands, without ever showing them.

Beau looked to have a very strong hand. Likely six of one kind of suit. She may have to bow to him. But her hand, although she had purposefully squandered better during this session, was also very strong.

The trick would be playing those cards in the right order to win.

She watched which card Lord Chester played and from what area of his hand. Hearts then. She did that in turn for everyone, while at the same time keeping a tally on which cards were played, her mind brimming with diamonds, hearts, clubs, and spades.

She had never pushed her talent so far or for so long.

They played seven games, all of them in sober, solemn silence. The banter was gone; the counters were piling up on both sides.

Soon they were in the final game.

Everything came down to the fact that Harriet was certain nobody had played the ace of hearts. It was the trump suit, and this was the final hand.

They were tied and whoever played this card would win the trick and the game. She was sure it was Beau. He had been playing determinedly, in a style that suggested she should subject her game to him.

It went against the grain to cede her game, because what if she was wrong? What if he *didn't* have the ace at all? When Lord Chester played a two of hearts, it was decision time. Should she play her low card and allow Beau the win, or blow it all completely if he didn't have that ace at all?

In for a penny …

She threw her low card onto the pile and looked at him expectantly.

He didn't smile. Her heart sank into the floor and she braced herself. They would lose. She could read him and with each card he put down, his demeanor worsened.

She'd failed him. By trusting he had a hand better than hers, she'd failed them both.

She threw her last card down and looked at him. "I'm sorry."

"Oh, you will be." It was flatly said and sent a chill down her spine.

Mr. Wosley triumphantly placed a king of hearts, sharing a

jubilant smile with Lord Chester. They thought they were in front on the final straight.

Then Beau nonchalantly threw down the ace of hearts. "Our game and match, I believe, gentlemen."

Their gazes whipped around as they took in the ace lying on the top of the deck. "Well, blow me down," Lord Chester said. "I thought that card had been played."

"No, because it was in my hand." Though his voice was even, she could see the thunder in his eyes, in the set of his mouth.

She leaned back, heart pounding and hands shaking. "That's more than enough gambling for me. Forever, I think." He hadn't forgiven her play despite their win.

Wosley's lip curled as Beau drew in his markers. "You won't allow me my revenge?"

She shook her head. "Not tonight, my lord. My heart will not take any more and my mind is all scattered."

"Come now, gentlemen," Beau said. "You've won more than this from me some nights."

Lord Chester paused and then nodded. "Very well." He looked at Harriet, his gaze moving down to her chest. "Ten thousand each, eh. That will buy you a stable of steppers at Tattersalls—if your young cousin is allowed entry."

"He is of age."

"Yes, but is he of the right sex?"

"I certainly hope so," Beau replied. "I've known him since we were children."

Lord Chester nodded, but appeared unconvinced.

Harriet sighed dramatically "My father calls me his soft lad and sent me to town to make me more manly. I *am* trying … but not very successfully, it would seem."

At this, Mr. Wosley clapped his friend on the shoulder and said, "Let him be. It sounds like you're being a poor sport."

"Well, I am not. I lose this amount regularly and make it all back the following night." He stood and so they all stood, too. Lord Chester bowed, and took a notebook and pencil from his pocket, scratching out an I.O.U. and signing it before handing it to his partner, who signed it too. "We'll call upon you tomorrow morning, if that suits, Beaufort?"

Beaufort nodded. "That last game could have gone either way, and I played the rubber like I did not have the ace up my sleeve, so to speak."

"It was good play. I think, perhaps, we were both taken in by the young man and forgot that we had a true gamester at the table with him."

Harriet was happy enough to have them think that, even though she'd worked harder than she ever had to *make* them think it.

The older men left the table and Harriet turned to Beau. "Shall we go?"

"We should," he said flatly. His shoulders were stiff, the line of his mouth flat.

He was *incandescently* angry.

He didn't turn to look at her, just led the way out and started walking down St. James Street. "I can't talk to you right now."

Harriet strode after him, understanding his anger but still hoping for the best. "Because you are so happy you might kiss me?"

"Let's just get home," Beau growled.

"I know it was a risk, but we won." She followed for a few steps more when he said nothing. "Doesn't that make it all worthwhile?"

"No." He stopped and turned, his face controlled fury. "You staked *four times* everything we had. You could have ruined me. I would have been just another anecdote that mothers told their sons so they'd be wary of gaming hells. I'm angry at you, and I'm angry at me for trusting you."

"But we didn't lose! We couldn't. You had the ace."

"And you knew that? With absolute certainty?"

She hesitated and then forged on quickly, "One can never be absolutely certain, Beau, but I suspected, very *strongly* suspected, based on the flow of the cards. I spent the first hour just figuring out their methods and tells. When I was as sure as I could be, I made the play."

"And how many times have your parents gambled everything you had, right down to your dowry and the clothes on your back, because they were as certain as they could be?"

He would compare her to them? She stopped, her stomach seeming to cave away. "What happened to 'if we lose, I'll buy you coffee at The Palace'?"

"That was losing everything we had in our pockets. Not everything we have in the world."

"So I did the *wrong* thing winning?" She couldn't keep the sharpness from her voice, and shook her head. "No. I did what I promised I would. I got you out of debt. No more debt, do you see? It's gone. We should be dancing down the street and drinking champagne right now. Instead, here we are, arguing over methods I *warned* you might be necessary."

"I thought ..." he started and then stopped himself.

"You thought what, precisely? That I would only ever do exactly as you wanted? Allow my talent to fly within the bounds of your expectations? It doesn't work that way. You set it free, it's going to fly as high as it can, even if there is the risk of touching the sun. I am not my parents for they do not have this talent I have." She clenched her fists and stepped toward him. "You either trust me, or you don't. You don't just trust me when it suits you."

"I trusted you to do the right thing. Not to lose your head entirely!" He thrust a hand through his hair. "I almost died when you said ten thousand pounds! Where would I find that kind of money? Because it would be my debt of honor to pay. You don't understand …"

"I *did* understand the risk. But I also understood the reward and trusted my talent. But even when I use it correctly, it *always* gets me in trouble." She stormed off down St. James Street, leaving him in her wake. Well, in a way. Each time she turned around he was a few yards behind her, like a storm cloud following her home.

It was only when she was halfway to Mayfair that she realized his house was not her home. It would *never* be her home. She had money now, and she wouldn't be beholden to a man who didn't appreciate all she'd done for him. That was the true way to ruin.

But she couldn't go home. Donovan would find her. And she couldn't go to Mariah because that would just put her sister in harm's way. No, she had to strike out on her own.

"I will leave as soon as our money comes through—as long as you do not mind me impinging on your hospitality a little longer."

"Of course not, but there is no need to make hasty—"

She cut him off. "I will not stay with someone who cannot trust me. Once I have my portion of the winnings, I shall find accommodation elsewhere and you will be free of me."

Not wanting to go back home with him, she marched off, ignoring her stupid heart as it complained how much it hurt.

CHAPTER 27

IN WHICH THE LAST HURRAH IS CANCELED

"Still won't talk to you, sir?" Merrick waited for Beau at the bottom of the stairs.

Beau's legs ached from traipsing up and down the stairs all day, begging Harriet to talk to him. It was hard to apologize to a door, but he'd tried multiple times. He could swear the wood sighed at him in disgust.

Since Merrick was grinning, Beau glared at him with each step. The household was *far* too amused by his predicament. "What a gross impertinence for you to ask. But no, she speaks only to tell me to go away. And now nothing. Perhaps she escaped out the window while we weren't looking."

Merrick seemed to consider it. "She is an enterprising young lady. But no, Mrs. Pearce brought her lunch, and then after lunch I saw her slip out to take Sooty for a walk, so ..."

"You might have told me *that* earlier." He sighed. "I deserve it, I suppose. But I'll need a stiff drink with dinner."

"We all will, sir."

"How rude. You go too far, my man." He reached the bottom step as Merrick bowed an apology.

But when he rose, there was a twinkle in his major-domo's eye. "Never did the course of love run smooth, my lord. Miss Harriet is worth a little groveling, don't you think?"

"Miss Harriet is not even giving me the *chance* to grovel."

"And you so talented in that respect. It's a crying shame." Merrick fought to hide his grin.

"*Way* too far, Merrick." Good lord, his staff had entirely mutinied. "Did you see her return from walking Sooty?"

His major-domo, who knew all the comings and goings, shook his head, and then his light-hearted mood was replaced with a frown. "No, come to think of it."

It explained why she hadn't answered even when he told her Lord Chester arrived with their payment.

It was two o'clock. Harriet loved the park and could sit there for hours so everything was likely fine. It wasn't late enough to start worrying. But unless she was under his roof, worry he would.

"Shall I send someone to check the room, and then the park if she's not there, sir?"

Beau hesitated, then shook his head. He'd already made enough errors. Stalking her in the park might be the last straw. "Let's wait a little longer."

The front door closed, and a brisk footfall made him turn around, hoping for Harriet. "Mother."

She had been out all morning, which was a blessing when he'd made such a fool of himself all day. But it meant he hadn't had the chance to tell her they could now pay their debt.

Merrick bowed to them both and withdrew.

He'd dreamed of telling her news like this for years, and worked so hard toward it. Now the time was here, and it felt bittersweet.

"I have good news."

"Oh? Do tell." She rubbed her hands together, eager to hear something positive.

"Our moneylender, Mr. Donovan, otherwise known as Jinx, is meeting with me this afternoon, and I have the entire amount of our debt to pay him. Plus some left over to help us start again."

Her hand flew to her heart. "Please, don't jest."

"No jesting. We're free." Despite his heartache, the priceless awe on her face had him grinning.

"We can stop the parties? Tonight? Now?" She looked around wildly, the white feather on her turban trembling.

"Tonight will be our last hurrah." He exhaled, the finality sinking in.

She held out both hands to him. "But how?" Then she shook her head. "Oh, I don't care how. I'm just so very glad you did it. We are free! You are wonderful."

"I would love to take the credit," he said, "but Harriet won this money for us. We spent an entire night at a gaming hell staking increasingly hair-raising amounts until there was enough to pay it all off."

Mother blinked. "But why would she do that? *How* did she do that?"

"Dressed in breeches and fooling probably nobody. And she did it for me." *And then I got furiously, stupidly, angry with her over it.*

She looked at him shrewdly. "Because she is in love with you."

"She saw the chance to secure our futures." He looked down at his feet, because that wasn't the whole truth. "Yes, she also did it because she is in love with me." *Or was.*

"Ah, well. It was to be expected, I suppose." She paused. "And are her feelings returned?"

Beau looked her in the eye so he could see her reaction. "What would you say if I said yes?"

The front door opened, and she whirled around without answering him. "Why, is that Mr. Daniels? Has he come to help you with the legalities? I must greet him."

She may not have answered, but her wide, shocked eyes told him everything he needed to know. He would have to pursue Harriet without his mother's blessing.

So be it.

Merrick returned. "I have put Mr. Daniels in the drawing room for you, my lord. And thank goodness this is the last party. We can all sleep good and proper now."

"You've got good ears, Merrick. Could you do me the honor of telling the staff? Make sure they know nobody will lose their position."

Merrick nodded. "But the job will be different now, won't it?"

Beau grinned. "Already missing the opportunity to pull a cork or two?"

His major-domo raised a bushy eyebrow. "I still will, just not on her ladyship's doorstep. It's not seemly."

No, it wasn't, and he was glad to be rid of the business.

But even better, he would have the pleasure of watching Jinx arrive, not realizing it would be the last payment he'd ever get from Beau.

Mr. Daniels was an insurance policy of sorts. It would be imprudent to enter a meeting like this with Jinx without the full support of the family solicitor. He had sent all the legal documents to Daniels that morning so that there was no way Jinx could sink his claws into Beau for even a moment longer.

"Very good. I am expecting Mr. Jinx at any moment. Please send him into my study, but do not leave him alone." He hesitated. "And if you could remove the jade phoenix and anything else of value, I would most appreciate it." He was a fool once to leave something of such value in Jinx's company. Not twice. "And have tea sent down for Mr. Daniels and me."

It had been Daniels who sat down with him the day after his father's funeral and outlined the horrid ways in which they were drowning in debt. He had done so with practicality, but also with empathy. And once he had outlined problems, he also had drawn up a list of suggestions to help Beau dig the family out of the quagmire. He owed Daniels more than he could say, for standing by the family and for helping.

Over tea, he and the elderly solicitor talked about the contracts. Mr. Daniels was slim and sprightly, with hair that was still thick and brown, despite his age. Only his papery skin and the lines around his eyes gave his age away.

"There is no clause for early repayment, which means you are free to repay the amount with no penalty." Daniels tipped three spoons of sugar into his teacup.

Beau left his own cup of tea untouched. His stomach was too jittery to enjoy it. "So you're certain the final repayment is correct?"

Mr. Daniels took a sip of his tea and his shoulders relaxed. "I have had three sets of eyes over it, just to be certain."

"So if I hand this amount over ..."

"And get him to sign the receipt I have drafted ..."

"I'll be free." Just the thought had his stomach leaping in anticipation. Free.

"You'll be free."

They shared a smile, and Beau couldn't help the spurt of jubilation. *Careful, nothing ever goes to plan with Jinx.*

Daniels eyed the tray of madeleines but did not reach for one. Was it because Beau himself was not eating? "Please eat these lovely cakes or cook will be most displeased."

The solicitor immediately put two on a small plate, which he placed on the side table with a satisfied smile. "I must admit that since Mrs. Daniels passed away, my cake situation has left much to be desired. We always had help in the kitchen, but she did so love baking."

They sat in companionable silence until a knock on the door announced that Mr. Jinx had arrived and was being shown through to the study.

He turned to Mr. Daniels. "Are you ready to meet the up-and-coming king of the underworld? I have no doubt this man will be ruling all the criminals in London before the decade closes out."

"I can't say it will be an honor, my lord. But, in my line of work, one meets with all different kinds." His gray eyes were sharp and amused. Beau hoped he would keep that amusement and that Jinx would not do anything to offend the man who had helped his family so diligently. Or he'd have to plant him the facer he'd been itching to for five years.

He entered the study first, to find Jinx had once again seated himself at Beau's desk, with the same two thugs on either side.

Mr. Daniels bristled at Jinx's presumption, but Beau just smiled. *I never have to see you again after today. Do what you want.* "Playing the lord again?"

Jinx frowned. "Why have you called me here, when your payment is not due? And who is this?" He motioned to Mr. Daniels.

"My solicitor." He turned to Mr. Daniels. "Mr. Daniels, allow me to introduce Mr. Jinx to you."

Daniels frowned at Jinx. "Is that your actual name, sir?"

Jinx stood and held out his hand to Mr. Daniels. "My name is Donovan. I'm always pleased to meet gentlemen of the law. People with my interests need to keep on the right side of it." He looked to Beau. "Why have you invited your solicitor here today, Beaufort?"

Beau walked to the window and looked out on Portman Square. He looked as far down the square as he could. Still no sign of Harri and Sooty. She loved to walk, true, but it was unusual for her to be gone so long. Though perhaps she had seen Jinx enter and was staying far away.

And he couldn't say he blamed her.

"Because it is an important day, and I wanted everything to be in order," he said, almost absently. "You see, I am in the lucky position of being able to pay out the entire loan today. I had Mr. Daniels look over our contract to make sure we calculated the correct amount so that we can sign it off right here."

Jinx's eyes widened in shock. "You gave no notice. Notice must be given of a final payment."

Mr. Daniels flicked over the pages of the contract. "Nowhere does it state that Lord Beaufort must give such notice. All that is required is the payment of the outstanding principal, and any interest amounts until the day of payment. As you can see from these workings—which you are welcome to take away with you, of course—Daniels, Delong, & Carruthers have calculated interest for the rest of the month and included that in the payment as a small bonus to you."

Beau put the bag, made of cheesecloth, on the desk. Such a simple bag for so much wealth. He took out the stacks of bank notes and lined them up on the desk for Jinx to inspect. "Please check it, but I assure you it's all there." Then he took the workings from Mr. Daniels' hand, and the receipt, and put them next to the bills. "If you could please sign the receipt."

Jinx was quiet for a few moments as he read down the page, getting a small notebook and pencil from his pocket and doing quick calculations. The speed at which he did it suggested a fine mind for figures. Which was no surprise.

Then he shrugged, but even that nonchalance could not hide his annoyance. His gaze darted around the room as though searching for an argument. But it was a simple transaction, and he obviously knew the contract held nothing in it to stop its closure. He signed the receipt and pushed it across the desk.

"It was one of my earlier contracts. I'm sure I've plugged up this kind of nonsense now." He stretched his neck both ways, resulting in an audible bone crunching sound. "I suppose this money will come in handy. After all, within the next twenty-four hours, I will have a wife to take care of. I'm going to collect her now, in fact. Then I'll keep her nice and safe until the deed is done."

Beau frowned. Jinx couldn't mean Harri. She would never marry him. Of her own volition, that was. The phrase 'nice and safe' had the hair on his arms prickling.

"Maybe I'll invite you to the wedding," Jinx continued. "After all, she was hosting at your parties until last night. It's not like you weren't acquainted. Better luck next time there, Beaufort. I guess I win after all, don't I?"

Harriet would never agree to marry Jinx, but would Jinx hold something over the people she loved to force her? Beau's world stilled, though his heartbeat was so loud in his ears it was all he could hear.

"What have you done to her?" His voice was so low it was almost a growl.

"Nothing!" Jinx said, with a sly grin. "There is a long-standing agreement with her parents. They were about to be off to Marshalsea when I loaned them blunt. Much more legally tight than that monstrosity." He flicked a finger on their contract. "She could renege, I suppose, but the cost to her family would be steep. Truchard even got Sir Charles to sign guarantee documents. I think he thought he was investing in the canals." He laughed, like nothing had ever amused him as much. "Francis Truchard even puts me to shame with his wiliness. I'll be glad to see them off to America next week."

If Jinx held Mariah's wellbeing over Harri's head, she would probably comply. "She'll be deeply unhappy with you."

He gave Beau a nasty smile. "She'll come around soon enough. My mum always said I was a handsome devil. I guess that finally paid off."

Beau looked at Jinx. He *was* a handsome enough fellow. If you liked the look of a man who'd had his nose broken a few times. But Beau could never quite get past the deadness in his eyes. And the thought of him even being in the same room as Harriet, much less touching her, made his blood boil.

"I'm not sure why you want her. She is a stickler for the rules, you know. That's why she was the perfect hostess. Nobody got away with anything."

Jinx nodded, as though Beau's comment had only satisfied him further. "Yes, she will guard my new business well. I see a very prosperous future, and it has nothing to do with whether she can cheat at cards like her parents do. There are better uses for her mind than that. She'll earn her keep."

Beau took a step forward before he could stop himself, but Jinx just gave him a sly smile. "Can you believe what you let slip through your fingers, Beaufort? She's solid gold, that girl."

He wagged a finger, his shiny gold signet ring gleaming. "I should warn you, if you go anywhere near her, I will ruin you."

Beau's anger tightened and again he had to resist the urge to retaliate. "I should like to see you try."

"Me too." Jinx got up and sauntered around the desk, then clapped Beau on the shoulder. "Remember, dear boy, it only takes one word in the wrong ear to bring this whole house of cards down."

With that, he picked up the bag of money, swinging it around and whistling as he headed for the door. At the last moment, he half turned and said, "Oh, do you have anything belonging to Miss Truchard here? She left with just the clothes on her back, wouldn't you know it."

Because she hadn't planned to leave. He had to find her, save her, as she had him.

"She is welcome to come and retrieve it," Beau said tightly, feeling more and more sure she would be unable to do so.

"My men will take them now." He motioned for them to jump to it. "They'll wait."

"No, they will not. Leave now or be assisted out."

Merrick appeared as though by magic, flanked by footmen.

Jinx shrugged a beefy shoulder. "It matters not. There's nothing here I can't replace."

After he left, Beau stared thoughtfully after him. They might do well to cancel tonight's party. One last hurrah wasn't worth the risk of Jinx informing on him.

"And good riddance to unpleasant company," Mr. Daniels said.

"I am hard-pressed not to agree." He ushered Mr. Daniels to the door, hoping he wouldn't notice he was being hustled out. "Thank you for your help today. Your level head meant it all went off smoothly."

Merrick helped the solicitor on with his coat and handed him his gloves. He put his hat on his head and offered his hand to Beau. "I am glad to be of service, and thrilled to see you out of the hole your father dug."

They shook hands, and Merrick closed the door behind him.

"Merrick?"

"Yes, my lord?"

"I am canceling tonight's party. Tell everyone and have someone stationed out front tonight to let people know."

"Very good, my lord. Might I enquire why? Everyone was looking forward to one last party."

"Because I have a future wife to rescue."

"Ho, ho!" Merrick replied, smiling broadly to reveal a golden incisor and missing teeth in his bottom row. "Wait till they hear about this below stairs!"

Beau clapped him on the shoulder. "You should smile more often, my good man."

"Bring her home, and I promise I will."

CHAPTER 28

MISTAKES WERE MADE

Harriet took a deep breath. How was she back here at the park, even more miserable than the time before?

Well, strike that, a little *less* miserable. Because at least now she had thousands of pounds and wasn't trapped. Her winnings might already have been delivered to Beau. Then she could find a cottage to live and write in. Far away from the gaming hells of London.

It was a good plan, so why did it sound so dreary?

"You'll come with me, won't you, Sooty boy?" There was no reply, of course, but she got a lick on her hand when she tried to pat him.

Someone called her name, and she turned to see Mother and Father waving at her. Harriet sighed. Brilliant. They'd found her. Her first instinct was to pick Sooty up and leave. But they were in a public space. Perhaps this was the best place to see them.

As they approached, Sooty started barking, so Harriet spent the time she should have greeted them in calming him.

She looked up, not feeling very calm herself. "What are you doing here?"

They were, as usual, dressed to perfection. Mother was striking in a very modish navy pelisse with gold frogging and a military hat, while Father had a lighter blue superfine coat and shirt points so high he could barely move his neck. They looked dressed to parade Rotten Row. Perhaps they were, since she wasn't so far from there. Had they stumbled on her by accident?

"Oh, lovely greeting!" Mother said. "You leave without a word, and when we finally track you down, you ask what *we're* doing here?"

"I left you a note. I'm perfectly fine." She hoped her red-rimmed eyes wouldn't give her away.

"A note! Unnatural child. We're leaving for America next week, and we're worried about you. You may be the family's bad penny, but we still need to see you settled." Mother straightened her hat, toying with the gold braid that buttoned under her chin. Obviously, she'd had time to shop amidst all her worry.

Harriet snorted. "If I'm a bad penny, you two are rattling around in the coin purse with me."

Father scowled, lifting his chin in the air. "I am *not* the one who left the safety of my home to be a croupier in a gaming hell."

Who had told them? She swallowed. Donovan, of course.

Mother stepped forward and placed a hand on her arm. "Your father asked the captain if there is a berth for you, and there is not. Donovan will look after you—"

"I am not marrying Mr. Donovan. I have not—and will not —agree to such a thing. You cannot make me." Sooty snuggled closer to her leg.

Mother looked off in the distance, then back to Harriet, smiling sadly. "I'm sorry you feel that way. I hope you will forgive us in the fullness of time."

She frowned. "What do you mean?"

Mother stepped aside, to reveal Jinx and his two henchmen approaching.

"Dash it. What have you done?"

Harriet stepped back, ready to run, but Father reached out and gripped her arm. "This was a done deed, long ago. You *will* marry Mr. Donovan."

She tried to shake him off. "I will *not*."

Sooty growled, showing what a superior dog he was.

Father held her tight. She should have stayed at Beau's where it was safe. But was anywhere safe from this man? She suspected not.

Mr. Donovan stopped in front of her, looked her up and down, and smiled. "Ah, there she is! Excellent. Willing or not, you're coming with me."

That was when she realized he intended to take her *now*.

She turned her gaze to her mother. "You can't do this."

Mother rolled her eyes. "Do what? Send you off to a life of riches and comfort? Oh dear, how could we?"

Harriet backed up a step, but she was trapped. "Where are we going?"

"A simple ride in the park," he said with a coaxing smile. "Come now, I don't have all day. Although, perhaps I do now that I have twelve thousand pounds in my pocket."

"Lord Beaufort paid you?" That meant he'd have her money, too. Not that it mattered. Beau likely had no idea she was gone and certainly no idea that she was now in trouble— deep trouble. By the time he did, well, it might be all too late. She glanced down at Sooty. If he could find his way home he could be her only hope. It wasn't far, and thank goodness she had walked him to this park every day. She took off her bonnet then bent down, releasing the lead from his collar and throwing her bonnet as far as she could. "Good boy, go home."

With luck, his love of chewing hats would mean he didn't come back to her, but made off with his prize.

She cheered him as he raced toward a gathering of pigeons, his bonnet trophy in his mouth, making them fly into the gray sky. *Good boy. Go back to Beau.*

"I hate dogs." Donovan grabbed her hand. "The good Beau has indeed paid all that he owes, but if you don't want me to ruin him entirely, you'll come quietly. I've let him go thus far, but I'd rather not."

"What do you mean?" she whispered in horror. Her heart thumped painfully at the thought of Donovan hurting him.

"My dear, it would only take a whisper in the wrong ear—the ear of a Bow Street runner, perhaps—to bring his whole illegal gaming den down. I must confess, I am tempted—very tempted—to do it, since you seem to regard him so highly. It annoys me."

She swallowed heavily. Beau might have it in his power to stop the parties now, but how quickly would he do it? *Please be clever, Beau. I can't go with this man.* "I'm sure you can resist such a temptation, Mr. Donovan, especially if you want us to have any kind of working *friendship*." She let the word hang there and watched to see if he understood.

He simply smiled. "Come, let's take a drive in the park. It's a lovely day and I find I don't spend enough time in the daylight, being a creature of the night."

"Dear Mr. Donovan," Mother said. "Let us say goodbye to our daughter. It may be years, if ever that we see her again."

She dashed away a non-existent tear, came to Harriet and enveloped her in an unwanted embrace.

"And that will be too soon, Mrs. Truchard," she whispered in her ear.

Then Harriet stepped back. "Help! I'm being abducted!" she yelled as loud as her lungs would allow.

Father laughed and looked to the people who littered the park. "She's fine! We're her parents and she doesn't want to go back to boarding school. Nobody is abducting her."

"I'm not fine, someone tell Bow Street!" Then she screamed again as Donovan pulled her into the carriage. She didn't stop even when he shut the door.

"Silly girl." Donovan pulled her to him roughly and put a hand over her mouth. "Stop, or I'll make you stop."

His hand was cold and she stopped screaming just so he'd remove it. The carriage took a slow drive up Rotten Row, exiting the park at the western end. It didn't turn back toward her parents' house. Not that she'd expected him to. They had given her care over to him.

He finally removed his hand and she shivered. "Where are we going?"

"Smart as a button," he said, smiling broadly.

There was always something off with his smiles, she realized. Then it hit her. They never quite reached his eyes. Like he was saying and doing all the right things, but not feeling any of them.

"I thought I might sway your opinion by showing you my house. We have just completed the refurbishment. Although it will be my place of business, I have claimed the top floor for myself and my wife. Adams did the internal fitting of it. I would like your opinion. Especially since you have just spent time at Beaufort's."

He'd just abducted her from the park and now he wanted her opinion on curtains and soft furnishings? Harriet shook her head and blinked, trying to understand. Was violence such a normal occurrence for him that it could happen in and around daily life? She *must* escape him. Who knew what else he'd just take in his stride to get what he wanted?

"Do say you'll tell me if it is in good taste or not." He stared out the window. "Beaufort told me my waistcoats were not the thing and now I second-guess myself. I need the Ton to find the surroundings appropriate or my business will fail."

Even though Beau had been in Jinx's power, he had still taunted him. Her heart twisted. If only she could turn back time and talk to him when he'd come to the top of the stairs. "The Ton can find entertainment at a cockfight. As long as they can throw their money away, they don't care."

He laughed, and for once it seemed genuine. "Life won't be boring with you, that's for certain."

"I have not agreed to be part of your life, sir, no matter what my parents might have said and no matter how many times you take me off the street."

"But you will. Eventually. You will have little choice." The carriage stopped outside a large mansion on Piccadilly. "Don't mind the scaffolds. They'll come off later this week when the mortar is set."

"It makes no difference to me," she said. She stared at the scaffolds on the building. *Could I climb down those to escape?*

He took her arm and led her into the marble-floored foyer, which was furnished with thick carpets and small groups of plush red velvet chairs. A large chandelier hung in the void, and sunlight entered from the domed ceiling above, casting a thousand small rainbows around them. It was most definitely—surprisingly—tasteful. Surely Carlton House itself could not have been more opulent than Mr. Donovan's mansion.

"Oh, my," she said, before she could stop herself. So much money had been plowed by Donovan into the mansion. A gambling house like this could take on White's and Brooks's easily.

"A good reaction." He led the way up the stairs. "But let me show you the private apartments. They are even more beautiful. Perhaps this will convince you. I mean you no harm, you know."

Alone with him? No. "We are unchaperoned. I would rather not." Harriet looked around, trying to find any avenue for escape. But his men were behind her and his grip on her arm was too strong to wrench free from.

When they finally reached the third floor, he fished in his pocket for a key. "I have this room locked because many precious items have been purchased for it." He gave her a small smile that failed to reach his eyes. "I hope you like it."

"It does not matter if I do or not."

"Untrue, given I furnished it with you in mind."

He opened the door and bid her to enter. She balked momentarily, but maybe she could look quickly, tell him it was beautiful, then ask to use the water closet and make her escape. He couldn't stop her running. If she was fast enough.

It was a large room, with arched windows that seemed to be up in the clouds, with a beautiful view of London rooftops and the sky. It was decorated in the Chinoiserie fashion, with delicate wall hangings of pink flowers, green leaves and pagodas. The bed was large and four-posted, made of gilded bamboo, with a fluffy mattress. "Very pretty. Now, I need to use the …"

The door closed and the key turned.

Her heart leapt and she spun around. Donovan was *not* in the room with her. Her relief was so fierce her knees buckled, and she gripped the dresser to remain upright.

But she *was* trapped.

"Donovan!" she yelled, even as her mind said, over and over, *this could have been worse, Harri. At least he's not locked in here with you.* "Donovan, let me out right now."

"You can have anything you want, but you can't come out until you agree to marry me, and only then to meet the parson."

"This is the only way you can get a wife? By kidnapping one?" Her voice rose to a high-pitched squeak.

He just laughed, which infuriated her even more.

"It's the only way I can get the wife I want. You'll soon see that what I have here to offer you is better than anything you can find out there. We'll have a wonderful life, you and I. You just need time to think about it."

She yelled at him, incoherent words that didn't even make sense to her, but words like 'hate' and 'monster' were definitely bandied around. She even smashed some of his precious items.

"I'll leave you to calm down. I'm not a monster, I just know what I want. You'll come to admire that about me in time. We'll tell our grandchildren this story."

There was silence for a moment, but she heard no departing footfall. "And before you think of jumping out the window, there are no tall trees anywhere near the house for security reasons and no way down without a thirty-foot drop. Oh, and the windows only open five inches. Enough for air, but not much else."

Well, she could always cover her hand in a sheet and

smash her way through the window. *If* she could figure a way down.

"I will *never* marry you. Not if you sail the sea of No-way, land on the shores of No-how, and cross the land of Never-more."

"How dramatic," he drawled. And then left.

She immediately opened the drawers and then the wardrobe, looking for anything she could use to escape. All she found were her belongings, all here no doubt thanks to her mother. *Mr. Donovan will take good care of you*, she'd said, having already delivered all her belongings to her captor.

She slumped on the bed. There had to be some way to escape. At some point they would have to bring her a tray of food, and then they'd have to take it away. If she hadn't broken that ugly vase earlier, she could have used it over someone's head.

A dog barked, and it sounded awfully familiar. Just like Sooty. She went to the window and pulled back the curtain to see her dear little dog in the back lane, barking into the air, her bonnet trampled on the cobblestones next to him.

He'd followed her, rather than go home.

Hope was lost.

CHAPTER 29

If Beau thought he would search for Harriet by himself, he was soon disabused of the notion.

He descended the stairs having vested himself in his greatcoat with a pistol in his pocket and a rapier hidden in his walking cane.

A gentleman could never be too prepared. He only hoped he didn't have to use any of it, and found her on her favorite park bench, feeding the ducks.

There were mumbling voices on the ground floor. He walked toward them to find Merrick flanked by every footman of the house, all dressed to go out.

"And what is this?"

"Your search party, my lord," Merrick replied. They broke out in cheers. "We'll bring her back."

"And that scamp that chewed my slipper," someone added.

They were rallying around him, like they always had. If he weren't so angry at Jinx, it would make him teary. "You are the best team a man could have. Thank you."

They cheered again.

It was nice that they were so enthusiastic and merry, a far cry from the desperation he currently indulged in. Like Harriet was slipping away each moment he didn't know where she was.

"Where to first, my lord?"

"Half of you come with me to Green Park. She has a favorite bench there. With any luck, she is still there, and we can reach her before Jinx does. The rest of you can go to Hyde Park, which is closer and where she walks Sooty. Look for her first, but then ask questions." He turned to Merrick. "What was she wearing when she left?"

"That lovely blue gown she has, and a chip straw bonnet."

A chip straw bonnet, tied under her chin with a large blue satin bow. He knew the one. His heart clenched as he remembered how pretty she looked in it.

"Plus Sooty, who is quite memorable on his own. Somebody will remember her. Let's take a few maids with us so that we can talk to the governesses that spend time with their charges in the park."

"Good idea," Merrick said.

Beau looked around at the group gathered around him. "Right, this is a twenty-minute walk for those of us going to Green Park. I will take my curricle and anyone who will fit. Feel free to make use of the town horses in the stable."

"And if Jinx already has her?" Merrick asked.

"Then we see if anyone saw what happened. We may get their direction, or at the very least discover more. Meet back here as soon as possible."

They set off directly, with Beau reaching Green Park before those who set out on foot. "This will be quicker if I drive around."

Her usual bench, the place where she looked over the small

reservoir, was empty. There was no barking in the air. Sooty wasn't chasing anything. But beyond that, he couldn't *feel* her close by. He'd never realized how much his senses lifted if she was in the area.

She wasn't.

"I'll pull up and ask these ladies if they've seen anything."

Ten minutes later, it was obvious nobody had seen Harriet, although some people recognized her description from other days.

They gathered near the gate to the park. "Let's go to Hyde Park and see if our men are still there."

He drove there with a sinking feeling. It was getting late in the afternoon and soon anyone who might have seen Harriet would be leaving the park. Then he would have to get his team out of their livery and onto the town to see if he could discover where Jinx lived.

Someone would know.

He arrived at Hyde Park to see his men dotted around, speaking to people. All the way from Rotten Row, to the Serpentine, they were intercepting ladies and gentlemen.

Which firstly meant they hadn't found Harriet. But if each of them got a little information, surely it would lead them in the right direction? His heart had not stopped pounding since Jinx's visit and he now had a monumental headache.

When he drove his curricle near the Serpentine, a place she would most definitely have visited, his staff ran across the grass and along the paths to come to him.

"She was here, my lord," Derek, one of his footmen said. "Many people saw her."

Anthony ran to them, and stopped in front of Beau, his cheeks flushed. "I just spoke to a governess who saw her being bundled into a carriage. Said she screamed, but a man said they were her parents, and that she was fine, just didn't want to go back to her boarding school when they asked him about it." He coughed, then bent over and put his hands on his knees.

"The scoundrel," Beau said. "How long ago?"

"Not long. The parents did not get into the carriage, apparently."

Merrick had joined the group and patted Anthony on the back. "Good work. They might still be here."

"They are Mr. and Mrs. Taylor from my bulletin board, if anyone has looked at it."

Merrick's eyes widened. "Are they now? Poor Miss Harriet, with thieves for parents." He turned to the group, which had grown to ten returned staff members. "Now, we're looking for an attractive older lady with black hair who looks a little like our Miss Harri, and a gent who is just shy of six feet, with the same red hair our girl has. If you see them, come fetch us. Don't engage them yourself." He turned to Beau, a question in his eyes.

"Perfect," Beau said.

Now he would have to put his skills to the test, because he had never met them, only stared at inky portraits on his wall.

With two footmen perched on the back and Merrick beside him, he drove his curricle toward the gate of the park. The one they would use to reach the Truchard house on Half Moon Street.

"No sight of them," he said.

Merrick pointed into the distance. "There?"

A couple walked with arms linked down Curzon Street. That was the right direction. He looked around him. "Might be. Let's go."

He handed the ribbons to Merrick, who maneuvered the

traffic with the same agility and brute strength he'd once brought to the boxing ring. "Steady on," Beau said with a grin.

"Never thought I'd see the day you'd let me drive the grays," he said with relish.

"Me either. Pull up behind them, then circle the block and come back for me." Beau said.

Merrick slowed the team down and pulled up just behind Mr. and Mrs. Truchard. Beau jumped out of the curricle and walked down the footpath behind them. He took a deep breath. He had to get a hold of his anger at them and concentrate on getting information from them. Harriet, and not her parents, must be the objective.

He increased his speed and came up level. "Mr. and Mrs. Truchard, I presume?"

Mrs. Truchard's hand flew to her breast like she'd received a fright, but Mr. Truchard looked at him knowingly. "Beaufort. The spitting image of your father. How do you do?"

How very polite and civilized. Very well. "Oh well enough, all things taken into consideration. I hear old Jinx has taken off with your daughter?"

"They are affianced," Mrs. Truchard said stiffly.

"So I heard. My congratulations. You must be thrilled to have fired her off so well."

They both narrowed their eyes, not trusting his good wishes. "You doubt me, but while I am grateful for your daughter's help, I am just glad to see her not hanging after me, if you know what I mean. M'mother was not at all impressed." That part at least, was true.

"Ha!" said Mr. Truchard. "Old Theodora Astley would despise being related to us. We did you a favor, didn't we?" There was an element of 'what's it worth to you' in the way he said it.

"I'm appreciative. But, you know, your dear daughter has left with something that belongs to me."

"That's not like Harriet. She doesn't have a dishonest bone in her body." Mrs. Truchard played with the braid on her bonnet.

"What was it?" Mr. Truchard asked.

"My dog. A little black terrier. Had him for years and I don't want to give him up."

"Oh," they both said at the same time. Then Mr. Truchard added, "She did have a dog."

She glanced at her husband, then back to Beau. "It ran after her carriage. Heard her voice, I think."

Heard her screaming, more like. "Where does Mr. Donovan reside? I'm sure he won't want my dog."

Mrs. Truchard arched an eyebrow. "He has the most *beautiful* house on Piccadilly. Under scaffolds at the moment, but it will be better than anything in Mayfair. I'm sure even Carlton House will be quite cast into the shade!"

"Louisa," Mr. Truchard said darkly.

"Apologies. I do rattle on. But I might be able to help?"

Ah, and here it came. The grab for money.

"I could fetch him for you," she continued. "Although I could only go later this evening."

It could be a backup plan if he was unable to locate the house. He could follow her there. "If you could fetch him for me, I'd be most grateful."

"How grateful?" Mr. Truchard asked, now fully in line with his wife's idea.

"Fifty pounds grateful? Something to make your travel to America go a little smoother?"

"One hundred and I'll do it," Mrs. Truchard said.

Beau held out his hand for her to shake. "Agreed."

"I'll take that emerald stick pin in your cravat as insurance," she said archly. The same pin Harriet had refused to take, because she thought he'd already paid her enough.

"No need." He fished into the pocket of his coat and pulled out a roll of banknotes. "Here is a twenty-pound deposit. You can keep that either way. But bring me Sooty and you can have the rest. Alive and unharmed, mind!"

She smiled, and it was so close to flirtatious that he squirmed. "But of course! You're on Portman Square, I believe?"

My, my, how well informed they were. They likely knew exactly where Harriet had been the entire time. "That's correct. I'll be waiting there for you." Beau turned to Mr. Truchard. "Lovely doing business with you."

Lovely of you to give me Jinx's address. Piccadilly was a long road, but the properties that had been recently overhauled were few. It was hard to keep the bounce out of his step as he strode away from them.

It took a few minutes for Merrick to pull up alongside him. Beau jumped in. "To Piccadilly, then drive along slowly. We're looking for a mansion that's scaffolded." The aristocracy may have left the street in the seventeenth century, but their grand houses remained, now flanked by coffeehouses, shops and taverns. One of those was bound to be owned by Jinx.

When they reached the thoroughfare, Merrick slowed. In the distance, a dog, a very yappy dog, was barking as though his life depended on it.

"I know that bark," Merrick said.

"Hopefully. Let me out here," Beau said. "Will you go around the block again for me?"

"I could do that all day if I get to drive these grays," Merrick said, taking off into the traffic.

Beau followed the sound of the barking around the corner and into the mews running parallel. There, Sooty was running in circles at the gate of a large house that had scaffolding all around it.

Found. Sooty must have followed her carriage until it entered the mews and the gates were closed to him.

It was five houses in from the corner.

"Sooty," he said in a tone that brooked no disobedience. The little dog turned at his voice and ran to him. "Good boy." He picked him up and received a lick to the nose. "You're relieved I'm here. Don't deny it."

No denials were heard.

"Come, let's drop you home so I can go to Bow Street. The two of us aren't enough. We need armed backup."

CHAPTER 30

IN WHICH SOME PLANS SUCCEED AND
SOME FAIL

The sun had set hours ago, and Harriet opened the wardrobe to pack a small bag. It felt silly, but it was the only productive thing she could think of doing. Her good things were at Beaufort's, but what she had left behind at Half Moon Street was still useful. Especially if she was to strike out on her own.

Her clothing and possessions had been lovingly folded and put in the drawers by staff who obviously thought she was firstly, not a victim of kidnap, and secondly, going to be the new Mrs. Donovan. If she'd still had her gems in her smelling salts bottle, Jinx would likely have taken them for his own, so it was lucky she had spent them all on Bertie.

She buckled her bag. Now she was ready to flee at any opportune moment. All she had to do was hope one presented itself.

Mr. Donovan—or Jinx as she now called him in her head because the criminal moniker suited him better—had not visited for hours. Perhaps he had forgotten she was up here altogether.

But alas, she was not so lucky. It was funny how she recognized his footsteps on the stairs already. Her stomach tightened, and she put the bag in the wardrobe then closed the door quietly. After moving quickly across to the chair by the window, she picked up her book, and pretended to read by the candlelight.

He didn't bother knocking, just unlocked the door and stepped in. "Ah, there you are. A picture by candlelight. What are you reading?"

She had not been reading, so had no idea, so she lifted the cover so he could see it. "Poetry!" he exclaimed. "I would not have picked you for a poetry person. More of a *Winning at Whist* kind of person, am I right?"

"Who told you that?" She aimed for an air of insouciance, but heaven knew if she succeeded.

"The same person who told me what time the parties are at their busiest, for when the authorities arrive tonight. His cousin is a fount of knowledge."

"Been working with him long?"

"Long enough."

That explained a lot. Poor Beau. "I take it you were with him the day I was celebrating my brother's good fortune at Dolly's?"

It would certainly explain the empty tankard she'd seen at his table.

"Indeed, but I have no use for him now." He studied her long enough to make her uncomfortable. "I'd love to know how Lord Beaufort landed himself so much money in such a brief space of time in order to pay off that debt. I'm mightily peeved by it, I don't mind telling you."

He suspected her involvement. She swallowed and said, as

evenly as she could, "You'd prefer to keep him in your thrall longer?"

"I would have preferred to keep him there forever, my dear, and I was a good few steps toward him needing to borrow more money from me when you entered the scene. Saw straight through all of it, didn't you?"

Did he mean he had a hand in creating the ring of fraud at Beaufort's? It made perfect sense. Thomas wasn't smart enough to do something so organized. So no, she had not seen the bigger picture, only the smaller one. But let him think what he wanted.

"It wasn't hard." She shrugged. "When you grow up a Truchard, spotting a cheat is nursery fare."

He slapped his hand on his knee. "That is precisely why we are so perfect together."

"No, Mr. Donovan, it is precisely why we are not. You think criminal activity is a valid method of advancement. I do not. It is vile."

"Vile? How can you, when your own parents …?" He left the rest of the sentence unsaid.

"When my own parents are such crooks themselves? Precisely. Not only do I think it's vile, I won't be a part of it. Why do you think they are so happy to be rid of me? Because I have not helped them. Not a jot."

"You'll jolly well help me." There was a dangerous glitter in his eye. "Our family fortune depends on it. I'm playing nice now, but I won't if you thwart me."

She rolled her eyes. A daring move, considering how badly her stomach was turning. "You don't need to cheat to make a fortune. I will tell you what I told Beaufort. You just have to stop private play in your public club. Everyone must play with you, or your employees, as bank. Then whenever someone loses, they lose to you."

"But then when they win, I lose."

"Yes, but you don't offer games where the odds aren't stacked in your favor, regardless. So when they win, you win too."

He frowned, his thick eyebrows drawing together. "Huh."

"If you run the percentages, you will find you come out firmly in profit. Even simple sums in my head show that. No underhand dealing necessary."

"I don't think there has ever been a simple sum in your head, my dear, and for the record, I never wanted you to fleece people on my behalf." The excited expression on his face only confirmed she should not have shared such a gem. "We will make a formidable team, you and I."

She sighed. "Once again, I have not agreed to marry you."

He reached out and drew a finger along her cheek. "Even after I spend the night with you?"

Her stomach seized. He wouldn't, would he? Goose bumps raised on her arms. "Surely you have women falling all over you without coercing one."

He shrugged. "Needs must, my dear. But later on. I have a very special plan for tonight."

He rose and bent to kiss her cheek. She retreated as far as the chair would allow, but his lips still brushed her skin. She shuddered. How could one man's lips feel so different from another's?

Then he left, having no qualms about leaving her alone.

He'd built a fortress, after all.

"I must admit," Beau said, "when I told you it was Jinx who kidnapped Miss Truchard, I didn't expect you to punch the air like you'd just won a lottery."

Richard Wolfe, principal Bow Street enquiry officer, smiled, and it was entirely malevolent. "I've been waiting for him to put a foot wrong. Any foot will do."

"I think kidnapping a lady shouting *Help! I'm being abducted!* should suffice."

"Thank you for thinking of me," Wolfe said. "This will be most satisfying. When I heard he'd refurbished an opulent mansion on Piccadilly with his ill-gotten gains, I could see him slipping from my fingers. The place will be a money-laundering behemoth if he ever gets it off the ground, and we'd be hard-pressed to prove it."

"Happy to be of service. Lord knows I will owe you my future happiness if you can get Harriet out of there."

Their hackney turned into Piccadilly. The sun had set hours ago, and luxurious carriages traveled along the thoroughfare toward whatever entertainment the evening held.

"Just remember what I said." Wolfe turned to Beau.

"You handle everything. I am not allowed to confront Jinx, bait him, or gloat over his arrest. You make this hard."

"Good," Wolfe said. "Can I have your word?"

"Of course, dammit."

"You are in attendance for Miss Truchard alone."

"Understood."

The carriage pulled up, and Wolfe tugged the brim of his hat. "Let's go then."

When they got to the footpath, the door opened and Jinx himself came down the stairs.

His frown was clear, even in the lamplight. "Lord Beaufort. What are you doing here? And with Bow Street, no less.

Shouldn't you be, oh I don't know, taking care of business? Just a thought."

"What business?" Beau winked at him. *We're coming, Harriet!*

Jinx looked at Wolfe. "He runs an illegal gambling den, did you know? Some of your colleagues are currently raiding his house in Portland Square to shut it down. You should follow them over."

So he'd been right. Jinx had organized to ruin him just because he was annoyed he'd paid the debt off. But Merrick was waiting for them, and he'd made sure everything had been cleared away. He'd given Mother a very special errand, so she was out of the house too.

Beau smiled. "They will find nothing. The only cards I play these days are with friends."

Jinx narrowed his eyes. "A step ahead, eh, Beaufort? It matters not." But his clenched jaw suggested it *did* matter, and that he knew he was outfoxed. "Then why are you here?"

Richard Wolfe stepped forward. "We have received reports a woman was kidnapped and seen bundled into your carriage. We suspect she is being held here."

"I don't need to kidnap a lady to have her want me, officer. The only women you'll find in the house behind me are maids and cooks."

"Then you won't mind us searching the premises?"

"If you have a warrant to search it; otherwise, yes, I do." He crossed his arms over his chest.

Wolfe put his hand in his pocket and brandished a folded piece of paper. "Like this one?" He smiled like the Wolfe he was named for. "I've been waiting a long time for this, Jinx."

"Have you? It was ill-advised to come here alone. I don't want you coming inside."

"Nevertheless, I will," Wolfe replied, stepping forward.

Beau strode behind Wolfe to follow him into the house.

Jinx put a hand up to block him. "Not you, Beaufort. You don't have a warrant."

"He's with me," Wolfe said, striding up the steps and through the open door.

Beau followed, but as he walked down the hall, Jinx pulled him by the back of the collar and dragged him back toward the door. "I said *not you*."

Instead of trying to right himself, Beau stepped backward with Jinx's momentum, barreling him into the wall. Then, in the most ungentlemanly way possible, he smacked his head against Jinx, hearing a horrible and yet satisfying crack, which could only be his nose.

Jinx hollered some indistinguishable swear words and soon enough his lackeys joined him in the hall, ready to fight.

"Stand down, gentlemen, unless you want to get on the wrong side of Bow Street," Wolfe said.

They looked at Richard, then at their employer. "Your orders, sir?"

Jinx slumped against the wall, his nose bloody. "Nothing to lose, my boys. Have at 'em, and a bonus if you can put them back out on the street."

One of the thugs pulled a pistol from his pocket, wild eyed.

"Stand down, gents, or you'll be attacking an officer." Wolfe pulled a wooden staff from his belt and shot a glance at Beau. "I rescind my orders to you."

Beau smiled and pulled his rapier from the walking cane. "A bit late, but very well."

Harriet leaped from the armchair. Was that a gun shot? A male voice yelled, and then others joined in. She might be putting herself in greater danger, but this was her chance.

"Help! I'm locked in here!" She pounded the door as hard as she could, the sound echoing. Would it be heard over all the noise downstairs?

The voices—mostly male, and one cockney female—got louder, closer.

For all she knew, this kind of hullabaloo was a daily occurrence at Mr. Donovan's house.

Footsteps thundered up the stairs. They didn't stop at the first landing but continued up to the second. A flutter of hope started in her chest. She kept pounding, kept screaming.

"Next floor," an authoritative voice said. Footsteps thumped on the stairs.

They were coming for her. "I'm here! Oh please, I'm here."

"Where are the keys to this door?"

A few moments later, the key turned in the lock. The door swung open, revealing a Bow Street runner and a furious Donovan, his nose bleeding and clutching his arm, which looked very much like it had received a gunshot wound.

No Beau.

Disappointment swept through her.

"Thank you." Harriet said, picking up her bag. "I can't tell you how relieved I am to see you."

"Are you unhurt, Miss Truchard?" The law officer looked her up and down. "Did anyone take advantage of you?"

"Not yet, but I think you have rescued me in the nick of time. Mr. Donovan threatened that if I would not agree to marry him, he would force himself on me so that I would have to." She shuddered.

"And you were abducted?" The man was tall, with sandy

blond hair and the look of someone who had seen much. He spoke like a gentleman and was definitely in charge of the situation.

"She came of her own accord," Donovan shouted. "Tell them, Harriet, or it will go badly for your parents."

"I won't lie to a law officer," Harriet said, then nodded at the Bow Street runner. "I was pushed into his carriage against my will. He brought me to this house and locked me in here, telling me I couldn't come out until I agreed to marry him."

The Bow Street runner nodded. "We will need to take a full statement, but for now, miss, you can go home."

Home. Did she actually have one?

They ushered her down the stairs and there, at the bottom, pacing back and forth with a rapier in his hand, was Beau. He *had* come!

Her heart took flight, and the spring in her step made it feel like floating.

He nodded to the Bow Street runner, then took her elbow and led her outside. His carriage waited out the front, horses restless and stomping.

"I must accompany Mr. Wolfe, but we will talk when I get home." He hesitated, his gaze searching hers. "Please stay there until I return."

She nodded, tempted to say she would stay forever if only he asked, but somehow held it back. It was an impossible dream, given who her family was. He took her valise and then held out a hand, his fingers warm against hers as he helped her into the carriage. But she was not alone inside.

"Lady Beaufort?" she said, in shock.

The viscountess sat in the corner of the luxurious carriage, both hands atop a silver-handled walking cane. She wore a very modish gown of lavender silk, with a turban to match.

Every inch of her person was dressed to intimidate and impress her wealth and rank.

"Get in, Miss Truchard. Let's get you away from here posthaste."

Harriet settled into the squab facing backward as the carriage took off into the traffic of Piccadilly. "I don't understand—why are you here?"

"I am here because my son thought you might need company on the way home. I think he thought you might run away." Her mouth was pursed, as though she was deciding what to say next.

Did she wish to warn Harriet away from Beau? Harriet should put her mind at rest, even as she broke her own heart all over again.

"If you mean to warn me away from your son, my lady, then save your breath. I would never take advantage of his good nature and I wouldn't accept an offer even if he made it."

"You wouldn't?" Her eyebrows shot up. "Why ever not? Don't you hold him in high esteem?"

"The highest. Which is why I would not want him saddled with my connections." She took a deep breath, prepared to brave it all. "My family—"

"I know your family, Harriet Truchard," Lady Beaufort cut in. "I have always known them. You are the daughter of Francis Truchard. I was in my second season when your mother ran away with your father. I was there for the whole sordid series of events that led to them escaping to the continent all those years ago. We called them the Infamous Pair, did you know? I have heard too many stories of what they've been up to since and I know, as well as you do, that their pictures are on the wall of my son's study."

"You knew them?" Harriet asked faintly. It wasn't just gossip for Lady Beaufort.

"Your father once played my future husband and cheated him of over a thousand pounds. As he did many of our friends before we saw him for what he was. I have been in horror at the fact that a Truchard was living under our roof and involved in our parties since the first time Beau told me your name. It was I who gave him your family's history and warned him against you."

Harriet couldn't control her shock. She didn't just know of her family, she'd *warned* Beau to stay away. But he hadn't listened.

"But nothing could shake my son's conviction of your honesty and integrity," she continued. "He himself is living proof that children can differ greatly from their parents and so, my dear, are you. You have proven to be everything he said you were. You have saved my family, and Beau is a different man since he met you. He even smiles. And since his happiness is paramount to me … If events conspire to make you my new daughter, you will be a most welcome and cherished member of our family. So the question is, do you love my son?"

"Oh," was all Harriet could say. After a few moments, she found her voice. "Yes. From the very first time I met him."

Lady Beaufort gave a small smile, disbelief evident. "What could he have possibly done that first time to make you so sure?"

Harriet took a deep breath and exhaled, remembering that fateful morning. "Why, he bought me a pile of books at the Temple of the Muses," she said with a smile. "The surest way to a young lady's heart."

"Ah well, whatever you decide, know that I will not stand in your way."

His mother's blessing was lovely, but until she saw Beau, she couldn't pin her hopes on it. She had saved him, and he had returned the favor, but that did not mean he trusted her.

CHAPTER 31

ODDS OR EVENS?

W hen they arrived back in Portman Square, Mr. Merrick took their bonnets and bowed to her ladyship. Then his severe countenance cracked, and Harriet was surprised to see a row of crooked gappy teeth, with one golden incisor. "I see you have retrieved the precious goods. Well done, my lady. Well done indeed."

"It was masterful, Merrick." She handed him her walking cane.

"You are never anything less," he replied solemnly. "While you were gone, Bow Street visited here, as Lord Beaufort suspected they would. It was unfortunate that they found our ballroom dark and her ladyship away from home."

"What conclusion did they come to?"

"That they had been sent on a merry chase. They left here scowling and complaining of the waste of time."

"Excellent work."

They shared a moment of mutual approval before Lady Beaufort remembered her son. "And Beaufort has gone to Bow Street to be witness for Mr. Wolfe. All is in hand."

Merrick inclined his head. "Very good, my lady."

Lady Beaufort turned to Harriet. "I find I am quite fatigued from the exertion, my dear. Would you forgive me if I retire for the evening? You could await Beaufort in the drawing room and, of course, your attic room will be ready for you if he is too late." She turned to the major-domo. "Will you organize the kitchen to send a supper tray for both of us?"

"Of course."

Harriet curtsied. "That would be lovely."

But the chairs in the drawing room were not comfortable, whereas there was a sofa in Beau's study. The day had been so long and if there was somewhere she could both wait for Beau and close her eyes, it would be bliss. So, after Lady Beaufort ascended the stairs, Harriet chased after Merrick.

"I will wait in the study, if that is acceptable?" She glanced at Merrick, who was regarding her indulgently.

"Wherever Miss would like. I recollect the sofa in there is the most comfortable in the house and matches the chair I had brought to your room. Many are the times I've stumbled upon Lord Beaufort sleeping there after a very late night." He smiled. "I will return shortly."

"Thank you, Merrick." She looked around her, at the rooms that would normally be bustling with guests. "I am so glad Lord Beaufort stopped the card party."

Merrick nodded. "And a good thing, too. As I said to her ladyship, we were visited by Bow Street tonight and if he hadn't cancelled at the last minute, yours truly would be in custody as we speak."

"But you are not responsible for the parties, Mr. Merrick." It hardly seemed fair that he would be arrested when he was just the man at the door.

"No, Miss, but I would have said I was. Not that his lordship needs to know that." He waved the idea away. "It's a moot point now, as Lord Beaufort was ahead of that rascal Jinx who informed on him."

"I believe *he* may be the one spending the evening in custody," Harriet said with relish.

Merrick smiled once again, proving it was a strange night indeed. "Couldn't happen to a nicer fellow."

Harriet went to the study, where a fire blazed in the hearth, and candelabra were lit, giving the room a soft glow. It was like the room was staying up late, waiting for the master to return home.

Someone had put the E.O. wheel on Beau's desk, likely to remove any hint of gambling before they found a proper home for it. She went to it, put a ball on the wheel and spun, watching it bounce over the letters that were gilded into the circumference of the wheel, E, O, all the way around. Even, odd, even, odd. Life had felt like that for months, one moment high, the next so low she thought she'd never dig her way out.

The ball finished its spin on O, that is, odd. Harriet smiled ruefully. "Sounds correct. I do feel odd."

Harriet walked over to the sofa and sank into it. *I should wait for my supper before I close my eyes.*

Her eyes disagreed, and she was woken some time later by Merrick pushing the door open with her supper tray. "Now I've woken you. I'm so sorry, Miss Truchard."

"Harriet, please, Merrick."

He nodded. "Harriet." He placed the tray on the small side table and backed away. "Cook says she's happy to have you back."

Harriet looked at the supper laid out on the tray. Broth, a thick slice of bread with butter, and an apple tart. A glass of

Madeira was nestled in the corner. "This is perfect. Please thank Mrs. Barrett for me."

When he left, Harriet ate the supper with more speed than was seemly, and when the last drop of Madeira was gone, she sat back on the sofa. *Much better.*

She closed her eyes again, only to awaken when someone cleared their throat at the door.

Her eyes sprang open, heart racing.

Beau. Looking tired, his clothes crumpled and torn, and a scrape across his cheek.

She resisted the urge to walk across to him, to hug him, hold him. He was not hers, no matter what his mother implied. "What happened to your cheek?"

Beau walked toward her, in a manner that suggested he had all day. Every step made Harriet's heart beat faster.

"After I saw you into the carriage and went back inside, Jinx unwisely decided to exact a little revenge with some fisticuffs. But I am well able to defend myself." He took a deep, satisfied breath. "I should not have enjoyed it so much."

She couldn't help a smile. "I do hope you landed a few good blows."

He rubbed his hand up his neck. "More than a few."

"Excellent." She pushed the table with the supper tray aside and stood.

"More so given now he will also be charged with assault and battery." Two more steps and he was now close enough to take her hands in his. Her breath hitched when he did. "Are you truly fine? He did not hurt you?"

Did he touch her is what Beau meant. She shook her head. "He never got the chance, thanks to you."

"Thanks to Sooty," he corrected. "Hearing him bark meant

we didn't have to waste time searching. Now, to the matter at hand—"

"I assure you," she cut in, her voice shaky, though she wasn't sure if it was due to his continued hold on her hand or the thought of leaving him, "you do not owe me a thing. I will find alternate accommodation as soon I have my funds."

His eyes glittered in what seemed like amusement. "Will you now? And abandon Sooty all over again? After his valiant part in saving you?"

His mood was strange. She couldn't quite pick it. Was he angry with her? Teasing her? "I ... perhaps you could mind him for me until I am properly settled?"

He raised his eyebrows. "No."

"Just no?" She stared at him, confused.

He released her hands, then stepped back and hollered Merrick's name. A moment later there was a sudden barking and a scampering of claws on the parquetry floor and Sooty made a grand entrance, skidding to a halt at her feet.

"You can't just love a dog and then leave it without a word, you know, my dear," Beau said. "Not the done thing. Your love makes a promise to them. That you'll be there, that they can safely love you back without fear of abandonment."

As she stared into his eyes, she realized, with a singing heart, that he wasn't talking about the dog.

Oh my ...

Uncertain as to whether she could believe what her heart was saying, she crouched and gave Sooty the affection he was asking for. "There now, little one. I'm here. I heard you were very brave."

"He hasn't eaten since he got home. Just sat on your bed, apparently."

She looked up at him, her mouth twitching. "Seems a little dramatic."

"Aren't we all when love is involved?"

She wondered again where he was going with all this, and why he just didn't get to the point.

He walked to his desk and pulled a large envelope from his top drawer. "Come then, let me give you your winnings. Then you can make a proper choice."

He opened the envelope and put the stack of pound notes on the table. "We won twenty, I owed twelve, but I had two in my bank here that we no longer needed, so this ten thousand pounds is yours. Enough to keep you a long time if you're frugal. Long enough to write a few more books, I should think."

"And the choice?" she said.

"Isn't that obvious?"

"No." But her breathless voice said otherwise.

"You lie, Harriet," his gaze twinkled.

"It's just that it's such a bad idea, Beau. I have no family connections, no upbringing. I don't play the harp or pianoforte with any skill. You shouldn't marry me."

"Who are you to tell me what is best for me? Don't let stubbornness impede your future happiness."

Was that what she was doing? Had she decided she was no good for Beau when he should decide for himself?

He lifted her hands to his lips, brushing them over her knuckles. He was so close that she could breathe him in and feel the heat of him.

Oh, how she ached for him to hold her.

"So forget all that. But before you do make the decision, let me say this. I apologize for my behavior the other—"

"No," she cut in. "We had an agreement. I should not have broken it."

He dropped her hands. "Yes, but you did it with the best intentions and I was given fair warning. I should have trusted you. I most certainly shouldn't have gotten so angry with you." His lips twisted in an endearing manner. "I was just as angry at myself, if truth be told."

"Why were you angry at yourself?" she asked in disbelief. "You had every right—"

"I was angry at the position *my* desperation had put you in. You should not—"

"And would not have, for anyone else."

"I hope you never have to again." He caught her hand again, and pulled her into his embrace. "Your life is your own from this point on. You are safe from Jinx. Your parents will be gone, and Bertie is off on his own adventures. You can do as you wish."

She pulled away slightly, a mischievous smile twitching her lips. "Which brings us back to this choice you keep mentioning."

"Indeed it does."

"Is this choice between you and the dog? I can have either?"

"More me *and* the dog, or, you and the dog, but no me."

"Such a tough decision." She pretended to give it serious thought. "Perhaps we should make one final wager."

He raised a lazy eyebrow, amusement on his lips and love in his eyes. "And what shall we play? You can beat me at most anything."

She motioned to the E.O. wheel sitting on the desk, a lost relic of a time that would never be repeated. Not in this house. "One final spin of the wheel to decide our fate. What say you?"

"What are we staking?"

"Our futures." She walked across and picked up a red token. "If E spins up, I win you, and Sooty, and we marry and live happily ever after."

He took a counter and put it on the opposite square. "And if it lands on O?"

"Then you win me, and Sooty, and we marry and live happily ever after."

"It sounds like you have this outcome loaded, my love."

Love. He'd called her *love*. Happiness all but burst from her.

"I did once warn you that I very rarely lose."

He laughed and spun the wheel.

It landed on E.

"You win," Beau said, and pulled her into his arms.

EPILOGUE

WHERE HAPPILY EVER AFTER THROWS
PUNCTUALITY FROM THE WINDOW

I t was strange to think that a large noble mansion could
feel like home. Soon the beautiful furniture, large airy
rooms and parquetry floor were as familiar to Harriet as a
pair of slippers.

Her books were in the library, her personal sitting room
had a desk beneath the window where she wrote her newest
manuscript *Victory with Vingt-et-un*.

But best of all, she was with Beau every day, and every
night.

Tonight, as was his custom, he was lounging in a chair in
the corner of their bedroom, legs stretched out, as she
finished her toilette for this very important night. His gaze
never left her and when her maid finished with her hair and
left the room, he rose and strolled over to stand behind her at
her dressing table.

"I'm very happy for Emmeline," she said to divert herself
from his heated gaze. It was his sister's debut ball. She had
wasted no time after their quiet wedding ceremony at St.

George's in coming to town, bringing their little brother, Benedict, in tow.

"She seems happy with herself," he replied, brushing his fingers up her neck and smiling when she shivered. "Never has a young lady planned her own come out in the space of six weeks."

"She was determined to debut before the season ended."

"We'd barely finished the last of our wedding cake before she descended. But it's nice to have them all here."

The country estate was still leased out, but now the rent from it was filling the coffers rather than going straight to Jinx. When the lease ran out next year, they would be able to take it back over.

"I was thinking," Harriet said, throwing Beau a sly glance.

"Always dangerous" he said, but he leaned down and kissed her behind the ear, then whispered. "What were you thinking, love?"

"We have my ten thousand pounds."

He straightened. "You do." He had refused to let her put it into their joint funds.

"And we have some very clever friends." She caught his glance in the mirror with a mischievous grin, a risky thing since it often made him carry her away, making them late for whatever outing they had planned.

"That we do. It has warmed my heart to see you becoming so close to them." The last six weeks had been filled with trips to Kensington for picnics, nights at the theater, and so many long dinners.

"What with Daphne's perfumes, Mandeville's spice trade, Templeton and Diana's horse breeding and Charis's home decoration, surely there is some way we can forge a collective to invest in our futures and bring us all wealth."

Beau stroked his chin, obviously thinking. "Ah, you think to make your ten thousand—"

"*Our* ten thousand," she corrected.

He nodded with a smile. "Very well. *Our* ten thousand as a seed to grow their businesses?"

"Precisely! Could you gather them tonight and suggest it?"

He laughed. "Why would I do that when you are the one whose head dances with figures, and who probably has pages of workings on possible investment options and returns?"

She glanced at the black notebook on the dressing table, so he reached forward, snatching it and flicking through the rows of columns filled with numbers. "As I thought." His expression was equal parts pride and teasing.

"It seems my head for numbers is good for more than just gambling."

"No surprise to anyone who knows you. But what would we offer in the collective?"

Harriet took a deep breath, stood, and took his hands. "A friend of Bertie's has a brother who is a stockbroker, and I have been speaking to him about investing on the 'change. I took a little money a few weeks ago and invested in some shares. I think I can make good choices if I do enough research and choose investments that have strong future possibilities."

"Huh," Beau said. "I like it. But I also like the idea of diversifying our investments with our friend's capabilities. What about Charles and Mariah? With the baby on the way, it's good to set up future wealth."

"Perfect." To say her relationship with Mariah had gone from strength to strength in the absence of their parents was putting it mildly.

"I have recently been researching the science behind steam engines."

"Oh dear," Beau said, his face falling. He took a fortifying deep breath.

"What?" She hoped he hadn't agreed too soon and actually didn't like the idea.

"I'm afraid the thought of you surrounded by research papers, maybe with those little spectacles perched on the end of your nose is …"

"No, Beau, we have to go downstairs. The guests will arrive soon!"

"… is very enticing to me. I'm sorry, Harri. There's nothing for it." He picked her up and carried her away. "We'll just have to be late."

THE END

Thank you for reading *A Talent for Trouble*.
If you'd like to hear about my new releases, I have a newsletter!
https://www.robynchalmers.com/newsletter

Reader reviews mean the world to me, let me know what you thought!

If you enjoyed this regency romance, you might also enjoy:

A Whiff of Scandal in which Miss Daphne Davenport risks all to save her family from ruin.

A Dash of Daring in which Miss Diana Kingsley enters a curricle race to win back her favorite horse, but ends up with more than she bargained for!

A Song of Secrets in which opera singer Sarah is the very last person the vicar of Seven Oaks should fall in love with.

A Lady Made for Mischief in which Charis is invited to redecorate a London mansion—but finds making over her ladyship's grumpy son far more enticing.

ALSO BY ROBYN CHALMERS

ABOUT THE AUTHOR

Robyn Chalmers is an emerging author of sweet regency romance.

She lives in a country town in southern Australia with her family and a white fluffy dog. She reads a lot, walks a lot and has way too many books.

When not reading, you can find her writing her favorite kind of novel–Regency romance.

She loves hearing from readers and you can find her on Facebook, and posting bad photos of donuts on Instagram.

facebook.com/authorrobynchalmers
instagram.com/robyn_chalmers_author

Made in the USA
Las Vegas, NV
12 August 2023

76002632R00184